BBC

DOCTOR WHO

CITY OF DEATH

THE CHANGING FACE OF DOCTOR WHO
This book portrays the fourth incarnation of Doctor Who,
whose physical appearance later changed when he lost an
argument with gravity.

THE CHANGING FACE OF SCAROTH
This book portrays the twelfth and final incarnation of Scaroth,
last of the Jagaroth

DOCTOR WHO

CITY OF DEATH

Douglas Adams & James Goss

From an original story by David Fisher

BOOKS

10 9 8 7 6 5 4 3 2 1

BBC Books, an imprint of Ebury Publishing
20 Vauxhall Bridge Road, London SW1V 2SA

BBC Books is part of the Penguin Random House group of companies whose addresses
can be found at global.penguinrandomhouse.com

 Penguin
Random House
UK

Original script © Completely Unexpected Productions Ltd and David Fisher 2015
This novelization © James Goss 2015

Completely Unexpected Productions Ltd, David Fisher and James Goss have asserted
their right to be identified as the authors of this Work in accordance with the Copyright,
Designs and Patents Act 1988

Doctor Who is a BBC Wales production for BBC One.
Executive producers: Steven Moffat and Brian Minchin

First published by BBC Books in 2015

www.eburypublishing.co.uk

A CIP catalogue record for this book is available from the British Library

ISBN 978 1 849 90675 3

Editorial Director: Albert DePetrillo
Series Consultant: Justin Richards
Project Editor: Steve Tribe
Cover design: Two Associates © Woodlands Books Ltd
Production: Alex Goddard

Printed and bound in Great Britain by Clays Ltd, St Ives PLC

Penguin Random House is committed to a sustainable future for our business, our readers
and our planet. This book is made from Forest Stewardship Council® certified paper.

MIX
Paper from
responsible sources
FSC
www.fsc.org   FSC® C018179

PART ONE

'One's emotions are intensified in Paris – one can be more happy and also more unhappy here than in any other place … There is nobody so miserable as a Parisian in exile.'

Nancy Mitford, *The Pursuit Of Love*

CHAPTER ONE
ALL ROADS
LEAD TO PARIS

It was Tuesday and life didn't happen. Wednesday would be quite a different matter.

Scaroth, last of the Jagaroth, was in for a surprise. For one thing, he had no idea he was about to become the last of the Jagaroth.

If you'd asked him about the Jagaroth a mere, say, twenty soneds ago, he'd have shrugged and told you they were a savage and warlike race and that, if you weren't happy about that, you should meet the other guys.

By and large, all life in the universe was pretty savage and warlike. Show me a race of philosophers and poets, said Scaroth, and I'll show you lunch. It would, however, be unfair to say the Jagaroth were completely without accomplishments. They did build very nice-looking spaceships, although they were not necessarily very good ones. There was a lot to recommend the *Sephiroth*. A vast sphere rested on three claws. It suggested formidable menace whilst evoking the kind of insect you'd not care to find in your bed. The tripod arrangement of the legs also meant that it could land on anything.

Which was ironic, as right now it couldn't take off from anything. Something had gone very badly wrong in the drive unit almost as soon as they'd landed in this desolation. They'd been hunting a Racnoss energy signal and had made planetfall, hoping for one more victory. Just one more victory.

The Jagaroth had devoted themselves to killing. There was nothing else they'd leave behind them. No history, no literature, and no statues. As a species they'd never achieved anything other than wiping out life.

The problem was that every other life form was equally dedicated to the same goal. So successful had everyone been that there really wasn't that much life left in the universe. The Jagaroth were one of the last ones standing and, even then, not by much. When the Jagaroth talked about their fearsome battle fleet, the *Sephiroth* was pretty much it. Or, actually, just *it*.

Scaroth, pilot of the *Sephiroth*, battle fleet of the Jagaroth, worried about this. Nice-looking spaceships, frankly mediocre drive systems, rhyming names, and, oh yes, a frankly lunatic determination to keep going.

Hence the voices of his shipmates that filled his command pod from across the ship.

'Twenty soneds to warp thrust.' Someone was counting down.

'Thrust against planet surface set to power three.' And someone down in engineering was really keen on getting off this rock.

'Negative,' Scaroth snapped back quickly. 'Power three too severe.' Warp thrust was used to speed between the stars, not for lift-off. Even from a thinly atmosphered, low-gravity dead world. There were too many things which could go wrong. Warp thrust from a planet's surface had not been tested. 'At power three this is suicide.'

The voices urging him on fell silent at that. Of course they would.

'Please advise,' he said curtly.

Eventually that keen voice in engineering came on the line. 'Scaroth, it must be power three. It must be.'

Typical. The refuge of the Jagaroth in definite absolutes. Scaroth twisted his face into a cynical expression. Well, as cynical an expression as could be conveyed by a face that was a mass of writhing green tentacles grouped around a single eye.

As pilot, Scaroth was in charge. The one to push the button. If history remembered this at all, it would be his fault. He knew that it was a stupid decision, but then again, from an evolutionary point of view, the Jagaroth had made a lot of fairly stupid decisions.

'Ten soneds to warp thrust,' prompted the countdown. Was there a trace of desperation in the voice?

Scaroth ran his green hands over the terminal. If the *Sephiroth* had been working properly, warp control would have been a mass of status read-outs, all of which he had had been carefully trained to simultaneously process. Instead, most of the panels flashed up requesting urgent software updates, or were simply blank.

Scaroth was relying on his instincts and the voices filling the module. And the rest of the crew seemed happy to leave it up to him.

'Advise!' he repeated, hoping to hear someone speaking sense.

The response that came was weary. 'Scaroth, the Jagaroth are in your hands. Without secondary engines we must use our main warp thrust. You know this. It is our only hope. *You* are our only hope.'

11

Thanks for that, thought Scaroth, his tentacles now positively quivering with cynicism. 'And I'm the only one directly in the warp field!' In other words, I'll be the first one to go. 'I know the dangers.' That was as close as a Jagaroth had ever come to asking for a rethink. Once they committed to an idea, no matter how lethal or ludicrous, the Jagaroth stuck to it.

Confirming his thoughts, the countdown came back on, sounding quite determinedly chipper. Whatever, something was going to happen now. 'Three soneds... two... one...' went the voice, as though unaware that the soned's days as a unit of measurement were about to be very firmly over.

Scaroth had a last attempt. 'What will happen if...?' It all goes wrong? If the atmosphere and gravity combine with the warp thrust to do something really unexpected and horrible? Starting with me.

Ah well. What's the use? Arguing with the Jagaroth had only ever ended in death.

Scaroth pressed the button.

At full power, the *Sephiroth* glided majestically up from the surface of the desolation. The idea of staying a moment longer here had appalled the crew. Why stay here on a dead world fiddling with repairs when we could go somewhere else and maybe wipe out another species? The omens were good. A tiny fluctuation caused by a fuel leakage seemed to right itself. As the sphere rose, the claw-like legs tucked themselves neatly up underneath. For a moment the sphere hovered there, glowing with energy, magnificent, expectant.

Then it shattered.

Directly inside the warp field, Scaroth was both intimately aware of the ship falling into itself and also strangely removed from the experience. Nothing seemed certain except that everything hurt. And the voices of the Jagaroth were still filling warp control.

There was no sense that they realised they had made a terrible mistake, that they'd made him press the button. Simply that they now expected him to do something about it.

'Help us Scaroth! Help us!' they pleaded. As if there was anything he could do now. 'The fate of the Jagaroth is with you! Help us! You are our only hope!'

The screaming voices cut off and, for a brief moment, Scaroth could enjoy his agony in relative silence.

I'm the last of the Jagaroth, he thought. For as long as that lasts.

The warp field finally, mercifully collapsed. The fragments of the ship, squeezed into place by impossible forces, finally felt free to fling themselves in burning splendour far and wide across the surface of the dead planet.

Scaroth died. And then the surprising thing happened.

That'll do, thought Leonardo.

Like most works of genius, it had arrived almost without being noticed.

One moment there it wasn't, the next there it was, somehow squeezing itself between the towers of paper and the dangling models that filled the cramped study.

Leonardo sat back in his chair and surveyed the painting, brush still in his hand. The brush hovered near the lip of the easel, not quite being laid to rest. He surveyed his work. Was that really it? Was there anything more that needed doing to it?

Finally, he tugged his eyes away from the painting. He looked over to the visitor snoring in the corner, boots up on the model of the dam designed for Machiavelli. Leonardo briefly toyed with the visitor's suggestions, no doubt kindly meant, about the portrait's face.

But no, he thought. He would come back to the painting, of course he would come back to it. That was his problem. Never quite able to finish anything. But yes, she would certainly do for now.

He let his brush fall, excitement turning into a vague sense of anti-climax and now what.

Deciding that tonight would be a drinking night, he poured himself a cup of cheap wine, and sipped it fearfully. Perhaps he'd buy something better tomorrow, but he probably wouldn't. He gazed out through the arched window at the stars and the city slumbering beneath them. His eyes wandered across the squares of Florence. God alone knows what they'll make of this on the forums, he thought. He knew that tomorrow all the whispering would be about his latest painting. Some would say it was a disappointment. Others would say he should stop dividing his time between painting and inventing. No doubt a few would say it was a triumphant return to form.

Ah well, let them. He was happy with it. More or less.

His visitor shifted in his slumber, and Leonardo wondered about the portrait's face again.

No. Leave her be. For the moment.

He rocked back in his chair, enjoying the wine as much as was humanly possible, and drinking in the painting. She had been a struggle, and, while he wasn't quite at the top of the mountain, the struggle had definitely been worth it.

Thank the Lord he wouldn't have to go through that again.

William Shakespeare was cheating at croquet. His visitor frowned and, while the Bard wasn't looking, subtly scuffed his ball closer to a hoop. He looked up. Well, bless him if

William hadn't done the same thing. The two smiled at each other politely.

'Patrons!' exclaimed Shakespeare, changing the subject.

His visited nodded and clucked sympathetically.

'This one's very keen,' continued the Bard. 'I tried out some of my new stuff on him last night. Normally that sends them scurrying away for weeks, but this one's promised he's coming back at the weekend. So he must have more.' He angled his mallet and sent the ball bouncing merrily across his lawn, neatly avoiding his visitor's scarf, which was unaccountably trailing across its path. The ball sailed through a hoop and smacked against the post. Shakespeare smirked.

'Oh, well done,' applauded his guest insincerely.

'He was very nice about a bit I was pleased with.' Shakespeare waited, both for a dramatic pause and for his visitor to miss his shot. 'Ah yes,' he announced with a studied spontaneity which explained why he'd given up acting. '*I could be bounded in a nutshell and count myself a king of infinite space, were it not that I had bad dreams.* Yes, that was it. He said it spoke to him and he couldn't wait to find out how it ends. Pah! Wonder what his bad dreams are, eh? Probably nothing much. Oh poor you, that is a shame.' As his visitor muffed his shot completely.

All thoughts of his patron's bad dreams banished, Shakespeare got on with winning the game.

It was said that the Nazis loved art as much as they loved a joke. Curiously, however, as they'd stormed into Paris they'd filled their lavish hotel suites with as much art as they could lay their hands on. And, when they'd swept out of Paris the first thing they'd done was to take their art with them. And the last thing they'd done was to forget to settle their hotel bills.

The train had been loaded by the Wehrmacht in the dead of night. It was one of the final ones to leave Paris, rattling slowly through the north-eastern suburbs, windowless metal containers baking in the summer heat. Behind the train came the steady, self-important crump of the American army. Ahead of the train lay Germany.

Inside one of the carriages was a very young German soldier, his poise stiff, even if his uniform was several sizes too large. His posture didn't waver, not even when the train juddered to an abrupt and unexpected halt just outside Aulnay. The tracks ahead were gone, blown up by the Resistance.

The young soldier could hear gunfire, shouts and footsteps walking down the track towards his carriage. He pulled out his gun and waited. The young soldier made a list of his options. He could fight his way out (unlikely), he could shoot himself (practical), he could set fire to the cargo (regrettable). For once, he took no action, and simply stood to attention as the bolts were undone and the container door slid to one side.

A flashlight landed on his handsome, perfectly Aryan face. The soldier tensed, just a little, expecting the shot that would end his life.

It did not come.

'Good evening,' The voice behind the flashlight sounded endlessly amused. 'Well, it all seems to be in order.' The light played over the contents of the carriage, some neatly in crates, the rest stacked up against walls. The carriage was full of paintings. 'Tell me, what do you think of it?'

'I'm sorry?'

'I said,' the voice purred, 'what do you make of it all?'

The soldier found his voice. 'It is all excellent.'

'Yes, it is, isn't it?' the man's voice laughed. 'And it's mine.' The tone shifted just a little, addressing him like a hotel porter. 'Thank you for looking after it so well…' A pause. A question.

'Hermann, sir.'

He could hear the man nod. 'Thank you for looking after it, Hermann.'

Major Gaston Palewski glared at the mountain. It did not explode.

Perhaps, just perhaps, they should not have named the bomb Beryl. He'd never cared for the name. Major Palewski groaned with annoyance.

'Give it time, my dear Gaston,' oozed the smartly dressed man at his side. Nothing ever seemed to rattle him. A fellow of infinite patience. In some ways so terribly French, in others so terribly not.

Around the Major, people checked watches, squinted through binoculars, lit cigarettes and tutted. It felt pretty much like a Parisian café, only they were all stood roasting on a plain in the Saharan desert.

'Not really sure I need to be here,' muttered the Major. 'Rubberstamping exercise.'

'Oh, I think you do.' The man was enthusing again. His smile was indelible. 'Nuclear power is almost the greatest force this world has ever known.'

'Almost?' Gaston raised an eyebrow.

'Well, who knows?' His companion frowned, but his smile did not go away. 'It's certainly the greatest achievement of humanity. Before you build all those power stations, I think you really do need to see a nuclear explosion for yourself.'

Well yes, Gaston had always liked fireworks. Even during the war, he had enjoyed watching barrage lighting up the night sky. But this was different. He felt a moment's unease at the presence of the genial man at his side. There were rumours about him, about his family – who were they really? Had they been *collabos* during the war? But there were rumours about everyone's family, and this was the new France, after all. Perhaps it needed people like this. Especially if the Palewski Plan was to succeed. The Major wanted France to be at the forefront of nuclear energy, and this man had convinced him to build even more power stations than the country currently needed. 'We have to think of the future, Gaston,' he'd assured him.

Well, why not, thought Gaston. Something to be remembered by.

He glared at the mountain again, and it exploded at last. Just not in the way it was expected to. Instead of shooting up into the air, a vast jet of flame shot horizontally across the plain, blazing towards them. The light seared their eyes. Even the Major flinched and screamed, backing futilely away from the fireball.

As quickly as it had appeared, the flame vanished, replaced by a choking black cloud that washed over them.

When eventually Gaston straightened up, he realised his companion had remained standing throughout, and was now dabbing black smuts off his white linen suit. He was smiling broadly.

'An impressive demonstration, I'm sure you'll agree,' he laughed.

'But…' Gaston could not find his voice. He coughed, clearing ash from his lungs. 'That was not supposed to happen! Was that safe?'

'Oh, perfectly.' His companion folded away his handkerchief into his top pocket. 'Perfectly.'

Gaston would not be the only person there to die of leukaemia, killed by a bomb called Beryl.

Heidi found most of Daddy's clients stiflingly boring. But not this one. Already her visitor had taught her that she had been wrong about something. No one had ever done that before.

Heidi had grown up thinking that money was dull and that people with a lot of it were even duller. Their clothes were dull, their conversation was dull, even their vices were dull. And her father put up with all of it. Because he ran one of the most exclusive banks in Switzerland and it was his job to somehow find these tedious people interesting.

It had been all right when she was young, but now she was coming of age, she'd realised to her horror that he was planning on marrying her off to one of them. Her mistake, she realised, was never rebelling when she had had the opportunity. There had been a point, somewhere, when she had still had a chance. Perhaps when her expensive finishing school, well, finished and before the emptiness of the rest of her life began. She could have hopped on a tiresomely punctual Swiss train and gone somewhere, anywhere other than Switzerland. She wouldn't have starved. Daddy, whatever his faults, would have made sure of that.

But instead she had come home and waited by his side, working in the family business. Most Swiss banks are, in their own quiet way, family concerns. Clients liked that sense of continuity. Heidi and her father would go to the airport to meet people off planes that were never late, and arrive in a restaurant in perfect time for their reservation. The plates would be cold, the conversation empty, and each evening would stretch on until she wondered if she should stab herself with a butter knife or just marry one of them to get it all over with. When her father had first insisted he accompanied her, she wondered if he was grooming her to take over the bank. Now she realised that she was simply an asset he was looking at realising. That was certainly how her father's clients regarded her.

She had an office. As it was mainly for show, she had

made the most of it, ripping out the wooden panelling and filling it with sharp steel furniture and fragile glass tables. There was even a desk toy, on which, pulling back one little steel ball would send another eleven flying off and ticking back. Little planets, knocking into each other. Back and forth until even they gave up and fell still, waiting for something else to happen.

Heidi could tell the client was impressed by her taste. He took in the room, rather than her. She liked that. When he looked at her it was almost as though he was assessing her as another gorgeously perfect piece of furniture, approving both the cut of her trouser suit, and the cut of her hair.

This client was definitely different. For one thing he was fun. And for another, he was a fraud. Her father hadn't noticed, but then her father was a great one for appearances and hunches. Heidi wasn't. She enjoyed thorough research. She had a whole folder lying in front of her on the glass table. This man had come to the bank with the details of a vault which hadn't been opened for a very long time. It wasn't unheard of for a vault to be passed down through a family without being visited for several generations, but it was certainly unusual. All the paperwork for this vault was perfectly in order. That was the problem, as far as she was concerned.

In such cases, the paperwork was never in order. There was always some small thing awry, some tiny detail that the bank would need to help smooth over. But not in this case. It was all in complete Swiss order – even down to the original documents just happening to provide information that matched the slightly revised requirements brought in after all that fuss caused by those nice Germans salting so much of other people's money away. Unless this handsome man sat across from her, smiling that charming smile, was somehow on speaking terms with his long-dead relatives, that was impossible. Which clearly meant that he was a fraud.

A fraud who was sitting back, insolently at home in her chrome and leather chair, his legs crossed, an exquisitely cobbled-shoe tapping the air gently, waiting for her verdict.

She had him. She could send him to prison for life. He was a fraud come to steal money from her father's bank. Now that, thought Heidi, would be interesting. She couldn't help smiling, couldn't hold in a little laugh at the thought.

The fraud looked at her, and he smiled too, laughing along with her. No, more than that – he winked. He knew. He knew that she'd seen through him. And he didn't care.

Heidi let him lean forward across the desk, face reflected in its surface as he lit her cigarette for her. With a toss of her long blonde hair, she leaned forward too, regarding this charming man thoughtfully. There was already an intimacy between them. A shared joke. One thing her father had taught her was that it was always fatal to get caught up in emotion. Her family prided itself on its tact, grace, and caution.

Heidi had long been planning on rebelling. Here was a man come to rob her father's bank. And she was going to let him. Because it would be fun.

'So,' she said to him coolly, 'how much money would you like to steal?'

The man didn't even blink. 'All of it,' he said.

'Now what?' Harrison Mandel thought. Having found himself suddenly, embarrassingly rich, he had no idea what to do next.

As was increasingly the case in the world, his problems had been caused by a computer. Harrison had invented one. Or rather, Harrison had come across some letters belonging to Ada Lovelace. A lot of people knew that Byron's daughter had invented the first programming language. Many people discounted her actual language, preferring to patronisingly applaud her efforts. While her contemporaries had been trying to dance in corsets or write novels about dancing in corsets, Ada had invented computer programming, whilst wearing a corset. The problem with her audacious attempts at programming was that they just fell a little bit flat when fed into an actual computer.

That was, until Harrison Mandel had found her correspondence with an Italian polymath. Harrison realised that the letters described a rather different kind of computer to any that had ever been built. Perhaps, Harrison figured, the letters were an elaborate game between tutor and student, an attempt to invent two sides of a coin by post.

Whatever, Harrison had been so diverted by this discovery that he sat down and built the computer they described. It was surprisingly easy. The jottings by Lovelace and her Italian were simpler to follow than the instructions that came with his wardrobe. They might almost have been written deliberately with that intention.

He fed in Lovelace's code, figuring that at most it probably wouldn't even compile and that would be that. But it had worked, and worked brilliantly. The problem lay in what to do next.

The Americans had ordered ten thousand. The Russians had ordered twenty. There's just the one, he'd protested, adamant that this was a discovery that belonged to the world. When he'd refused, things had suddenly started going a little awry in his life. As though he was wandering through a Laurel and Hardy film. Pianos really did fall out of windows near him. Cars mysteriously failed to stop at crossings.

Nervous, Harrison decided the best, and certainly the

safest thing would be to sell it after all, but to a private bidder. Let them deal with the Russians and the Americans. The offer he received was so ludicrous, he'd said yes.

When his sudden, embarrassing riches were merely impending, his only problem was how to quantify them. He'd idly flicked through a newspaper, and noticed the headlines about the recent sale of a hitherto unknown Van Gogh, the kind of art treasure that only obscenely wealthy people sold to each other to convince themselves that they were cultured people. He looked at the painting reproduced splotchily in newsprint and thought, 'I'll be worth exactly that.'

It was a funny feeling. On the one hand his life's worth equated exactly to one of the treasures of the world. On the other hand he was worth exactly as much as a sheet of pasteboard daubed with cheap colours by a lunatic between one hangover and the next.

He kept staring at the picture. He could not work out how he felt about it. Harrison had never really been moved by art. He'd paid money to go to museums and look at things. But all the time he'd been preoccupied by everything else. The perfume of the woman next to him, the way his left foot always ached more than his right, the distant smell of the café, the hilarious faces of people pretending to be transported by aesthetic rapture. The pictures themselves did nothing for Harrison other than fill up the walls. What were they for? Come to think of it, what was *he* for?

Now that he was suddenly and embarrassingly rich and wondering what to do with his life, Harrison Mandel found himself pondering art and pondering what he was missing out on. An idea struck him. Surely there was only one place in the world to find out about art?

Nikolai couldn't possibly eat any more. No matter how hard both his host and the waiter pressed him, he waved away, with a good-hearted show of reluctance, both a final sorbet and another round of the cheeseboard.

His host topped up his wine personally, smiling with delight at his appreciation of the vintage. The sommelier rushed over to suggest a no doubt delightful dessert wine, but Nikolai, to much good-hearted laughter by all, waved the fellow away.

Everyone agreed he had acquitted himself excellently. Praise was heaped on his judicious choices from the menu, and a few regretful chuckles were had about roads not taken. Ah well, all agreed, there'd be plenty of time. Maxim's wasn't going anywhere.

His host took care of the frankly extraordinary bill and then went off to fetch their car. Slowly, Nikolai heaved his considerable bulk off the banquette, nodded to the waiters like old friends, and then waddled slowly over to the window to savour once more that magnificent view.

His host returned, and they shook on the deal, before Hermann, that exquisitely dressed chauffeur, handed him into the car. Of course it would be a Rolls Royce Silver Ghost, of course it would be.

He settled his head back against the reassuring leather upholstery and marvelled again as Haussmann's floodlit boulevards whipped by.

Yes, thought Professor Kerensky, I'm going to enjoy working in Paris.

If it hadn't been for Swansea, none of it would have happened.

Some agents in the Department could push back their chairs after one drink too many, ruefully recalling their nemeses, and they would talk of Geneva, Monte Carlo, Tangier and Berlin. Names you could conjure with. Locales that spelt allure, style, romance and tragedy. In the world of the Department, it was all right to fail if you did so somewhere with subtitles.

But Duggan? His downfall was Swansea. Ironically, he had never even been to Swansea. But that's where the Department's expenses desk sat. Probably on its own in a car park. As much as Duggan ever imagined anything, he imagined it rained a lot in Swansea.

Duggan had had a hot lead, a trail that pointed to a shipping container in Ghent. He knew he had to get there quickly before the evidence vanished for ever. This was the kind of urgency that required a helicopter, a private jet, or even a hovercraft. But that desk in Swansea had its limits, and those limits were a cheap hotel and an early ferry.

If only, Duggan thought later, they could have allowed him another two pounds. He could have got a hotel that wasn't so abysmally cheap. Then he could at least have had a proper night's sleep. Every cheap hotel, along with a thin pillow and a chipped tooth glass, includes someone called Barry, who pops in at 3 a.m. to shout out his own name and slam some doors. If only Barry could have done that at 5 a.m., then Duggan wouldn't have missed the early sailing. As it was, Duggan slept through his alarm and was left to prowl the harbour miserably for hours, becoming briefly convinced he was being tailed in Woolworths, before passing some time in a café where they served you your tea with a greasy thumbprint on the mug.

Duggan had always been a man of limited emotions, but later, on the evening ferry crossing, he found himself toying with some new ones. His constant companions Anger and Annoyance were shuffling over to make room for Apprehension. He kept checking his watch, brushing aside the sleeve of his crumpled raincoat and staring at the dial. Time was doing two things simultaneously – it was crawling by very slowly but it was also racing past. The ferry lurched through the waves to Ghent with all the hurry of a Sunday rail replacement bus service. Meanwhile, on the distant docks a shipping container could be emptied at any moment.

Inside the container was the smoking gun, the hot potato, the reward for the last eighteen months of gruelling work. Work that had taken him nowhere near Geneva, Monte Carlo, Tangier or Berlin. He'd fought his way into, and out of, an auction house in Aberdeen, and traded blows with toughs in a dull town in Norway. He'd made a lot of trouble, but Duggan knew that trouble was how you got noticed. If you were walking into a spider's web, he'd told his chief, you'd best do it as an angry wasp.

His chief had nodded seriously at that and told him that his heart was in the right place but his foot was best off in his mouth.

Finally, Ghent loomed on the horizon like a hangover. The sun was setting over the harbour's unpromising skyline. The air was turning cold and some rain had popped over from Swansea. Duggan shivered, pulled up his raincoat and made his way to the docks. He hurried through the maze of iron boxes, guided by the tip-off he'd torn out of that terrified oculist. Was that really only yesterday? He glanced again at his watch, rubbing at an egg stain on his sleeve. It was fine. He would be just in time. It was always about time, this job.

There were a couple of guards on duty at the dock. Of course there were. He made swift work of them. Maybe they were in the gang's pockets, maybe they weren't, but, at the end of a miserable day, Duggan didn't care. He didn't have time to find out and hitting them made him feel better.

He didn't linger over the padlock either. He carried tools with him that were as useful for ironmongery as they were for interviewing suspects. As he unlatched the door,

Duggan's mind tried out another new emotion. Trepidation. No, he didn't like it.

If luck was on his side and hard work was to be rewarded, then inside this container would be everything he'd need. Its contents had been gradually moved here from all over Europe. People had died getting each object here. This shipping container was one of the most audacious clearing houses in history, and, if Duggan was right, even with that missed ferry, he'd got here just in time. With luck, he'd even have caught them red-handed.

The door swung open. The container was empty. Apart, that was, from an empty champagne bottle sat on the floor. Resting against it was a note, also, no doubt, completely lacking in fingerprints. The note read: 'Sorry to have missed you.'

At the lazy end of time there was a box. People have variously described this box as small and blue or vast and white, depending on how they looked at it. An estate agent once described it as deceptively spacious before bursting into tears. A mechanic in the spacedock of Centrum IV once had a look at the engines and was still scratching his head and sucking air through his jaws several years later. A scientist had called it impossible. A philosopher had called it annoying. Genghis Khan had thrown an army at it with little success. His grandson had won it at backgammon. It had flown through black holes, it had crashed into bus stops, but right now, it was idling.

Inside the box was a complicated hexagonal mushroom where computing and thought met in a series of wonky switches and some big, red, juicy buttons. A hand emerged from underneath the mushroom holding a spanner. Flinging it carelessly to one side, the hand hastily edged its way past some dials (all either at 'Zero' or 'Danger!'), flirted with some switches and then settled on the juiciest and reddest of the buttons. The hand formed itself into a fist and thumped the button heartily, as if it were part of a fairground game.

And, in many ways, it was. The Randomiser was, at heart, the most important fruit machine the universe had ever known. A single press would fling the little-blue big-white box somewhere and somewhen in the universe, completely at random and without a thought for the chaotic consequences which would inevitably follow.

For a single moment the box hung perfectly still in space and time, paused between here and now. And then, with a triumphant laugh at dimensions collapsing and rules being torn apart, the box pirouetted away.

The TARDIS was on its way.

CHAPTER TWO
ISN'T IT
NICE?

'Nice, isn't it?'

The overheard phrase made Harrison Mandel nod unconsciously. He'd been about to join in with the crowd of sightseers who were all outdoing each other in superlatives (especially the Americans). Really, he thought, the Eiffel Tower was just very high up.

The journey in the jolting, crowded lift had been as mildly terrifying as a Ferris wheel, one that smelt of French tobacco and diesel oil. The tower itself was thunderingly solid but also spoke volumes about the Parisian spirit of defiance. Put up in a hurry for the 1889 World Fair, it had lingered magnificently. It had survived two world wars and quite a few letter-writing campaigns. The criss-cross lattice of ironwork dominated the Paris skyline, but with an air, just an air, that at any moment it might hoist up its stumpy little legs and stomp off to bring some glamour to Bruges.

The thing about the view from the Eiffel Tower was that it gave you a perfect vista across Paris, across the orderly boulevards, the haphazard jumble of palaces and squares and even a few peeps towards the disappointing humdrumness of the suburbs that, by mutual agreement, left the tourists alone. The one thing you couldn't see from the Eiffel Tower was the Eiffel Tower, which seemed a bit of a shame. If ever a building had been designed to be seen from a great height, it was that one. The best you could do was peer down through its legs, feel a bit giddy, and then go and buy some postcards.

Harrison stood next to a gasping tour party. The Italians were terribly excited, a Japanese couple treated the occasion to a couple of flashbulbs, and the Canadians said that, actually, they had a tower of their own that was a bit higher, but no one was interested. Harrison hung back, squinting down at Elena. He'd bumped into her at a party (now he was very rich, he always seemed to be at parties) and she'd instantly spotted how miserable he was. Elena was everything that Harrison wasn't. She was confident, glamorous and demonstrative. She'd wrapped him in a hug and said how sorry she was that he seemed so down. This surprised him. After all, he thought, I don't look that bad, do I? 'This is one of my greatest friends,' she'd announced to two bankers and an aspidistra, 'The poor darling needs cheering up.'

Paris had followed, much to Harrison's bemusement. He didn't actually think that Elena was one of his greatest friends. She'd always seemed very nice, in a hugs and scarves indoors way, but he remained unconvinced that she had actually ever given him a second thought. She was beautiful, intense and exciting. Harrison was more of a punctuation mark, and not one of the ones that invited comment.

'Come see me in Paris, darling,' she'd enthused, 'And I'll show you Life.' He hoped, he really hoped, that her offer wasn't to do with his money. Was she hoping for marriage? He'd nervously raised the subject over dinner on his first night and she'd looked, for a moment, disappointed and cross. She'd reached over the table and tapped him on the nose (she was the kind of person who tapped people on the nose, whether or not there were wine glasses in the way). 'Harrison, yes, you have an awful lot of money. But you have no excitement. *Rien*. Why should I marry to be bored?' Harrison felt both relieved and a little disappointed, but she laughed that wonderful laugh that said that everything would be all right.

They took a boat trip down the Seine, gliding between floodlit arches and he'd ventured to tell her it was heavenly. She'd tapped him on the nose again. 'You don't mean that. *Bien sûr*, you are enjoying it. It is pretty. But you are not...' She paused, her arms trying to find the right word somewhere in the warm night air. 'You are not enraptured. The deal is I will keep showing you all of Paris until you see something that you find truly beautiful. *Non?*'

So here he was, stood on top of the Eiffel Tower. He could see, a long way down, Elena, reading a book and waiting for him. She'd declined to come up with him, declaring that while Parisians adored their Tower, actually going up it was a little *gauche*. He thought she'd have been disappointed if he'd told her he had found it delightful.

Harrison glanced over at the two people next to him, every inch in love, if not with each other then certainly with life itself. They were both grinning like schoolchildren. Actually, she was dressed exactly like a schoolgirl, with a short navy skirt, silk blouse tied with a red ribbon, and a neat straw hat perched on golden hair that was on very good terms with the breeze.

He was the kind of man you could only meet in Paris, with a long coat, an even longer scarf, and a lot of curling hair. The overall impression was of a man who had been completely knitted. Apart from the teeth. You could see a lot of the teeth because the man was always laughing.

If only, thought Harrison, that was me.

'Nice, isn't it?' the Doctor said, waiting for a reaction from Romana.

The Doctor spent a lot of time waiting for a reaction from Romana. Sometimes even K-9, his robot dog, could be more enthusiastic. Romana and the Doctor were both Time Lords from the planet Gallifrey. He'd long ago left behind that world of august domes and hushed cloisters, running away to see the universe, accidentally saving most of it as he went. Romana had joined him fairly recently (was it a few weeks or a few years?). A mere stripling of 125 she had come to him fresh out of the Academy and still had a lot of unlearning to do.

Initially he'd worried that Romana wasn't enjoying travelling with him at all. She even occasionally referred to their trips as 'missions' which made his teeth itch. 'Romana,' he'd said to her, 'there are far too many people who take the universe too seriously. Don't be one of them.' She'd simply nodded, very seriously.

She'd kept travelling with him and he was beginning to worry glumly that she wasn't enjoying it one bit. Normally when his companions weren't having fun they'd tell him so quite brutally. Often by getting married or, in one case, wandering off halfway through a rather thrilling battle with a supercomputer in the Post Office Tower. But no, Romana stuck with him. Terribly serious, terribly efficient, but just a little bit of a pill.

And then, one day, just to prove him wrong, she'd regenerated for the fun of it. The Doctor had regenerated many times and for a variety of reasons (one day he feared meeting someone who'd list them all in order), but he'd never dared change bodies for a laugh. That had rather impressed him. It was one thing to be able to renew one's body at a time of deadly crisis. It was quite another to take the legs in a bit. In their game of pan-dimensional one-upmanship, Romana might just have won.

Worse, she had regenerated so easily. Whenever the Doctor did it, it was the closest he'd ever got to having a hangover. He'd spend days thrashing around feeling sorry for himself (mental note: next time, must try a bacon sandwich). Romana had regenerated with barely a shrug, before trotting off to defeat the Daleks.

That was the problem with this new Romana. Even the outfits were amazing. Suddenly, for the first time in his many lives, the Doctor rather feared that he was no longer the cool one.

Which was why he'd been hoping to land somewhere impressive. He'd felt a tiny bit of a thrill when the Randomiser had picked Paris. Never fails.

'Well, I think it's nice,' the Doctor repeated, hopefully.

Romana looked around and nodded. The Doctor's hearts sank just a little towards his boots.

'Well, it's not quite as you described it,' Romana said eventually, with a smile that could just have been polite.

'Oh?' the Doctor said carefully. The TARDIS was parked around the corner. With a bit of luck they could be back there in ten minutes and on their way somewhere else. Yes, that was it. Call it a misfire, blame the drift compensators and try again. Paris. Bad idea.

Romana looked around again, sniffing the air, and her cautious smile broadened. 'No. It's so much better.'

That was a relief. 'It's the only place in the universe where you can truly relax,' said the Doctor, truly relaxing.

'It's marvellous!' Romana sniffed the air again, getting a lot from it. Petrol fumes, wood smoke, rain on pavements, and, more than that, animals and vegetables being roasted over minerals. She exhaled. 'Ah, that bouquet!'

'What Paris has,' the Doctor said, warming to his subject, 'is an ethos, a life, a…'

'Bouquet?' suggested Romana, being genuinely helpful.

'A spirit all of its own that must be savoured. Like a wine, it has a…'

'Bouquet?'

'It has a bouquet.' Having fished around and failed to find a better word, the Doctor borrowed hers and pronounced it definitively. 'A bouquet. Exactly. Just like a good wine,' He couldn't help offering a bit of seasoned advice. One traveller to another. 'Of course, you have to pick one of the vintage years…'

'What year is this?' asked Romana, a suspicion forming in her mind. 'I forgot to check.'

'Ah yes, well…' Caught out, the Doctor narrowed his eyes at a passing seagull. 'It's 1979 actually. More of a table wine, shall we say? The randomiser is a useful device but it lacks true discrimination.' For a moment he was lost in surprisingly fond memories of the French Revolution and Robot Napoleon the Twelfth. Then he grinned, a broad Welcome Mat of a grin. 'Shall we sip it and see?'

'I'd be delighted.'

Turning away from the view, Romana couldn't help smiling, partly with relief. The Doctor's definition of a 'vintage year' undoubtedly meant alien invasion, several bloodbaths and an exploding stately home. Just for once she could do without all that. Just for once, it would be nice to land somewhere and just have fun. What was it that humans called it? A holiday. Yes, that was it.

'Shall we take the lift or fly?'

The Doctor sucked a finger and stuck it in the air, testing the wind speed. It had been a while, but, well… He glanced around at the tourists they were sharing the viewing platform with. The Japanese photographers, the chattering Italians, the slightly glum-looking Englishman. Well, yes, it might cheer him up. 'Let's not be ostentatious,' he cautioned Romana.

'All right, then,' she nodded. 'Let's fly.'

Tempting. But no. 'That would look silly.' The Doctor grinned again. 'We'll take the lift.'

So, they went and stood inside a box that was, for once, exactly the same size inside as outside.

'Where are we going?' asked Romana.

'Are you speaking philosophically or geographically?' The Doctor watched as the ground, that lovely exciting ground of Paris slid gently closer.

'Philosophically.'

'Then we're going to lunch,' he said firmly.

'Lunch!' Romana repeated, giggling happily. They so rarely got a chance to stop for food. Her last meal had been what the TARDIS food machine had sworn blind wasn't a British Rail cheese and pickle sandwich, but Romana had remained unconvinced.

'I know a place that does a bouillabaisse that'll curl your hair.' That is, thought the Doctor, if it was still there. Hmm. It had been one of the few sensible recommendations Catherine de Medici had ever given him.

'Bouillabaisse.' Romana lit up. 'Yum yum.'

The Doctor and Romana were very firmly on holiday.

Most people agreed that Count Scarlioni was the most charming man they'd ever met. Even those who died during the encounter.

He could fill a room with laughter, gliding through it with a nod here, a wink there, and a beam for everyone. Hostesses clamoured to have him at salons. Ambassadors yearned for him at receptions. Curators begged him to gallery openings. And he'd always come, lighting up the occasion with that ever-present smile of his, which *Paris Match* had once called 'the second most famous smile in Paris'. This was a man, everyone agreed, who really loved people.

The one person who did not find Count Scarlioni charming was the Count himself. Sometimes he'd wander the vast corridors of his château, touching the ancient art treasures, the rare and beautiful *objets*, the priceless bric-a-brac, and, when he was absolutely sure he was quite alone, he'd pause in front of a mirror and look at himself. At his almost perfectly handsome face. At that smile.

When she'd first met him, the Countess had asked him about that smile. It was as if he was in on some glorious private joke. She wanted so desperately to share it. He'd leaned forward across the table and told her:

'I'm the greatest art thief the world has ever known.'

He'd laughed. And she'd laughed too. But something in his eye told her that, audacious, daring and true as that was, that wasn't quite the reason for his smile.

Most people wondered what they were put on this Earth to do. Count Scarlioni knew. The problem was, it was quite fiddly.

The Count lived in one of the most unique addresses in Paris. At the edge of the Marais, in between two scrupulously neat boulevards showing off Baron Haussman's work at its finest, was a handsome estate. Over every inch of it sprawled a château. Not the slightly boxy stripped down *Hôtel Particulier* versions that most nobles made do with for their *pied à terre*, but a full-sized palace, high walls ranged with turrets and balustrades. Mazes filled the courtyards, peacocks strolled in the grounds, and deer were sometimes glimpsed among the trees. History had failed to notice the Château – the Germans had failed to occupy it, floods hadn't touched it, the mobs of the Revolution had somehow missed it. The Château was so huge that, even though *tout Paris* had been to parties there, no one dared claim to have seen all of it.

Some people called it the House of Questions, because there were so many questions about it. When had it been built? How had it survived for so long? Who were its previous owners? Who, really, was its present owner? And, of course, why did no one who lived there ever have any answers?

A particularly poisonous gossip columnist had once cornered Count Scarlioni at a party and confided that she, and she alone, had coined the phrase. How simply wonderful wasn't it that all of society had taken it up! How wonderful, the Count had agreed with a thin smile. Curiously, when the columnist vanished soon afterwards, no one had asked any questions.

A question that a few people had had answered over the years was 'What were the cellars like?' The answers had varied over the years. For once, the tiresome clutter of bottles and leftovers from the Inquisition had been cleared a little to one side. Everything makes way for progress, including the Count's wine collection. The space was now taken up by a uniquely powerful and very large computer and an awful lot of technology. In contrast to the beautiful dust gathering on the exquisite bottles of wine, the equipment was gleamingly new. It sang to itself, reels of computer tape taking up the melody while pinwheel printers handled the chorus and an oscilloscope chipped in with a merry descant.

In pathetic contrast to brand new and singing with happiness, Professor Kerensky slumped somewhere in the middle of it. His thin, frail figure tottered unsteadily between the banks of equipment. Occasionally he'd grab hold of something expensive just for support. He'd rapidly developed a quite reasonable terror of his employer whilst simultaneously being exhilarated and exhausted by the work.

Today, Kerensky was almost at breaking point, and had reached it courtesy of some paperwork. To be precise, a set of bills printed in red and with FINAL DEMAND stamped on them. It had initially amazed him that he could receive post in his basement. Then it had horrified him as every envelope served only to make him more miserable.

The one good thing about the last few months was the weight loss. If my doctor could see me now, Kerenskey told himself as he cut yet another new notch in the frayed leather belt. Then again, there was the exhaustion, and also the vitamin D deficiency that came from never leaving the cellars. I think I may just surprise everyone by dying of scurvy, he thought.

Today was the day of Kerensky's last stand. He was going to make the Count listen to reason. This was proving harder than he'd thought. The Count had many years of experience sailing through parties ignoring awkward questions, and he didn't see the point in breaking the habit now.

If Kerensky looked like a half-dead morsel brought in by the Château's cat, then Count Carlos Scarlioni himself provided a glorious contrast. He always did. He was a man for whom the words suave and louche had been invented. His face was handsome, thin and quite excitingly cruel. His hair was blonde. His tight suit told you exactly what expensive tailoring looked like, whilst also being in a shade of white that dared you to pour wine on it. His face, almost like a mask, was set in a permanent smile. Kerensky had at first found that smile charming. Now he found it terrifying.

The worst thing about the Count's smile was that it never ever reached the eyes. His eyes focused on you with the cold accuracy of a microscope or the sights of a gun, and let the rest of the face get on with the smiling. Today, that smile said that it was thoroughly bored.

'But…' These days Kerensky began most sentences with *but*. The Count found it a tiresome habit that he really should be bothered to correct. 'I can proceed no further, Count! Research costs money. If you want results we must have money.'

Money? Ah yes, thought the Count. Who had invented money in the first place? Well, that had been a mistake. Here was Kerensky waving some pieces of paper at him and the only way to make him shut up (short of shooting him) was to give him some more pieces of paper. How utterly dull.

'I assure you, Professor…' Count Scarlioni spoke with a drawl that told you how much better educated he was than you. It was a voice that came with a mind that was already firmly made up. 'Money is no problem.'

Rather like Kerensky himself, that wouldn't work any more. 'But, so you tell me, Count, so you tell me every day!' He waved the sheaf of bills around again, warming to his subject as though he were delivering a lecture at the university. He paused then, thinking fondly of the formal dinners and less fondly of his colleagues. He imagined they were all wondering how they could possibly cope without him. 'Money is no problem? What do you want me to do about these equipment invoices? Write "money is no problem" across them and send them back?'

Would that work? wondered the Count briefly. He leaned back against a piece of equipment which, judging by Kerensky's horrified expression, really shouldn't be leaned against. Good. Languidly he reached into his jacket pocket, removing a bundle of paper that had been causing a rather irritating bulge. It was as fat as a cookbook. 'Will a million francs ease the "immediate cash flow problem"?' Like most things the Count said, you could hear the ironic quotation marks. He peeled off just enough to render the bulge less annoying and handed them casually over to Kerensky. He resisted the impulse to fold them into paper aeroplanes. Now, that would be fun.

The tiny fool's face lit up as if the Count had done something not boring. He even made a strange little clucking noise. You could always tell people who'd never got used to being around money. They grew so tiresomely excited by the sight of it. 'But yes Count! Yes! That will help admirably!' Struck by a mundane thought, Kerensky paused and waggled a finger at him. The Count toyed with biting it off. 'But I will shortly need a great deal more.'

Just like a peasant. If you gave them bread they only came back and asked for more. Much better to just let them starve. 'Of course Professor, of course.' He twitched his smile up a notch. 'Nothing must stand in the way of the Work!'

He strode away to the corner of the laboratory, his hands tapping idly away on the side of the computer before making the tiniest of alterations to a dial. It annoyed Kerensky when he did that. It annoyed him even more that, invariably, it turned out to be right. Kerensky had long ago reached the horrid realisation that Count Scarlioni simply employed him because he couldn't be bothered doing it himself. It pulled him up. He, Kerensky, was an acclaimed genius, fought over by universities, wined and dined by conference organisers. He was a man whose opinion mattered, whose contribution to science was vital. Here, in this miserable cave in Paris he was about to make a breakthrough that would change the world for ever. And yet, and yet, he felt

40

as if he'd been hired to tidy an overgrown garden while the owner sat dozing in a deckchair with a long, cool drink. What would that drink be? His mind wandered dreamily away.

Yawning, Count Scarlioni reached a rope pull set into the wall and tugged it. Because the Count was in the cellar, it was answered immediately. The door at the top of the stone staircase creaked open and Hermann, the Count's darkly suited butler descended.

Kerensky had never dared strike up a conversation with Hermann. The man had a cultured, but recognisably German accent. His shoulders were broad, his hair had once been blonde, he had an athletic build which was untroubled by his advanced age. Kerensky had made a few educated guesses about how Hermann had spent his late teens and had swiftly decided against confirming them. He did not enjoy being alone in a room with Hermann.

Whereas the Count greeted Hermann like an old and valued friend, watching with delight as the timid figure of the Professor scuttled away to fuss around his computer.

Hermann approached, bowing. 'Your Excellency?'

The Count patted the slimmed-down bulge in his jacket as though it were a regrettably empty cigarette case. 'The Gainsborough didn't fetch enough,' he murmured. 'I think we'll have to sell one of the bibles.'

'Sir?' Hermann queried.

'Yes, the Gutenberg.' The Count was unable to keep a trace of sadness out of his voice.

'I think we should tread carefully.' Hermann was one of the few people who ever spoke plainly to the Count. Never excitingly, but always wisely. Hermann had, after all, quite a lot of experience in dealing with art. 'It would not be in our interests to draw too much attention to ourselves. Another rash of priceless art treasures on the market...' Hermann rubbed his neatly trimmed beard with regret. His lowered tone managed to convey that he thought it both careless and also tasteless.

Hermann was the only man the Count would take such criticism from. 'Yes. I know Hermann, I know. Sell it…' He paused, and flicked his smile into a grin. 'Discreetly.'

'Discreetly, sir?' Hermann raised both eyebrows. 'Sell a Gutenberg Bible discreetly?'

Hermann had a point. The Gutenberg Bible was the first bestseller in the history of publishing. Up until the 1450s bibles had been laboriously hand-doodled by bored, cold monks. Gutenberg changed all that. His were printed. It was the most exciting thing to happen to the Bible since it got a sequel.

These days the Gutenbergs were so rare that even the discovery of a stray page was a sensation. Only twenty-one complete copies were known to exist. Nestling next to the teasmade on the Count's bedside table was a twenty-second.

The Count mustered a noble smile. 'Well, sell it as discreetly as possible, Hermann. Just do it, will you?'

Knowing better than to argue, Hermann bowed. 'Yes, sir, of course, sir.' And climbed the stone stairs, closing the cellar door behind him. Because the Count was still down there, his exit was not followed by the click of the lock.

The regrettable bit of the day dealt with, the Count turned back to Kerensky. Neither knowing nor caring what a Gutenberg Bible was, the old fool was still burying himself in the wiring of a circuit board. Looked at from a few paces away, it was actually quite impressive what Kerensky had managed to put together. Not how he would have done it himself, but then, so few things were. The Count rubbed his hands together, his mood approaching glee. 'Good Professor, excellent. I do hope we are now ready to perform the next stage of the experiment.'

Concentrating on his circuit board, Kerensky entirely missed the vague threat. 'In two minutes, Count. Just two minutes,' he muttered, waving a hand in the Count's direction.

The Count drummed his fingers against a work bench, mildly impatient. A more patient man would have said, if you've waited so long for something, a couple more minutes cannot hurt. But the Count had long ago run out of patience.

CHAPTER THREE
A PAINTING
LIKE...

They never did find that place that did the bouillabaisse, but Romana didn't mind. The Doctor claimed that the streets of Paris were like the rooms of the TARDIS, always rearranging themselves when you weren't looking. Romana wasn't convinced about the analogy. She did think the Paris Metro could teach the Doctor's ship a few things about arriving late but stylishly.

Stepping into one of the Metro's stations was like running into the mouth of a metal Medusa, her copper green tentacles spun up into a ticket hall. The trains themselves wailed and hooted like busy behemoths as they raced between stations called things like Marcadet-Poissonniers, Tuileries and Trocadéro. Names that were so much fun the TARDIS's telepathic circuits simply refused to translate them.

Outside, the boulevards stretched before them, clogged with motorcars honking to each other. Only Paris, marvelled Romana, could make a traffic jam look festive.

Each car was a little tin sculpture, eschewing efficiency for sweeping lines, fussy details and cheery colours. Every road was blocked as though the cars had poured onto them in a tearing hurry to go somewhere and then decided 'but where, where is better than here?' before settling happily in for the long haul.

The leafy pavements were a delightful muddle of trees, dogs, cobbles and footworn steps that wound up to other streets, to cathedrals, or simply to a door with a cat cleaning itself slowly in the sun. The Doctor told Romana that they'd arrived at that blissful point between the invention of drains and wheelie luggage, so the streets of Paris would be at their best, and for once, he wasn't even fibbing slightly.

All in all, she was enjoying their holiday enormously. They dashed down the Champs-Élysées, for once running somewhere without deadly robots in pursuit. They considered taking in an exhibition ('Three million years of human history' said the over-dramatic poster. 'Poppycock,' said the Doctor). They stopped off at a bookshop, looking for Ernest Hemingway (the Doctor was evasive whether it was a book by him or the actual author). There was a poetry reading going on outside. Seemingly recognised by the owner, the Doctor couldn't resist a pressing invitation to give a performance of a Betelgeuse love song to rather polite applause. 'Don't drink the wine,' hissed the Doctor as drinks were passed around in unusual metal goblets which turned out to be tuna tins.

Finally they found themselves climbing the steps to Montmartre. The domes of the Sacré-Cœur smiled down on an impossibly quaint square filled with impossibly quaint cafés. Somehow they picked one and Romana found herself, for the first time in her life, forming the thought 'Quick bite to eat and then a spot of shopping later?'

The Doctor was in similarly joyous mood.

'It's taken years off you,' Romana confided. 'You barely look 750.'

He'd settled down in a quiet corner of the café, banging his legs up onto a chair and leaning far far back in his own. As a waiter wandered past, the Doctor murmured something which the waiter could not possibly have heard, and yet he came back automatically with a carafe of red wine, two glasses and some bread. Ignoring the wine, the Doctor pulled the book he'd just bought from his pocket, cut the leaves with a butter knife and flicked idly through it.

'Any good?' asked Romana, doing the French crossword.

'Not bad, bit boring in the middle.' The Doctor put the book back into his pocket and peered vaguely at Romana's crossword. He suggested a couple of answers, and, when they turned out to be wrong, helped himself to bread, and made a loud harrumph. The Doctor often made this noise. Usually it was the prelude to a pronouncement of doom, or to a confession about a small rewiring disaster. But, just this once, it was the terribly happy harrumph of a truly contented man.

The Doctor had the look of a man contemplating a nap. The café itself, like much of Paris, felt like an old friend who hadn't bothered tidying up when you'd popped round. Warm, welcoming and a slight smell of wet dog in the air.

The Doctor waved away the returning waiter, unfolded a hat and placed it over his face. Seeing him like this, Romana could barely believe that, when they'd first met, she'd found him a little intimidating. Also, worrying. It was still a bit frightening to realise that the fate of the universe was quite often in the hands of a man with no formal qualifications. Well, none worth counting. The Doctor tried out a gentle snore, seemed satisfied with the results, and produced another one.

Romana smiled and poured herself a glass of wine. She'd

heard so much about wine. She wondered what it would be like.

'Don't move,' muttered the Doctor from underneath his hat.

Romana froze, worried. Normally when the Doctor said that one of them (usually the Doctor) had stepped on a landmine or pulled a trip wire. 'Why?' she asked. 'What's the matter?'

'You might destroy a priceless work of art,' was the Doctor's puzzling response.

'What?'

The Doctor slid the hat from his face, speaking urgently to her from the corner of his mouth. 'That man over there.' The last time he'd used that tone, Davros had been threatening to unravel the universe. 'No! Don't look!' warned the Doctor.

'What's he doing?'

'Sketching you,' came the exciting answer.

Romana couldn't stop herself from turning around. As she did so, her sleeve caught her glass, knocking wine over the table. As she sprang to her feet to try and sort out the mess, she caught a brief glimpse of a man in a serious jumper, sat across from them in the café. He was scribbling furiously with charcoal on a pad of art paper.

He glanced up from his pad and noticed that Romana, instead of sitting serenely in her chair, was now scrubbing the floor with a napkin. A scowl crossed his face. Romana scrambled to get back into her chair, but she was too late. The man was already on his feet. Angrily, he tore the sheet from his pad, crumpling it up and throwing it at Romana's feet as he stomped from the café in disgust, without paying his bill.

'I told you not to look round.' Well, she'd not missed the Doctor's I-told-you-so tone.

'But I just wanted to see!' Romana, left with nothing but a dirty wet napkin, felt miserable.

'Well, it's too late, he's gone now,' squinting, the Doctor tossed a handful of coins expertly onto the artist's table.

'Pity. I wonder what he thought I looked like,' mused Romana.

She and the Doctor had the same thought at the same time. 'Well, he threw the drawing over there, so we can see how far he got.' The Doctor finished the sentence, feeling that he'd missed something.

Well, for one thing, the artist was sat back at his table, sketching away. Romana's glass of wine was also resolutely not spilt. She was staring at it in puzzled alarm.

'What?' she said as the Doctor spoke in a gabble.

'Romana, he's there again. The artist! We just saw him walk out but he's still there.'

Startled Romana spun round in her chair, knocking over her glass again as she did so. Hearing the noise, the artist glanced up from his pad and noticed that Romana was staring at him, mouth agape. A scowl crossed his face. He jumped to his feet, tore the sheet out of his pad, crumpling it up and throwing it at Romana's feet as he stomped from the café in disgust, without paying his bill.

Romana let the wine get on with spilling itself while she stared at where the artist had been. 'Doctor, what's happening?' she asked, slowly and carefully. The answer would probably be wrong, but it would at least be somewhere to start.

'I don't know,' the Doctor was shaking his head, trying to clear it, 'It was as if time slipped a groove for a second.'

'Hmm,' Romana said, bending down to pick up the drawing, saving it from the advancing puddle of wine. 'I'm going to have a look,' she ventured as she unfolded the crumpled sheet of paper. And stopped.

The Doctor stared at the sheet of paper.

Romana stared at the sheet of paper.

'Well,' said the Doctor after a bit too much of a pause, 'for a portrait of a Time Lady, that's not at all a bad likeness.'

The artist had drawn Romana with skill, getting her hat, her shoulders and even her hair beautifully correct. But he'd replaced her face with the shattered dial of a clock.

'That's extraordinary.' Romana smoothed out the creases of the picture.

'Isn't it?' the Doctor agreed casually.

A trace of worry crept into Romana's voice. 'I wonder why he did it like that. The fractured face of the clock.'

'Yes,' the Doctor nodded. 'It looks almost like he was trying to draw...' He stumbled and then found the phrase: 'Trying to draw a crack in time.'

Kerensky was, for once, too excited to feel tired. The expensive equipment in his laboratory was finally working. Perhaps not working properly, but definitely on the road to properly. If he could bear to stay here maybe another six months, then there was a chance of a real breakthrough. It would be expensive, but worth it. The Count had deep pockets. Kerensky stood back, marvelling at the machinery he'd built. They're going to name cities after me, he thought. He had so nearly done it.

'Time, Count, it will take time.'

'Time, time, time...' Count Scarlioni was thinking of anything but the future. He patted the Professor almost fondly on the shoulder. They'd nearly done it. He straightened up, tidying the corner of his expensive silk cravat. 'Nevertheless, Professor, a very impressive, if flawed, demonstration,' He watched the fool's face fall a little and cheered up. 'I am relying on you to make very fast progress now. The fate of many people is in our hands.'

Kerensky, clearly thinking of his own destiny, muttered solemnly, 'The world will have much to thank you for.'

'It will Professor, it will indeed.' For once, the Count's smile was purely for his own amusement. He scratched idly at a spot over his right eye which had, strangely, begun to itch. 'Now, how soon before we can run the next test?'

'The next one, Count?' Kerensky looked suddenly miserable. 'Well…' He ran some calculations through his exhausted brain. Allowing for a few hours of sleep, and some rewiring maybe –

'I want to see it today.' Count Scarlioni was very firm, his smile dangerous.

'Today?' Kerensky stared at a fused circuit. Why, to mend that alone would take…

'Yes, today.' The dangerous smile became exactly thirteen per cent more dangerous and twenty per cent firmer.

Kerensky was as baffled as he was concerned. 'Count, I think this is wonderful work, but I do not understand this obsessive urgency.'

For a moment it looked as though Count Scarlioni was going to give him a proper answer. Instead he tossed the Professor's words back at him. 'Time, Professor. It is all a matter of time.'

'There's something the matter with time,' the Doctor said.

Romana didn't answer. She was looking sadly at the sketch.

Feeling in need of a breath of fresh air, they had moved to sit outside the café. The air no longer seemed quite so warm, the afternoon no longer quite so welcoming.

As the chill spread, there were fewer people drinking out in the square. The exception was provided by two Englishman sharing what was clearly not their first bottle of wine. They were talking about how terrible it was working in television. One kept glancing over at the Doctor and shaking his head.

The puzzling drawing sat on the table between the Doctor and Romana. The Doctor was staring at it. I know where this is going, thought Romana sadly. The Doctor opened his mouth to speak. Oh, here we go.

'I think something is the matter with time,' he repeated.

Romana glanced up at the sky. It looked like rain.

'Didn't you feel it?' the Doctor pressed on.

'Well, just a twinge,' Romana admitted. 'I didn't like it.'

Just a twinge? Really? It had felt like falling off a rollercoaster and then back onto it again. An explanation presented itself to the Doctor. 'It must be because I've crossed the time fields so often. No one else seemed to notice anything at all.' He gave Romana a friendly grin. 'You and I exist in a special relationship to time. Perpetual outsiders.'

Definitely rain, thought Romana. In about two point three one minutes. 'Oh, don't be so portentous,' she said.

'Portentous?' The Doctor stabbed the drawing with his finger. 'Well, what do you make of that then?'

Romana ducked the question, wondering whether Paris sold umbrellas. 'At least on Gallifrey we can capture a good likeness. Computers can draw.'

Sometimes Romana could be so naïve! 'What? Computer pictures? You sit in Paris and you talk of computer pictures?' The Doctor sprang to his feet, folding the drawing away in a pocket (we'll never see that again, thought Romana) and strode through the square, startling a taxi driver. 'Come on,' his voice boomed over a car horn. 'I'll show you some real pictures done by real people.'

That was it with the Doctor. He'd only just convinced her there was a problem worth investigating, and now he'd completely forgotten all about it. Rassilon alone knew what his sock drawer must look like. 'But what about the time slip?' she called after him.

The Doctor was already striding down the sloping street back towards the city, his hands jammed into his pockets, scarf trailing through autumn leaves.

'Oh, let time look after itself for a change,' his voice drifted back to her. 'We're on holiday.'

The Louvre had once been a palace. Now, one bloody revolution later, it was an art gallery. That didn't strike Romana as particularly auspicious. If they were keeping any paintings worth talking about then they'd have surely built something specially. The Doctor was having none of it as they strode towards it through the rain.

'The Louvre. One of the greatest art galleries in the galaxy!'

'Nonsense!' Romana shot back at him. She may have been on shaky ground with computer pictures, but the Academy had had a reasonably good pan-cultural studies course. It certainly hadn't included a large cake with a rather disreputable-looking lead roof. 'What about the Acadamia Stellaris on Sirius Five?'

The Doctor made a noise. It wasn't complimentary.

'Or the Solarium Pinaquotheque at Strikian?'

The Doctor made the same growl that she'd heard Parisians make when tourists asked for directions.

She tried a third time. 'Or the Braxiatel Collection?'

The Doctor scowled. 'No, no, no, no. This the THE Gallery. The only gallery in the whole of the known universe which has a picture like...'

And then he showed her.

When Madame Henriette later recounted the story to her cats, she would remember the man's eyes. As terrifying as everything else about him was, his eyes seemed nice. Eyes that had been places. When she conducted her tours, she liked to think of them as exclusive and with a touch of luxury. Her guests (never customers, guests) looked to her for advice, a bit of valuable local insight into a few select treasures in the Louvre. There was so much to choose from, but she picked her way through with judicious consideration, pointing out artworks as though she was greeting favoured old friends.

She was good at reading the mood of her groups as she led them around the galleries. It was always the same. Genuine interest which segued into *politesse* (one had to do a few Dutch Masters, even if no one enjoyed them) and then mounting excitement as they ascended the majestic Daru Staircase before she finally let them approach The Painting. Sadly, the only reason most people ever really came to the Louvre. She sometimes wondered why they didn't move it to its own museum, which would give some of her favourite exhibits a real chance to breathe on their own. A little limelight never hurt anyone, did it?

She turned the corner, as she did so many times a day, getting ready to unveil the painting to another group of enquiring minds with cheap cameras. She was used to finding a small crowd around the painting, but she had never before found it dominated by one man. One man who had quite remarkable eyes and who was astonishingly cross.

The Doctor hadn't bothered with any of the other stuff ('Mostly rotting fruit and so on' he'd snapped). He'd just hurried her to the star exhibit, of this museum or any other. He'd stormed up to the painting, shooing aside some gawpers like pigeons, Romana following apologetically in his wake.

When he was three paces away from the painting he pointed at it. Ta da!

Romana followed the line of his excitedly pointing finger.

She could see a rectangular board that was 77 centimetres tall and 53 centimetres wide, housed in a frame that looked very pleased with itself. A lot of the paintings they'd dashed past had shown the grisly deaths of saints, or violent battles in heaven. This one showed an unremarkable woman who was merely sitting down. She was wearing a gown. She was sat on a balcony. Behind her was a landscape you wouldn't go on a walking holiday in. The woman, well, not much more than a girl really, looked about to say something. Possibly that she was a little bored.

'The Mona Lisa!' announced the Doctor proudly.

Chapter Four
Look to the Lady

Romana regarded the Mona Lisa. The Mona Lisa regarded her.

The Doctor was waiting for one of them to say something.

'Y-ess,' announced Romana eventually. 'It's quite good isn't it?'

'Quite good! Quite good!' Outraged, the Doctor was shouting now, and he really could shout. 'One of the priceless treasures of the universe *quite good*?'

Here he goes. Romana made frantic flapping gestures with her arms. They'd had such a lovely day and now, here he was attracting attention. There was the vaguely belligerent man three point four metres away to the right. There was the immaculately dressed woman, sat on a bench two point four metres behind them. They'd do for a start. 'The world, Doctor, the world,' Romana hissed.

'What are you talking about?' thundered the Doctor.

When the Doctor was like this, Romana concentrated more on the stray details. She calculated the weight of the strongly built meaty man. She estimated the thickness of the paint on the walls of the gallery and compared it to the mean average thickness of the paint on the canvases. She idly wondered why the stylish woman was turning her bracelet around her thin wrist so precisely. And she wondered why the Doctor could be such a childish buffoon when he got carried away with himself. 'Not "the universe" in public, Doctor,' she admonished. 'It only draws attention.'

'I don't care!' Sometimes the Doctor behaved like a child of eighty. 'This is one of the greatest treasures in the universe.' Rassilon help us all, he was starting to address the crowd. 'Let 'em stare. Let 'em gawp! Let 'em gape!'

Romana looked helplessly at the painting, wondering if there was something about it that she'd missed. Oh yes, there was. 'Why hasn't she got any eyebrows?' she asked.

Much has been written over the centuries about the Mona Lisa. Some critics have acclaimed it as the first portrait of an ordinary person just being ordinary. Others have claimed it contains mystical and hidden symbolism, from pyramids to a self-portrait of the artist. Some have speculated as to why the painting languished in relative obscurity until the turn of the twentieth century, when it suddenly rocketed in both fame and value. Very little has been written on the tricksy topic of exactly why Leonardo da Vinci left the eyebrows off. Possibly because, up until that precise moment in Paris, Earth 1979, no one had ever really spotted that this was a problem.

'What? Is that all you can say? No eyebrows! This is the Mona Lisa you're talking about.' The Doctor whipped around, startling someone from Portugal who was about to risk flouting the ban on flash photography. The Doctor glared at the painting. It was the same look he'd recently used against the Black Guardian while he was mending the universe (which he had done by switching it off and then back on again). 'The Mona... Good Lord, you're right, she hasn't got any eyebrows, has she? You know, I never noticed that before.'

Stumped, the Doctor ground to a halt.

Romana marked up her attempt at gently distracting the Doctor as a decided failure. He really could be terribly hard work. If only K-9 were here. He'd make a pithy remark about pigments, or his batteries would run down, or some tourists would try and buy him or something, anything. As it was they were very much the centre of attention. She'd already spotted seven surveillance cameras, fourteen thief-baffling devices and one security guard frantically stabbing a concealed button in the wall. The good news was that, thanks to the TARDIS's telepathic translation circuits, the French she was soon going to need for 'Please release my uncle from that straitjacket' would be impeccable.

It was at this point that several very remarkable things happened, spelling a sudden and complete end to the Doctor and Romana's plans for a holiday.

THING ONE

As Madame Henriette would later tell her cats, 'He was crowding the painting so. I am quite sure he was English.'

During the Liberation of Paris from the Germans, Madame Henriette had once hidden an English airman behind the water tank in the attic. It had been the most exciting period of her life, and also one of the most annoying, as, after he had gone, she found that he'd drunk all of her father's carefully hidden vintage wines. They'd survived searches, pillaging, and quite a lot of bombing, but not the English.

If the treasures of the Louvre were left unguarded, the Americans would try and buy them, the Japanese would photograph them, and the English would load them all cheerfully into the back of a taxi and then not tip the driver. That was Madame Henriette's considered opinion. What else was the British Museum other than the world's greatest display of kleptomania? Of course, there were some who argued that the Mona Lisa herself belonged to Italy, but that was different. After all, when one has lived in Paris for a while, does it not become one's true home?

As her discreet, select and deluxe tour approached the Mona Lisa, for once Madame Henriette wasn't actually looking at her. She was vaguely aware of discontent in the room, and hunting out the source of it while reciting the spiel that had long ago entered her dreams.

'And over here, ladies and gentlemen, we have possibly the most famous exhibit in this gallery.' Tiny pause for laughter. 'The Mona Lisa – La Gioconda – painted by Leonardo da Vinci –' and here she popped in the brackets. Everyone loved a date. Even if it became immediately forgotten. '(1452–1519).' Always went down well.

Then she stopped. The cause of the commotion was not the *Rosbif* in the tattered raincoat. Or the glamorous woman who appeared to have come to the Louvre to read *Le Figaro*. It certainly wasn't that wretched-looking schoolgirl. Nor the tourists itching to take a flash photograph. Or Claude, the security guard who was making frantic gestures with his bulbous nose.

No.

It was the *bobo* man with the eyes, standing pressed up against the Mona Lisa as though she had personally upset him.

Madame Henriette had dealt with this sort of situation before, using all of the tact and gentility with which she would direct her select guests to the bathrooms. She began with a gentle 'Excuse me, m'sieur...'

When that failed to attract his attention she tried tapping the man on the shoulder. He whirled round, halfway through muttering what sounded like 'I knew it! If only I'd told him,' then brought those eyes to bear on her. So dazzling was their ferocity she let out a little squeak. But no. This would be fine. She had once successfully moved on a party of Australians who were posing for pictures in front of the painting with their thumbs up. One man in a scarf would not be a problem.

'What?' the man bellowed.

'Excuse me, m'sieur, could you move along? Other people wish to enjoy the painting.'

The girl seemed not to have heard. 'What did she say?'

The man was about to reply when

THING TWO

The Countess wished her bracelet didn't make that noise. It wasn't a noise one could hear, but it was a noise one felt. As a piece of ornamentation it matched the gold necklace round her throat perfectly. The only differences were that the necklace didn't make a noise and was easy to take off. The bracelet had a funny clasp to it. Carlos kept offering to have it mended and then never got around to it. Ah well, there were so many other things to be done. So many things in which the bracelet would play an important part.

The Countess had never had a problem fitting in. It was one of the reasons Carlos said he adored her. She was capable of being at home in any room. Even here, in the most crowded gallery in the Louvre, she could look quite at ease, gently aloof, reading the paper and quietly noticing how many of the news stories were directly or indirectly about Carlos.

The rising pitch from the bracelet told her that its work was nearly done. She carefully and delicately turned it on her wrist, just a little, with a practised flick, and then turned the page of *Le Figaro*. Ah yes, here was a tiny little paragraph about that container in Ghent.

As she finished reading it she looked up, caught Duggan's eye and looked away, hiding a smile. He was, she supposed, handsome enough for an Englishman. If only he'd been a little more interesting, she would have invited him around for a drink. And he would have come. Everyone came when the Countess Scarlioni asked.

The world Heidi now lived in seemed so far away from the icy slopes of Switzerland. Nothing ran on time, the menus constantly changed at restaurants, and money was treated almost with contempt. She lived, it often felt, in an endless whirl of romance and excitement. That did not mean her life was unplanned. No, not at all.

She had been brought up to ignore commotions. They normally signified the problems of what the French called peasants and the Swiss called the unmoneyed. These struggles were rarely about beautiful things, and, if so, then what was the point of them?

And yet, this hubbub was becoming hard to remain detached from. For one thing, the security guard was looking around, wondering if the shouting of that buffoon bohemian was some kind of decoy. As if. Only an amateur would try something like that.

She spotted a quizzical arch in Duggan's eyebrow which she answered with a tiny shake of her head. How could you think so little of me?

Her bracelet beeped. Its work was done. Which was good. She could leave. She stood up, straightening out the pleats of her skirt and as she did so

THING THREE

Duggan was hating Paris. He knew he was drinking in the last chance saloon of his career, but why did that have to be Paris? True, when everything went wrong, at least blaming Paris would sound impressive.

'You won't like it,' the Chief had told him. 'You've no romance in your soul.'

Duggan disliked it when the Chief was right. He looked at Paris and he thought it would be all right if they spent a weekend cleaning it. It seemed to be a city of teenagers waiting for someone else to clean up after them. Even the dogs were prolifically lazy, turning every walk into a grimacing game of hopscotch.

His last hope had been that his hotel would at least have a view. Sadly, the best that Swansea had sprung for was a grim place behind the Gare du Nord that stank of guinea pigs.

But at least Paris allowed him to follow the Countess up close. He'd put two and two together and was, for once, convinced he'd reached four. There were rumours of a supremely audacious art theft being planned. All the sources for said rumours had later been found face down in the Seine. And the Countess Scarlioni had started spending a lot of time reading fashionable magazines in art galleries. He'd dutifully begun to trail after her like a faithful bloodhound, waiting for something to happen. And now this.

Duggan was trying to work it all out. Something was up. Something was definitely Up. What, he could not quite tell. But up it was. The Countess had to be involved. What utterly random coincidence would bring her to this room at the same time this children's entertainer started clowning around and shouting at the tour guide? Duggan would give the idiot one thing. It took a lot to rattle Madame Henriette.

He'd seen her coldly pluck chewing gum from the breast of a Rodin and return it to a trembling high school student from Ohio.

Yet here was this man, creating a scene, right in front of the Mona Lisa. And there was the Countess, watching him over the pages of her newspaper. The Countess. He never saw her in the same outfit twice. Every one fitted her perfectly. Every one showed off her style, and her beauty. Her thin, graceful figure flowed and wafted in summer and strode crisply through winter. She was watching him now. He returned her look, trying to work it out. That idiot had to be something to do with her. Unless, well, two options presented themselves. One was a rival operation, queering her pitch. Duggan quite liked that. The other, worrying notion, was that another agency was on the trail of the Countess. But who? He felt quite defensive about that, almost protective of her. She flashed him one of her rare smiles and got up to go. As she went, the ageing schoolgirl shuddered with embarrassment at the antics of the man in the scarf. Or was it a signal? Involuntarily, Duggan's hand slid to the handle of his gun as he

THING ONE

'Excuse me, m'sieur, could you move along? Other people wish to enjoy the painting.'

Startled, the Doctor spun round and carried on spinning.

Madame Henriette had entered the room and seen him there, blocking the view of the painting. Mustering her tiny, birdlike frame, she'd reached forward and tapped him, just tapped him, lightly on the shoulder, but this seemed to send him reeling across the gallery. She caught a mere flash of his eyes, but that would stay with her for ever. Glaring at her with confusion and horror.

The schoolgirl with him had her hand to her forehead,

wincing with pain. She was trying to reach out to the man, but there was no stopping him. He toppled against the flowing skirts of a woman as she got up from her bench. She cried out with surprise and fury as the man fell to her feet.

'Sorry madam, so terribly sorry,' the ill man bleated dazedly.

Startled, the woman seemed about to say something in reply, but then, much to Madame Henriette's confusion, another man entirely, the *Rosbif* who could do with everything he owned washing, stepped forward to help.

'Come on, stand back everyone.' Ah, she thought, there was no mistaking that tone. A *flic*.

The policeman picked up the stricken man casually with one arm, helping him to his feet. As he did so, the man collided with something in the policeman's terrible raincoat and let out a gasp.

'Are you all right?' the policeman asked tersely.

Rubbing his head, the injured man nodded weakly. 'Yes thank you. Just dented my head on the handle of your gun, that's all.'

The policeman cursed under his breath. The schoolgirl grimaced. The glamorous woman floated from the room, nodding to... well, Madame Henriette guessed it was a bodyguard. He followed her out. There was an air of menace in the room. Oh dear, this was most unfortunate. She looked over to her crowd of deluxe and select tourists. Commotion and the mention of the word 'gun' had brought out the cameras. Illicit flashbulbs popped, twisting the policeman's face into a fury. Claude, the security guard was moving forward, pushing the crowd to one side, vainly trying to stop them taking pictures. They simply took more of Claude. One of her party then noticed his Polaroid camera was missing and kicked up an awful fuss.

'Oh my dears,' Madame Henriette later confided to her cats, 'it was all so frightful.'

Sat miserably on the floor, rubbing his head and wishing the whole world would make its mind up what it was going to do, the Doctor groaned.

Romana leaned over him. 'Are you all right?'

The Doctor gave no reply.

She spoke rapidly to the ox-like man in the raincoat. 'Take no notice of him. He's just having one of his funny turns.'

The Doctor groaned again. 'Funny turn? The whole world took a funny turn.'

One day, Professor Kerensky was planning on writing a withering monograph on the relationship between science and money. When he was rich, of course.

Up until now, time had been the only dimension that had evaded the relentless march of progress. In other words, someone with money turning up and flinging cash at it. Without cash, the dimensions were egalitarian to a fault. Queen or kitchen maid, your progress through them was at a fairly steady rate. The advent of the horse had changed all that. Suddenly, simply by buying one, you could travel quite rapidly through rather more dimensions than you had perhaps intended. There was a reason why the horse was still used as a measure of speed. It was the first way that the rich had invented of cheating.

Cash had proved to be quite the best way to progress through a dimension in rapid comfort. If you were rich you could leap onto Concorde and arrive in New York with barely a chance to breathe in your champagne. If you had less money your options were more limited, irksome, and tiresomely lacking in champagne.

Time was the only dimension that had proved impervious to horses. Up until now, science had only allowed you to measure it. Money could get you to your destination faster and with a better pillow, but it could not alter the speed at which you travelled forward through the dimension of time. Nor could it increase the amount of time you had. Rich men, suddenly perceiving a lack of days remaining to dance around their money, threw frantic amounts of it at time, but time ignored them. Rich or poor, everyone travelled through time at a walking pace and in only one direction. In any other dimension, you could lose your keys and go back and do something about it. Time just moved you resolutely further away from your keys.

The best that science had managed so far was to come up with some very expensive ways of measuring time. Your wrist could tell you, with ruthless Swiss efficiency, how far away you were from your keys, but could do absolutely nothing about your terrible lack of keys.

Until Count Scarlioni had entered the life of Professor Kerensky, that was. For all Kerensky's mild terror of the man, for his vague threats and his awful smile, the Count had enabled him to wander into time and poke about a bit. Admittedly by flinging vast sums of money at the problem, but the thing about the Count was he knew exactly where to throw them.

When he'd first been approached, over that quite amazing dinner, Kerensky had warned the Count that you would need to be unimaginably wealthy to succeed in this project. A small amount of progress (he'd waggled a finger in a friendly way and the Count had smiled), yes a small amount could be achieved simply by burning through the fortunes of one very rich man. But, if you actually wanted to pull this project off, if you really wanted to take control of time, then, well, you may need to throw the achievements of the entire world into it.

'Yes Professor,' smiled the Count, 'That'll do nicely.'

Kerensky rubbed his eyes blearily, staring at the smoking ruins of yet another circuit board as the supercomputer behind him stuck out a long paper tongue of data at him. He was worried. On the one hand, the machine he was building was certainly powerful. On the other hand, it wasn't behaving quite how he had expected.

For once, however, the Count didn't seem that concerned. 'Excellent, Professor, excellent,' he declared, running a finger along the printout.

Kerensky was cautious, defensive. 'An unfortunate effect,' he observed.

The Count waved this away like false modesty after a piano recital. 'Not so, Professor. Not so. The work progresses well.' He flicked the ticker tape up into the air and it drifted down in a slow ribbon. Behind it, the Count adjusted his smile to a beam. 'Now, you must find a way of vastly increasing the time span.'

Increasing? Was he mad? Surely that was impossible. At the very least – 'But are you certain, Count? Einstein says that—'

'Pfft.' The Count flapped a hand dismissively. 'I am not employing Einstein, Professor,' He seized Kerensky in his arms and danced him around the laboratory, 'I! Am! Employing! You!' He released Kerensky, who, just for a moment, felt a little flush of delight. Was it true? Did this man really think he was better? Was that what he meant? The delight snapped off from the Count's face and he rubbed at his right eye. 'Now, please continue with the work.'

The abruptness of this hurt Kerensky. He could have stood to hear a little more about his own genius. Just a bit. Not flattery, of course not, just an awareness that his employer was properly cognisant of his abilities. They'd run two tests in a single day. One a fortnight, perhaps that was more realistic. But today had been a remarkable achievement! To gather the results they had, to be able to scoop up and hold a single droplet of time, even for a… oh, he couldn't say moment. They needed a unit of measurement. A Kerensky? Oh, that would be delightful. Test 1 had achieved 1 Kerensky. Test 2 had achieved 4 Kerenskys. No, wait. Was that ungenerous to his employer – should he offer him the measurement of the elongation of time? The Scarlioni Factor? And he himself would take the name of the device – the Kerensky Process. Maybe, maybe. But which guaranteed absolute immortality? James Watt's surname was still used whenever you changed a plug. The second had been around almost since the dawn of time as a measurement of it. To come up with a new term for that… well, that would be quite something. Should that not be his own name? Truly a daunting decision. Was that really what he wanted?

Actually, what Kerensky really wanted was far more simplistic. 'But, you are stretching me to the limit, Count,' he pleaded, balling his hands into his eyes and hoping neither of them fell out.

The Count, clearly still playful, clapped him on the shoulder. 'Only thus is true progress ever made, Professor. You as a scientist should be the first to appreciate that.'

Kerensky paused for two Kerenskys before replying . 'But I do, Count, I do. I appreciate many things. I appreciate sleep, regular meals, I appreciate walks in the country.'

The fool sounded like a lonely hearts advert, thought the Count. Perhaps he could, after all, afford to be generous. Why not? Today had been a good day. He tugged the bell pull and Hermann the butler appeared smoothly at the top of the flight of stairs.

'Ah, Hermann, would you please prepare for the Professor…' a vat of acid, some electrodes and a branding iron. All those Hermann could produce in a trice. The Count paused, making his smile seventeen per cent more celebratory. 'Half a dozen *escargots aux beurre*, followed by an Entrecôte Bordelaise *avec haricots et les pommes sauté*. Served directly here to the laboratory.' The Professor was drooling like a bloodhound. Bless him. 'Oh, with a bottle of the Chambertin – my own – oh, better make that half a bottle…' A confidential wink to the Professor, best of friends. 'We wouldn't want anything to get in the way of our work, would we, Professor?'

Hermann bowed. The Count's smile shone with maximum benevolence for all in the room. I can be a generous employer.

Delighted by the gluttonous visions conjured up by the Count, Kerensky pushed the envelope of his luck. 'But Count, I would really like to get some sleep…'

The smile snapped off and the Count turned on his heel, striding up the stairs out of the cavern. 'Hermann, cancel the wine! Bring the vitamin pill. We must press forward. I'll be upstairs.' Opening a bottle of something. I'll make sure you hear the cork pop.

CHAPTER FIVE
MIXED DOUBLES

Duggan wove through the streets of Paris, not letting his quarry out of sight for a moment. There was an art to surveillance which was actually pretty simple to learn – most people went through life without suspecting for a moment that they were being followed. Blameless, boring souls, they never looked over their shoulders as they pottered from the building society counter to the Co-Op till because there would be no reason for them to be followed. A camel could follow ninety-eight per cent of people and not be spotted. But there would be no point. It was the remaining two per cent you needed to be careful of. Half of them were guilty of something terribly mundane and domestic – adultery, fingers in the cash register, poisoning next door's goldfish. They'd glance over their shoulders, they'd boggle, they'd break down sobbing, waste police time, and only occasionally reveal that granny was under the patio. You could eliminate them fairly easily because they just looked Too Guilty. Which left a final one per cent. The carefully sly. Frequently their sheer casualness was a dead giveaway. No innocent person laid down a false trail, ducked into a shop and out the back, loitered near a payphone. Following them without being detected was tricky, but even someone with Duggan's bovine build could pull it off.

As his chief had told him wearily after yet another partially successful operation, 'Your problem is –' Actually, most pronouncements from the Chief started like that. 'Your problem is that you look like a policeman. Even disguised as a clown you'd look like a copper. As soon as anyone glimpses you, they'll start whistling the Z-Cars theme. They can't help it, any more than you can. Next time –' So, there would be a next time, eh? Good old Chief. '– just make sure you're not seen.'

Duggan had become an expert ducker. The excellent thing about Paris was that it was full of things to duck behind. Newspaper kiosks, flower markets, pissoirs. He peeped through a postcard rack, feeling just a little like Inspector Clouseau.

His quarry marched on, seemingly two people without a care in the world. Which was extremely suspicious given their recent behaviour and their rather hasty exit from the Louvre. If they'd really been innocent British tourists, they would be curled up in embarrassment at the side of the pavement, not striding through a bric-a-brac market, down towards a café on the banks of the Seine.

Duggan slunk after them, stealthily. Completely unaware that he was himself being followed.

Paris can be exceedingly subtle. The texture of foie gras, the flavour of cheese, the exact point that a road ends and a café begins. At some time an agreement had been reached between the Notre-Dame cathedral and the café opposite it. At a certain point between the two, cars could race through the plaza. A little further beyond that, with no appreciable change in the surface of the road, pedestrians could meander, and, a little further still, tables could perch quietly outside the café and make the most of the view.

Romana was unfamiliar with these subtle, smoky distinctions. To her it looked rather as though the Doctor had decided to sit down in the middle of a motorway. This did not surprise her one bit. He indicated that she pull up a chair opposite, and, a little uncertainly, she did.

A lorry did not run her over. Well, that was something.

Romana didn't need to say anything. Clearly, their holiday was over. Something was very wrong with Paris. Since travelling with the Doctor, Romana had grown used to sentences like this which would have previously seemed completely *outré*.

A waiter bustled out of the café and handed them a menu. Romana noticed ironically that they served bouillabaisse. Sadly, now was not the time for fish stew. She leaned forward. 'Doctor, you do know we're being followed?'

Running his fingers through the pastry section, the Doctor nodded grimly. 'Yes, all the way from the Louvre, by the idiot with the gun.'

Romana was slightly disappointed. 'Oh. You did notice.'

The Doctor buttered some crusty bread and popped it into his mouth airily. 'Of course I noticed.'

'What do you think he wants?'

'Look in your pocket,' said the Doctor surprisingly.

Romana did so.

'Other pocket.' The Doctor sounded just a little annoyed.

Romana fished out a bracelet.

The Doctor had the air of a conjurer delighting a children's party.

'What's that?' Romana wrinkled her nose.

'It's the bracelet that woman I bumped into was wearing,' the Doctor admitted bashfully.

'What? You mean you stole it from her?' This was a worrying new development. Perhaps it was a good job they hadn't gone shopping after all.

The Doctor flashed his most disarming grin. 'Look at it.'

Romana took the bracelet. It tingled slightly with an unmistakable energy. 'It's a micromeson scanner.'

The Doctor nodded approvingly. 'She was using it to produce a complete record of all the alarm systems round the Mona Lisa.'

'She wants to steal it?' Romana was surprised. I mean, it really didn't seem worth the fuss.

'It is a very pretty painting,' the Doctor offered.

Romana put the bracelet firmly down on the checked tablecloth. 'And this is a very sophisticated device for a level five civilisation.'

'That?' the Doctor huffed. 'That is never a product of Earth technology.'

'You mean an alien wants to steal the Mona Lisa?' Romana got to the end of the sentence and giggled.

The Doctor shrugged. 'It *is* a very pretty painting.'

He fell silent.

Romana picked the micromeson scanning bracelet up again. Was this really alien? It seemed so very old, and the carving suggested… she squinted, her eyes adjusted as the TARDIS's telepathic circuits struggled to render them and failed. If those were hieroglyphs then they were from an extremely ancient civilisation. Tricky.

'Romana…' The Doctor broke into her chain of thought.

'Mmm?' Romana didn't look up from rubbing her finger along the inlay. There was clearly a sophisticated internal power pack with a half-life decay of –

'Romana,' continued the Doctor airily, 'I think something

very odd's going on. For instance, you know that man who was following us?'

'Yes?' Romana was tracing the power threads back to their source.

'Well, he's standing behind me poking a gun into my back.'

Romana looked up.

The Doctor was not lying.

Duggan was in command, he was in control, he had the gun. Whatever the story of these two was, he'd get to the bottom of it.

Suddenly finding himself in the road, he stepped out of it to avoid a coach. He weaved around a group of tourists pushing past to taking pictures of the cathedral. As it wasn't on the map, they ignored his gun.

The Doctor and Romana were still sat at the table, placidly watching all of Paris go by.

Duggan's grip on his gun did not waver.

'Shall we go inside?' he suggested.

The café owner barely batted an eyelid when Duggan marched the Doctor and Romana in at gunpoint. The Doctor, who had his hands theatrically up in the air in surrender, favoured him with a friendly waggle of his fingers. 'Patron! Three glasses of water, please. And do make them doubles.'

Refusing to feel out of his depth, Duggan marched them over to a table in the corner. No escape. A chance to interrogate them. He waved his gun around the bar, not exactly pointing it at anyone, but ensuring that everyone was aware that he had a gun, was allowed to use it, and they really needn't bother calling the gendarmes. He was slightly disappointed to realise that no one was paying him the slightest bit of attention. Paris had a venerable history of ignoring tourists seeking attention.

The Doctor and Romana sat down opposite him, hands still politely in the air.

'I'm the Doctor,' announced the Doctor. 'This is Romana. I would shake hands, but... well.' He gestured to his hands, still, somehow insolently held in the air.

'Now then,' began Duggan, but the Doctor shushed him.

'No, no,' he whispered confidentially 'Let's wait for our waters.'

In the library of the House of Questions, the Countess was having to provide a lot of answers.

The Count was wearing his most dangerous smile. She hated Carlos when he was like this. He'd go from being the most charismatic, charming man she'd ever known to this strangely detached creature. She felt she was being observed down a microscope. A bacteria.

It brought out the worst in her. It reminded her of the clinical appraisals she'd been subjected to by her father's clients back in Switzerland. *Very pretty, but what is she thinking?*

When she was a little girl she'd shuddered. But now she became petulant. There was so much about Carlos she didn't know. Odd really. Now she wasn't wearing the bracelet, couldn't hear that inaudible buzzing, it almost felt as if her head was clearing.

When she'd first put the bracelet on, Carlos had been dismissive about the buzzing. 'A buzzing? Really, my dear? Pay no attention to it. Only the stupid can hear it.'

She'd never complained about it since, only...

Silly thought. She had never seen him clean his teeth. Why was that?

'And then?' the Count asked, finishing his crème de menthe.

She ignored the question, flicking through a book of such rareness that she enjoyed slowly folding down the corner of the page to mark where she'd got to. Then she wandered over to a table, pouring herself some champagne into a flute. She sipped at it, looking down at the peacocks in the gardens.

'And then?' repeated the Count. He was barely smiling at all now. A rare event.

The Countess shrugged. 'Oh, I followed that fool of a detective.'

'Why?'

Another shrug, a sip of champagne. It was too warm to be properly enjoyed, but who cared. 'Reasons.'

The Count leaned forward, seizing her wrist with surprising force. He took the glass from her hand, drained it, and then put it down. All the while, he kept gripping her arm.

'Do not play with me, my dear,' he breathed. As ever, his breath smelt of nothing.

It took an effort, but the Countess managed a twinkle. 'What else have I been doing all these years?'

The challenge hung in the air between them.

'Following instructions,' the Count replied, and the smile flicked back on his face. He walked over to a window, looking down into the courtyard where they had once had burned a cardinal alive. He inhaled deeply as though he could still smell the cooking fat. 'Continue with your story.'

The Countess crossed to a sofa, settling down in it, flicking through the pages of American *Vogue*. 'The detective, Duggan. He annoyed me. He's stopped watching me and started watching the painting.'

The Count clicked his tongue as he turned back from the view. He looked almost surprised, but his face seemed unable to quite manage the emotion. 'So... Duggan's shown a glimmering of intelligence at last.' He appraised the Countess's figure. Was he, she thought briefly, jealous? Was that it? 'Perhaps we should deal with him.' His smile warmed up. That was it! He was jealous! The Countess wondered if she would miss Duggan. Would the Count let her watch when he killed him? She felt a tiny thrill of pleasure.

One which the Count swiftly dispelled. Rubbing his right eye, he folded himself casually into a chair opposite her. He plucked the magazine from her hands, dropping it to the floor. He held her hands in his, staring into her eyes, his gaze a mixture of love and challenge. 'But no. I think Duggan is too stupid to bother us seriously. Don't you?'

'Except…' The Countess stood up, letting his hands fall away. Was she nervous? Perhaps. Just a little. She went over to the escritoire, its pigeonholes overflowing with invitations. *The Marquise would consider it an honour…' 'The Chief Auctioneer politely inquires…' 'M. President requests the pleasure…'* If only they knew. She toyed with a jewel-handled letter opener, picking at imaginary dirt under her fingernails. 'Something else happened today,' she began steadily. 'In front of the painting.'

'Oh yes?' the Count pretended only mild interest.

'A tall man I had not seen before fainted.'

The Count chuckled. It really was most unlike her to get distracted by overexcited tourists. He hoped this wasn't the first sign of nerves. That would be unfortunate. 'You are getting jumpy, my dear,' he purred. 'Probably overcome by your charms. A man can faint if he wants to.'

'Except…' The Countess put down the letter-opener and turned to face him, biting her lip. She was afraid to make the admission. 'Except that by the time he hit the ground he had somehow got the bracelet off my wrist.'

'What!' The Count sprang to his feet, genuinely

incredulous. He was staring at her arm. Why had he not noticed it before? He'd just taken it for granted. 'Wear it always,' he'd said when he'd first placed it on her wrist. 'Wear it always and think of me.' And she'd have had no choice in the matter. How had someone managed to release the isomorphic clasp? Clearly the pickpockets of Paris were excelling themselves. But still. He found he couldn't contain his anger and something else, something that felt like fear. 'And you let him take it?' he roared. He realised he was now towering over her, his smile furious. She was staring at him, the terror plain on her face. Well, good.

'I had no choice!' she broke away from him. 'There was a rush, confusion. Well-organised, I'm sure.'

'But by the heavens...' The Count's brain was catching up with the implications of this. Could Duggan possibly know about the bracelet? He doubted Duggan would even have the intelligence to comprehend what the bracelet really was if he was given a colouring book about it. 'That bracelet...' Well, this would not do. This would not do at all. If an idiot like Duggan was acting on a hunch, then they were all right. But if that bracelet fell into the hands of someone with a brain. Who could guess what it was. Or rather, what it could be...

The Countess was suddenly wreathed in cool smiles and warm reassurances. As though a maid had spilled soup on his favourite cravat and lost it at the dry cleaner's. 'Don't worry, my dear. We will get it back. The matter is in hand.'

The Count forced himself to nod. His right eye was itching abominably. He rearranged his features, making his smile thirteen per cent that's fine and thirty per cent more apology accepted. But deep inside, Count Scarlioni felt worried. Not just for himself. But for everyone. He realised he was still standing in the middle of the library, like a hero in a drawing room comedy. He made himself stride over to the marble fireplace, leaning nonchalantly against it. He lit a cigarette and smiled familiarly over at his wife.

'My dear,' he purred, 'I do trust you will be…'

As ever, she finished his sentence. 'Discreet?' She tapped her cigarette holder against the mantel. 'Of course.'

'What bracelet?' asked the Doctor innocently, a gun to his head.

You can be as rude as you like in a Paris restaurant so long as you don't insult your waiter. The appearance of two men with guns seemed to be testing this rule. But, unlike most tourists, they knew what they wanted as soon as they walked in, which marked them out as true Parisians. And they were only pointing a gun at foreigners, so live and let live. The customers of the bar had already turned a blind eye to one incident of people being held at gunpoint. Well, why not two?

The manners of Parisians are baffling. Waiting your turn and queuing are frowned upon. People are pitied for giving correct directions, and sneered at for insincere politeness. Yet, Parisians are also famed for their charm, their enthusiasm and their immense kindness. Such are the Parisians' contradictions between their good nature and their bad manners that the Japanese Embassy maintains a special helpline for tourists who find it all a bit much.

Romana, Duggan and the Doctor sat at their table. Duggan was waiting for the Doctor or the girl to react. But they didn't. Their hands were held placidly in the air as though they belonged there.

The two men (sharp faces, sharp suits) frisked them quickly. It took them seconds to find it.

'Ah,' remarked the Doctor. 'You mean that bracelet.'

The two men pocketed the bracelet, nodded politely to the waiter and left without another word.

The Doctor and Romana sat there, arms still in the air, seemingly without a care in the world.

'Romana, are you all right?' the Doctor asked.

'Oh, I'm just relaxing and enjoying Paris,' she said.

They put their arms down on the table, calmly waiting to see what would happen next. They turned to favour Duggan with identical, polite grins.

Duggan leaned back in his chair, applauding slowly and sarcastically.

'All right,' he sneered. 'Very good. Nicely staged but you don't fool me.'

The Doctor and Romana exchanged a quick glance. Romana considered their situation. Imminent threat to the fabric of space-time? Yes. Weapons pointed at them? Double yes. And now mistaken identity. If things ran according to her projection, they'd be locked up in a dungeon within the hour. 'What are you talking about?' asked the Doctor, courteously.

'Your men who were in here just now.' Duggan had perfected sounding bored from endless interrogations.

'My men?' The Doctor pointed to himself in a pantomime of outrage. 'Those thugs?'

'Your thugs,' Duggan nodded slowly. Now, my friend, now we're getting to it.

The Doctor pointed to the café door. 'Are you suggesting those men were in my employ?'

'That's exactly what I'm suggesting.'

'I don't know if you noticed –' the Doctor cleared his throat and leaned forward, confidential, sharing a secret – 'but those men were pointing a gun at me. I'm sorry, but if anyone in my employ did that, I'd sack them on the spot.'

Romana nodded solemnly.

Duggan was having none of it. 'Except that I know you arranged for them to hold you up as a bluff.' His tone was triumphant. 'You're trying to put me on a false scent.'

There was a pause.

'You're English, aren't you?' The Doctor rhymed it with stupid. Dismissing Duggan, he turned to le Patron. The café owner, who had so far displayed a magnificent unconcern for the goings-on in his café, materialised by the Doctor's side, solicitous for his every need. 'Patron! I thought I ordered three glasses of water!'

'M'sieur.' Le Patron scowled and went to run a tap.

Romana and the Doctor settled back to wait for their drinks.

Feeling snubbed, Duggan felt the urge to get violent. In about two minutes, maybe three, he would be very much enjoying hurting this man. 'Listen you,' he began. He always said this. Which was odd as there was rarely much to hear except the sound of his fists hitting things.

The Doctor could sense the mounting threat but was completely unconcerned by it. He'd noticed on the menu a slightly unusual ordering of the ingredients for a *Salade Niçoise*. Anchovies received undue prominence over the boiled egg. He wondered if this was deliberate, and if so, what difference that would make to the flavour. He held out a hand. Duggan shook it automatically.

'Let's start again,' said the Doctor. 'Where were we? Ah yes. I'm the Doctor. This is Romana. You are?'

'Duggan,' said Duggan. As they clearly weren't bothering to tell him their real names, he couldn't see why he should give them his first name.

Le Patron brought over three glasses of tap water, putting each one down on the table with a casual yet loud slam. '*Bonne dégustation*,' he muttered sourly as he slumped away. The Doctor toasted his retreating back, sipped the water and relaxed in his chair, beaming merrily.

I'll soon wipe that grin off your face, sunshine, thought

Duggan. He tried a direct question. Even if you got a denial, there was always some tell-tale giveaway.

'What's Scarlioni's angle?'

'Never heard of it.' The Doctor dismissed the question. He passed it over to Romana. 'You were good at geometry. Have you ever heard of anything called Scarlioni's angle?'

'Whose angle?' Romana shrugged facetiously. Duggan had never seen a facetious shrug before. He didn't like it.

'Scarlioni,' Duggan growled.

'Who's Scarlioni?' As though politely listening to a dull anecdote, the Doctor stifled a yawn.

This was too much. 'Count Scarlioni. Everyone in the world's heard of Count Scarlioni.'

'Ah well, we've only just landed on Earth.' The Doctor favoured Duggan with his broadest, most disarming grin.

And we're done. Duggan glared at them both, stood up, consigned them to the loonie bin. 'All right. I give up. Forget it. You're crazy.'

Duggan left and got on with his life. The Doctor and Romana drank their water and then got on with their holiday.

Only...

'Crazy?' the Doctor called after him. 'Indisputably. But crazy enough to steal the Mona Lisa?'

The café paused for just a second. Despite not paying any attention to these three ghastly tourists, everyone was dying to know what would happen next.

Duggan returned to the table. For once in his life, all the fight left him. He pulled out a heavy iron chair and slumped into it. The Doctor pushed a glass of water to him, and Duggan took it.

'Or, at any rate,' the Doctor beamed, 'are we crazy enough to be interested in someone who might want to steal it?'

*

The Count was surveying the bracelet. It was intact.

The two suits were standing to one side, as nervous as it was possible for gorillas in suits to look. Satisfied that all was in order, the Count laid the bracelet down on an exquisitely engraved table and smiled at them warmly.

'Good, thank you, you may go.'

The two suits left gratefully and without a word.

The Count leaned back in his chair, stifling a yawn. As he did so he caught Hermann's eye. The butler swept forward.

'Good,' sighed the Count. 'But not good enough. Kill them.'

'The detective and his friends, Excellency?' suggested Hermann.

'No Hermann, those two fools.' The Count jerked a thumb towards the door.

'With pleasure, Excellency.' Hermann bowed and went to kill them.

Hermann had originally thought he'd been hired to keep the Count's hands clean. He'd discovered that the Count, although exquisitely lazy, relished getting his hands dirty from time to time. But he was more than happy to leave the routine killing to Hermann. A situation which Hermann enjoyed considerably. For Hermann, no death was ever routine.

Magnificently unconcerned by all this, the Countess sat in a corner of the library, flicking idly through some unpublished scandal letters of the Marquise de Sévigné. The Count walked over to her, tapping the bracelet against the side of his face. Oddly, he didn't feel it.

'So,' he declaimed, 'one of them was interested in you and the painting, the other in this bracelet?'

The Countess didn't look up from her reading. 'Yes.'

'Hmm,' the Count said. 'I wish to meet them.'

'Of course,' the Countess said as casually as if he'd

suggested inviting extra guests for dinner. 'Just tell Hermann.'

'No, my dear,' purred the Count. 'You tell Hermann.'

The Countess put down her letters, rose with little grace and went to find Hermann.

Alone, the Count lifted the bracelet up to the light. Hopefully all the data within it was intact. He scratched at that itch above his right eye.

'So, do you work in crime as well?' asked Duggan.

'Work? Not as such, no.' The Doctor chuckled, swatting away the question. He'd tried having a job once. It had all been so terribly routine. Even the aliens had been expected to invade during office hours. He drained the last of his water and pushed his glass across the table to Duggan.

'Same again?' the detective asked.

'Well, if you're buying.'

It was Duggan's round. He ordered some more waters.

Le Patron heartily wished someone with a gun would turn up. What was it with the English and water? A century ago a man called Wallace had arrived in Paris, realised the city had no clean drinking water, and insisted on building fountains that provided it, free of charge, to whoever wanted it. Ever since, Parisians had regarded the English as unnecessarily obsessed with water. And here were three of them, taking up a table which could be used for the drinking of wine. No wonder people kept pointing guns at them.

Romana couldn't see what the fuss was about. She'd studied the History of Art on the Planet Earth extensively (well, she'd read a book about it that morning) and had emerged from the experience baffled.

Humans had been making art for almost as long as they'd been humans. The idea seemed to have come to them in a cave. Initially it had made up for a lack of language, providing an effective way of inviting your friends out for a pleasant afternoon's bison hunting simply by drawing one on a wall. The next step had been commemorative, drawing a picture of that afternoon's jolly good bison hunt to raise a smile on the long ice-age evenings. And then people had started drawing bison simply because they liked looking at bison.

After that, Romana thought it had all got out of hand. For a long time, art had been about great warriors and hunters and their food and that was fine. Then, unable to make up their minds about the existence of higher beings, humanity had started including them in their paintings. Quite a lot of these showed gods turning up to surprise young ladies in the bath. The resulting trouble allowed for even more paintings of glorious battles and nice meals.

Maybe it was because gods and food stopped being interesting, but art gradually turned its attention to other things – flowers, sunsets and the seaside and so on. This was all very well, as it was what people wanted to look at because it made them somehow feel good about themselves. But for some reason artists then decided that that wasn't the purpose of art at all, and started painting things that weren't so nice to look at.

As Romana had reached the end of her book on art, she'd decided that artists were now doing this to be deliberately annoying. It was no good asking them for pictures of flowers and sunsets and bison. Instead, art galleries were full of things which made people think and so made them unhappy. In Romana's experience, human beings were at their happiest when they weren't thinking. In their short lives they were so rarely happy that the idea of creating a leisure activity that deliberately made them miserable seemed rather mean.

Equally perverse was what humans valued in their art.

As it was all so terribly fragile, bits would fall off, get cut off, eaten or just generally damaged, and instead of throwing it away and making a new one, humans simply valued it all the more. As far as she could tell, humanity seemed to reward things for being old and mostly intact. They didn't even have to make that much sense. On that basis you may as well put the Doctor in a museum. Actually…

Duggan was in full flow, his face lit up with a rather piggy enthusiasm. 'So you can imagine the furore…'

'The what?' Romana tried to show that she was paying attention.

'The uproar.'

'Oh, the uproar.' She rested her head on her hand and stared through the café window. Outside, it looked as though Paris was having such a fun day, and all this sounded so complicated. Duggan was explaining how in recent months the whole Art World had been plunged into a furore and an uproar. Masterpieces that had apparently been missing for centuries just started turning up in auction houses across the world.

'All fakes of course,' interjected the Doctor airily.

'Well, they've got to be, haven't they?' said Duggan. 'Haven't they?'

'Are they?' Romana asked.

Duggan paused. 'They're very, very good ones. They stand up to every scientific test.' He made it sound as if there was something wrong with science.

The Doctor was finally, properly intrigued. 'And the only connection in all this is the Count?'

Duggan explained how the Count's name kept on cropping up. The great auction houses of Europe prided themselves on their discretion. Sellers were rarely named (for fear of revealing a reversal in the fortunes of a country, or worse, a famous family). Even so, it was sometimes possible to find out who was selling what. Very rarely would the Count ever directly be the vendor. Occasionally he would be acting on behalf of one of his many friends. Sometimes a piece was being sold by one of his dear friends. Maybe the Count would appear in an auction room on the Drouot to bid on some rarity (which cleared him, of course. It was unthinkable that Count Scarlioni would bid on his own auction even if he never won). Perhaps the Countess would be there, flicking ash as she leafed through the brochure, smoking through a cigarette holder and looking quite beautifully bored. Occasionally they would be spotted at a soirée, making a beeline for a boorish American billionaire, smiling pleasantries as they listened to tiresome anecdotes about frogs' legs and snails. Sometimes Hermann, the Count's right-hand man, would be seen driving back across from the Italian border. After one such trip, a hasty inspection at a garage had uncovered what might just have been a repaired bullet hole. Once, when the Count had been in Tokyo, Hermann had been to Buenos Aries. Visiting relatives, he had claimed.

'But nothing dirty can be proved,' Duggan concluded ruefully. 'The Count's absolutely clean. So clean he stinks.'

'He isn't clean any more.' The Doctor tapped the side of his nose. 'The Countess has that bracelet.'

Good point, thought Duggan. Or was it? The Doctor had, after all, stolen it. The Countess had simply retrieved it. And Duggan only had the Doctor's word that the bracelet was in any way unusual. What was it he'd said? Something about a hidden camera in it or something? Come to think of it, that sounded a bit fishy.

Suspicious of everyone and everything was Duggan's natural state. 'How much would you say that bracelet is worth?' he asked. What if the Doctor really had just been trying to steal it? What if he'd just traded confidential Department secrets with a Parisian pickpocket? Oh, that would look bad. The Chief would no doubt say something withering.

'What's the bracelet worth?' The Doctor lowered his voice mysteriously. 'Well, that rather depends on what you want to do with it.'

Romana coughed.

The Doctor straightened up, neatening his scarf. He nodded and waved, as though to an old acquaintance across a crowded room.

Two men in suits had come in. Two different men in suits. Holding guns.

Le Patron pointed immediately to the table of foreigners. The men nodded their thanks.

Everyone else in the bar suddenly looked elsewhere.

'Do you know –' the Doctor already had his hands in the air – 'I rather think we're being invited to leave. The dear Countess, I shouldn't wonder.'

Romana broke into a radiant smile and put her hands up enthusiastically. Sounded like fun.

Le Patron watched with relief as the foreigners were led out of his café at gunpoint. One of the men in suits nodded to him, and left a generous tip on their table. A true Frenchman.

Cinq à sept is a rich Parisian tradition you won't find in the guidebooks. Between the hours of 5 and 7 p.m., the city is at its most discreet. They are the hours when husbands announce they must, regrettably, work late, and when wives suddenly bump into an old friend in town and just have to have a catch-up. They are also the hours when certain hotels fill temporarily with the sounds of laughter and popping corks.

Between *cinq* and *sept*, the minds of all good Parisians are on anything other than the whereabouts of their spouses. To even ask would be unthinkable. And yet, this particular afternoon, the Countess was bored.

The Countess had nothing to do. She had ordered Duggan brought to the Château, she had watched Hermann executing his henchmen, and she had finished her letters. An empty patch of time stretched ahead of her. There was no sign of Carlos and nothing to do. So it was that some neglected wives took to eating chocolates and growing fat.

Idly, she tugged at a bell-pull and Hermann entered the library, his uniform surprisingly immaculate.

'My lady?' he enquired.

'Hermann, where is the Count?'

'Down in the laboratory, my lady.'

'With that professor again.' She didn't bother to hide her distaste. She knew she had no right to criticise his diversions. She knew it was all something to do with one of the Count's grand schemes. And yet, well, that windowless room, that terrible little man, and all that equipment. How frightfully dull.

'No, my Lady,' Hermann corrected her gently. 'The Professor is resting in his room.' Hermann had carried the exhausted man there himself.

'Oh. Thank you Hermann.' The Countess dismissed him, puzzled. What would Carlos be doing down in the cellar alone?

She wandered through the halls of the Château, past several Rembrandts, half a dozen Canalettos and a Matisse that could do with a clean. She ignored a dusty row of the Count's family portraits done in oils, a series of men, all with a strong resemblance – that same wonderfully bored smile. Her fingertips strayed over a collection of vases so beautiful a pasha had put out the potter's eyes so he could make no more. She didn't even see them. Rotten floorboards bounced beneath her feet as she traversed a corridor skirted with entwined marble lovers by Bartolini. She paused to use the proffered conch of a Michelangelo nymph as an ashtray, then crossed to a door leading down to the cellar. She had, she'd decided, come to see what Carlos's Great Project was all about.

The door was locked. Oh.

'Carlos?' she called. She rattled the handle.

Down in the cellar, the Countess's voice drifted through the wine racks, past the banks of the mighty computer and echoed off the great glass spires of the Professor's device.

But the Count did not hear her. Or if he did, she was not important. Not right now.

Count Carlos Scarlioni's right eye was twitching.

It had started as an itch. It had grown.

The Count had been wandering through the basement, altering a setting here, a dial there, really little more than tidying up (and, in the process, advancing the Professor's work by a good few months).

He'd caught up with his face in a shaving mirror. That smile.

He was struck by a thought, one that started to make sense of everything.

He'd always known and yet he'd never quite known.

He was transfixed by his own reflection. And yet it wasn't his reflection. Not really.

He scratched again at the skin above his right eyebrow.

He paused.

He touched the skin again, delicately. It felt, for the first time in his life, odd.

He caught sight of his smile. It was broad now. Eager for him to know.

He reached up to touch the skin again and instead of scratching, he tugged at it, curiously, wondering what would happen. With horrid ease, the skin came loose. He carried on pulling at it, a strip of it peeling away and opening out, falling across in the centre of his face. Curiously, he didn't feel any pain, or any sensation at all.

Count Carlos Scarlioni didn't feel anything as he pulled his face slowly, methodically apart. Piece by piece.

As he opened up the flesh, the voices came pouring out.

And this time, he knew what they were saying.

They were calling his name.

The last of his face fell away in ribbons to the floor. The Count continued to stare into the mirror.

There was no blood. There was no skull under the skin.

The single eye, the green tentacles that made up the true face of Scaroth, the last of the Jagaroth, stared back at him.

PART TWO

'I love Paris every moment.'

Cole Porter

CHAPTER SIX
PARIS
IN A DAY

The Count began to remember. The ship, the terrible sky of that lifeless world. Being caught in an explosion so endless it was still ongoing.

So, I'm the last of the Jagaroth, Scaroth thought. For as long as that lasts.

The warp field finally, mercifully, collapsed. The fragments of Scaroth's ship, squeezed into place by impossible forces, at last felt free to fling themselves in burning splendour far and wide across the surface of the dead planet.

Scaroth died. And then the surprising thing happened.

Pinioned by unimaginable forces at the heart of the warp field, Scaroth found himself very briefly sharing space with the entirety of time. The Jagaroth's last great achievement was time travel. Of a sort.

*

'It's sensational isn't it?' oozed Elena.

Harrison Mandel glanced around the gallery and wished for a nice cup of tea.

Elena had dragged him to a 'happening space'. It was somewhere beyond Montparnasse, a crumbling commune on the Boulevard Arago. He felt at any moment he was going to get his pocket picked. He really didn't want to be here. But Elena had been most insistent. She'd bought him a horrible glass of wine on the way in and that, at least, had made the whole thing slightly bearable.

The happening space was everything Harrison had dreaded. Smell of joss-sticks? Check. Ravi Shankar LP? Check. Coats that smelt of dead sheep? Check.

Someone was even playing the bongos.

The worst of it all was how impossibly young and pretty everyone seemed. Have I really got so old, thought Harrison? Have I forgotten how to have fun?

A girl danced passed him, giggling at precisely nothing and Harrison took another swig of his wine.

Someone started to perform a prose poem accompanied by a cello. Harrison shuddered.

They wove their way through the crowd. Someone offered round a tray full of fairy cakes. Harrison reached out for one. Elena placed her hand on his and steered him away. 'Are they drugged?' he asked.

'But no,' she gasped. 'They just have rats in the kitchen. Now, here we are.'

In a corner sat a man, drawing frantically, on the walls, on the floor and on sheet after sheet of paper, scribbling away with charcoal. He was a burly man with a beard. His pullover was threadbare and covered with black sooty smears.

'He is called Bourget,' breathed Elena. 'I just had to bring you. He's quite the sensation. Everyone says he's had a breakthrough. Look.'

All of Bourget's drawings were of people, their faces replaced with broken clocks.

'I don't know what to say,' admitted Harrison. 'Does nothing for me.'

'*Alors!* You must learn how to talk about art. We shall have to try and find you better words,' Elena clucked. 'Poor Bourget says he's seen through the cracks of time.'

What does that even mean? thought Harrison.

Bourget was hastily scrawling away like a man possessed. He'd seized a tourist's reproduction of the Mona Lisa and was sketching what looked to be a plate of calamari over it.

'How daring,' enthused Elena encouragingly. 'What he's done here is to set up a breathtaking conversation through a pop-art reappropriation of a standard form, don't you think?'

Hmmm, thought Harrison.

The Countess walked back through the empty halls of the Château. They kept a large number of servants, but, as was still the fashion in the very oldest of houses, they were rarely seen. A maid brought her café au lait to her room every morning, and Hermann took the Count's to his.

When she got back to the library, she wasn't surprised to find the ashtrays had been emptied and her papers tidied. She wasn't surprised because she didn't notice.

She sat down, toying idly with a Chinese puzzle box, her fingers working their way across the intricate inlay of the wooden surface. A twist here, a push against a slight indent there, a gentle pressure and then a slide… Such boxes could demand over a thousand steps before they would open, yet this one required just a couple of dozen. Even so, it had taken her a long time to learn the intricate sequence, like mastering a piano sonata. At moments of indecision, she found the box calming.

With a cough, Hermann announced his presence in the room. 'Countess, the people you wished to speak to are here.'

She nodded, cheering up enormously. This would be diverting at least. 'Show them in, Hermann, show them in.' She favoured Hermann with a warm smile. He'd stay and help, of course.

Hermann padded away to fetch her guests. The Countess noticed Carlos had left her bracelet on display on the table. That would never do. Swiftly she slotted it inside the puzzle box, sealed it, placed a cigarette in her holder, lit it, tucked her legs up under her on the sofa and settled back to relax and enjoy the interrogation.

She could hear footsteps. What would they be like? She struggled to remember them. Duggan, a man and a girl. Perhaps the man would share Duggan's somewhat bovine charms… And the woman? She fished around in her head for an image of English femininity and managed some sort of starched and dowdy librarian.

A tangled man in a scarf was thrown in by Hermann. He landed in a heap at her feet, startling her out of her reverie.

'I say!' exclaimed the man, springing up. 'What a wonderful butler, he's so violent.'

The Count was standing in a corridor. In front of him an elaborate mirror stretched from floor to ceiling, its golden frame blotched with the ages. He was looking at the duck-shell blue wall, at the frame, at anything other than the mirror. He was doing whatever he could to avoid staring incredulously at his face.

He'd stood in the laboratory, enraptured by the strangeness of his own reflection. His head had flooded with voices and thoughts, a tidal rush that would have overwhelmed him had he not already been lost.

He'd swept the little shaving mirror to the floor and then picked up the scraps of his discarded face from between the fragments of glass. He'd staggered up the stairs, the strips of flesh dangling from one hand. He'd paused in the corridor, to try and look at his head once more, but it was almost more than he could bear. How had he forgotten all this? How could he still not remember it clearly?

He heard voices again, and for once they weren't in his head. They were approaching rapidly and, for a moment, the Count felt something like panic. Then, as the voices turned into the library, he relaxed. His secret wasn't about to be discovered.

He looked down at the ribbons of flesh in his hands.

All that remained of the face of Carlos Scarlioni.

Hermann strode in, shoving Duggan with one hand while one of his men brought... Oh. Well, the girl was unexpected.

The Countess's enquiring stare was met and reflected right back at her. How young, how beautiful she is, thought the Countess generously, regarding the glowing tip of her cigarette. Watching her suffer would be most rewarding.

Duggan was struggling in Hermann's grasp. Always the barely tethered hound, so bad-tempered and stupid. Hermann brought up his gun to club him down, yet the strange man on the floor raised his hand in a casual wave, coincidentally blocking Hermann's swing.

'Thank you, Hermann,' the man announced. 'That will be all.' The rumpled bohemian remained kneeling, beaming at everyone, sizing up the room.

The Countess was happy to give him ground and enjoy the show. For the moment. Last month that very patch of carpet had been dominated by an equally boisterous railroad tycoon. They were still finding bits of him in the central heating furnace.

'Hello,' announced the man shuffling towards a chair. 'I'm the Doctor, this is Romana.'

The girl favoured her with a radiant beam.

'This is Duggan, you must be the Countess Scarlioni, and that is clearly a delightful Louis XV chair. Louis may not have been as good a ruler as his father, but his furniture was far nicer.' The Doctor dropped into it delicately, yet firmly. 'May I sit in it?' he asked.

He wiggled experimentally around in the chair, making himself at home. 'I say, haven't they worn well?' He fingered the upholstery and was pleased to discover it was original. He was less pleased to discover an entire fingernail which had been left behind by a Yakuza. The Doctor examined it briefly, flicked it away, and then patted the chair down, an expression of pure delight on his face.

'Doctor.' The Countess nodded graciously. 'You're being very pleasant with me.'

The Doctor looked embarrassed at the compliment. 'Ah, well, I'm a very pleasant fellow.'

The Countess got up from her chaise longue and strode towards him, waving her cigarette holder around. 'However, I did not invite you here for social reasons.'

'I know.' The Doctor looked crestfallen. 'I could tell that the moment you didn't offer us a drink.' She didn't even have a chance to stutter before he continued. 'Thank you, three glasses of water, please, do go easy on the ice.'

Hermann didn't move an inch, but he shifted his posture. A word, my lady, just give the word.

Not yet. But she knew she would enjoy seeing this man reduced to a whimpering animal.

She carried on talking, her words as precise as a piano recital. 'Doctor, the only reason you were brought here alive is to explain exactly why you stole my bracelet.'

'Ah.' The Doctor's face was a picture of bashful

remorse. 'Well, it's my job, you see. I'm a thief, Romana is my accomplice and Duggan here is the detective who has been kind enough to catch me.' He paused, judging her expression. 'That's his job,' he added. Still her expression did not waver. 'Our two lines of work dovetail beautifully.' He accompanied this with an elaborate gesture.

She rather fancied he was left-handed. She would let Hermann break that one last.

'Very interesting, Doctor. You see –' and here she allowed herself a moment of mock regret – 'I rather thought that Mr Duggan had been following me.'

'Well, now…' The Doctor looked between the two and raised an eyebrow. 'You're a beautiful woman, probably. I know! He was trying to summon up the courage to invite you out to dinner! Weren't you, Duggan?'

Duggan scowled. A pity. There had been a time when she might, just might have said yes. No matter.

'Who sent you?' she asked.

'Who sent me what?' The Doctor beamed facetiously.

The Countess had a tiny flutter at the back of her head that told her that she was not only losing control of the situation but she was also losing her temper. This never happened. Every shop girl in Galleries Lafayette knew that the Countess never shouted. But when she grew quiet, that was when you had to tread carefully.

She spoke, forcing a casual shrug of her wrist as she ground her cigarette into a marble ashtray. 'Doctor, the harder you try to convince me you are a fool, the more I am inclined to believe otherwise. It would be the work of a moment to have you killed.'

Hermann caught her eye. He was asking permission to be let off the leash.

That momentary distraction was enough for Romana to march past her and sit neatly down on the chaise longue, picking up the Chinese puzzle box with a pleased expression. 'Well, this is nice,' she said politely.

'Put it down,' the Countess snapped. She was being attacked on two fronts and the girl, the stupid girl was playing with things she didn't understand. It was all so unfair.

'It's one of those puzzle boxes isn't it?' Romana gave it a none too gentle shake.

The Countess winced. 'It is a very rare and precious Chinese puzzle box.' She didn't care how patronising she sounded. Carlos would be furious if it was damaged. 'You will not be able to open it. So put it down.'

Romana didn't seem to have heard her. She flicked the sides of the box apart as though she'd been doing it all day, and shook the bracelet out. 'Oh look!' she giggled.

The Doctor did not actually applaud. But he looked like he was thinking about it.

'Yes, very pretty, isn't it?' The voice came from the door. Lounging there, not a care in the world, favouring them all with the laziest of smiles, was Count Carlos Scarlioni. He looked magnificent, and gave every air of waiting to be asked what he wanted to drink. One hand was tucked neatly into his jacket pocket. The other flicked up, catching at a lock of stray hair. Nothing was out of place in the Count's life. 'Very pretty,' the Count repeated.

'Very,' agreed Romana. 'Where's it from?'

'From? It's not from anywhere.' The Count seemed chidingly puzzled by the question. 'It's mine.'

Duggan had only been to the theatre once. He had not enjoyed the experience. He'd spoken about it with his Chief. 'Maybe it's because I know when people are lying. Theatre is just people lying to each other in a room.'

'Maybe it's because you have no imagination,' the Chief had said.

Right now, Duggan felt as though he were in a play. At any moment, someone was going to come bounding through the French windows asking 'Anyone for tennis?' That seemed to happen in most plays. Well, it hadn't happened in *Othello*, but there was a play in sore need of some tennis.

To Duggan's eyes, everyone in the room was wearing a mask. The Doctor was suddenly playing the jolly burglar. Romana was every inch the naively bright schoolgirl. The Countess was pretending not to be annoyed by it all, and the Count… who was the Count playing? There was definitely something going on there. It was the first time that Duggan had actually met the Count face to face. They'd nodded to each other at art galleries and auctions. Duggan's nod had said, 'I know your game.' The Count's nod had been that of the well-fed fox to a chicken it could not be bothered to eat. 'Not today. But soon.'

But here, in his own house, the Count still seemed to be putting on an act, in front of everyone. Duggan could tell. They were all at it. The exception was Hermann the butler. There was someone Duggan could respect. They were each eyeing up the other, two old fighters, masters of the game, always on the lookout, ready to attack if the slightest opportunity presented itself. Duggan admired that. Were circumstances different, Hermann was a man he could drink a beer with.

(For his part, Hermann did not return the favour. Inasmuch as he was aware of Duggan, he despised him. He was rather more concerned about his master. Was he quite all right? For once the Count seemed almost ill at ease.)

The Count strode confidently across the room, fingers lingering over a few volumes left open on tables, before reaching the fireplace. One thing every good room should have is a solid fireplace. This one had once belonged to

Madame du Pompadour and was a rococo delight of *Bleu Fleuri* marble, with an elaborate frieze showing nymphs and shepherds hiding daintily from each other. The most important thing about it, right now, was that it was very solid. The Count leant heavily against it, making every effort to show that the movement was casual, taking every pain not to suggest how much of his weight the marble was supporting. He risked a glance in the mirror. Was his face right? Despite his every effort, his hand reached up involuntarily to check it again and he hastily converted it into a casual flick at his hair. He made his smile eighteen per cent more relaxed, jammed his hand back in his pocket and took pains to survey the room at his leisure.

It would, he thought, be so much easier to just have Hermann spray the room with bullets. Yes, he thought. A gesture with a single finger. Do it, and damn the consequences. Wipe the whole lot out. Start again.

But no.

The Count devoted himself to an inspection of his fingertips. Still propped up against the mantelpiece, he took in the room, his smile clearly saying 'Well, now I have arrived. We can begin.'

The Countess took her cue. 'My dear, these are the people who stole the bracelet from me in the Louvre.'

The Count was about to acknowledge them all with a masterful nod, when the Doctor broke in with a twinkling wave from his chair. 'Hullo there!'

The Count ignored him. He stared at the sun setting behind the Countess. 'How curious,' he mused, allowing his voice to take on an air of incredulity. 'A pair of thieves go into the Louvre and come out with... a bracelet.' And now he trained his eyes on the Doctor, slouching insolently across one of his favourite chairs. 'Is that really the most interesting thing you could find to steal?'

'I just thought it was awfully attractive, terribly unusual design.' The Doctor shrugged regretfully, 'Of course, it would have been very nice to steal one of the paintings instead, but I've tried it before and –' he rolled his eyes – 'all sorts of bells go off, which does disturb the concentration.'

'I can imagine,' the Count clucked with sympathy. 'So you stole this bracelet simply because it looked pretty?'

'Yes,' the Doctor agreed quickly. 'I think it is. Don't you?' He seemed terribly eager to hear the Count's reply.

The Count let a silence hang in the air. His wife waited for someone to light her cigarette, and then lit it herself. She glided closer to her husband, muttering in a stage whisper, 'I don't think he's quite as stupid as he seems.'

'My dear, no one could be as stupid as he seems.' The Count smiled knowingly back at her. Then he turned his smile almost completely off. He had so much else to do. So much else. And all he was getting from these people was noise. That itch was back. He resisted the urge to rub his forehead. 'This interview is at an end,' he announced.

'Good, good!' The Doctor leapt to his feet, rubbing his hands with glee. 'Well, we'll be off, then. A quick wander up the Champs-Élysées and perhaps a spot of dinner at Maxim's. What do you think, Romana?'

The girl sprang to her feet as well with a little bounce. 'Maxim's what?' she asked eagerly.

Hermann appeared at the Count's side. He nodded. Someone here could be relied upon to behave properly. 'Ah, Hermann! Would you kindly lock our friends in the cellar?'

The Doctor's face fell. The Count acknowledged him for a moment, if not as a peer then certainly as an almost worthwhile waste of time. His smile was charming and sarcastic in equal measure. 'I would hate to lose touch with such fascinating people.'

*

Duggan had had enough. Everyone was still talking without saying anything. It annoyed him. Here was this strange Doctor, and that smug girl, and they were alone in the room with the world's biggest art thief, and they weren't talking about that at all. Just blathering about a piece of jewellery and a wooden box. It was all a wasted opportunity, and what was worse, the Doctor was now happy to let them get locked up. Duggan saw his opportunity and he seized it with both hands.

He grabbed the chair recently vacated by the Doctor and hoisted it up into the air, ready to bring it crashing down on Hermann.

'Duggan, Duggan, Duggan!' The Doctor had seized his wrist lightly. To Duggan's amazement he couldn't move his arm at all. The Doctor was hissing in his ear, horrified. 'What do you think you're doing? That's a Louis XV!'

The Doctor had had to act quickly. For one thing, he'd seen Hermann's hand dart effortlessly to his gun. Duggan didn't stand a chance. And, for another, he really would have regretted the loss of that chair.

The moment was gone. Duggan traded a rueful expression with Hermann. What can you expect when I'm saddled with these amateurs?

Hermann barely noticed. Killing Duggan would have been a joy, but gunfire so near a Persian rug was always tiresome. The housemaids had proved themselves excellent at lifting bloodstains, but one day his luck would run out.

The Doctor released Duggan's wrist, and he dropped the chair with disgust.

He turned furiously on the Doctor, snarling, 'You're not just going to let them lock us up, are you?'

'Just try and behave like a civilised guest, won't you?' The Doctor's tone was coaxing.

Romana skipped over to the Doctor's side, her arms

jauntily in the air. 'Shall we go?' she asked brightly.

'Ah, Hermann,' The Doctor bowed with utter politeness to the butler. 'Would you show us to our cellar, please?'

The Doctor swept out of the room, followed with a bounce by Romana. Duggan threw another glare of angry apology at Hermann and traipsed after them.

If Duggan had lingered a little longer, he would have heard the Count make a remarkable confession. He and the Countess watched the Doctor go. If the Countess was annoyed at how the interview had gone, she did not show it. If the Count was still feeling uncomfortable in his own skin, he was at pains not to betray it. Instead he beckoned to her, and she came over. Obedient.

They stood for a moment, watching the sunset.

Then, very softly, Heidi kissed her husband on the lips. For an instant, it seemed as though he flinched, but then he smiled, taking her in his arms.

She offered him her wrist, and he slipped the bracelet back onto it. He smiled at her warmly.

'Be a little more careful with your trinkets, my dear,' he chided affectionately. 'After all, we still have a Mona Lisa to steal…'

CHAPTER SEVEN
LIES
BENEATH

It took Hermann longer than he'd expected to get his three prisoners to the basement. The Doctor was treating the march rather like a guided tour of a private art gallery. He would coo with delight at a Monet, and Romana would idly wonder if perhaps it could be displayed to a bit more advantage.

As they were marched through the Château's halls, it was almost as though Hermann wasn't even holding a gun to them. The Doctor was forever pointing out some treasure, or nipping off down a hallway, marvelling at the vast treasures of the Count's collection.

'What pretty paintings!' the Doctor marvelled as they passed through a corridor that would have made a curator faint. 'Don't you think they're pretty paintings, Romana?'

'Not particularly,' she replied. She seemed thoroughly uninterested.

Hurt, the Doctor turned to Hermann for his opinion, got nothing, so tried Duggan. 'I think they're very pretty. Don't you, Duggan?'

'Very pretty.' Duggan was learning that it was safest to humour the Doctor.

They walked through a dusty banqueting chamber, the Doctor ticking off the paintings as they passed them. 'Gainsborough, uh-huh… Rubens… ooh, a Rembrandt!' he whistled. 'Very, very pretty!'

Hermann ignored all this.

They'd reached an ancient oak door. Hermann unlocked the door, revealing a long flight of stone steps and a blast of cold air. He gestured with his gun. 'Down,' he said.

The Doctor did some of his best thinking at gunpoint, especially on his way down to a dungeon. Gunpoint and dungeons were both magical ingredients for some quite unexpectedly brilliant leaps of logic. The Château was quite astoundingly old. The trip to it in the back of a sealed Renault van had told the Doctor little more than that it was on a quiet, old street nestled between two of Baron Haussman's grand boulevards. This alone made its survival even more remarkable.

Parisians had spent much of their history finding one reason or another to tear down old bits of their city and then falling in love with whatever had somehow managed to survive. Even though the Germans hadn't bombed much of Paris, that hadn't stopped the post-liberation government from rebuilding large chunks of it. The city employed vast departments dedicated to identifying the nice bits and drawing up elaborate plans to replace them with shopping centres and motorways.

Baron Haussman had been quite the most insane example of this mania. It was to him that Paris owed its nickname of the City of Lights, thanks to the enormous gaps he'd knocked in the skyline, like a beggar's smile. He had tried to make Paris straight. Lanes that were designed for wandering and corners that invited a linger were swept away, replaced with rigidly straight boulevards. Under Haussman's regime, the ramshackle improvised grandeur of Paris was replaced with streets that were composed entirely of ordered ranks of buildings, identical in height, proportion and features. And yet somehow, marvelled the Doctor, this vast château had escaped Haussman's attention. By rights and probability it should be a car park by now.

Baron Haussman had been many things, of course, the Doctor remembered. He'd been a town planner, he'd been Napoleon's right-hand man, he'd been a lover, a collector, a schemer, and terribly dull company. He'd also been a criminal, a blackmailer and, actually, not even a baron at all. Not that Paris seemed to mind a fraudulent aristocrat or two. They'd not even paid much attention to his reforms of their streets. After he'd finished his grand boulevards, Parisians simply shrugged and then *flâneured* along them much as usual, still finding bits to wander through and corners to linger on. That was Paris. It survived.

'Tell me, Hermann,' the Doctor asked as they turned a corner and went down another flight of steps even more worn than the last, 'how long has this château been here?'

'Long enough.'

'Long enough! I like that. Really, that long?' There were a lot of stairs, the Doctor thought. They really were going a long way down. A rattle told him that the Metro went quite close by. Interesting that the Château hadn't been disturbed by that. All things considered, its survival was quite remarkable. 'And modernised, at least four or five hundred years ago?'

'May have been.'

'Really? Stimulating, how very stimulating.'

Modernised half a millennium ago? If you could call that modernisation. What would you call it, then? The steady accretion and evolution of a building that was quite remarkably old. He passed a bit of wood jutting out of a wall that was an improbable mixture of brick and stone and rock. It was as though they were descending into a cave. The wood was so old it was practically fossilised, as though a tiny fragment of mud hut remained. Imagine that, eh, a tiny bit of a prehistoric mud hut dating back to when people... when people...

The Doctor passed a bit of rock where someone had, a long time ago, carved a crude drawing of two people hunting a bison. One of the people had one eye and wild hair and was holding a spear. Surely this was just graffiti.

Imagine that, thought the Doctor. Imagine if the house had always been here and the city had simply grown up around it? Wouldn't that be funny?

The Doctor rather wanted to examine the drawing more. He turned to Hermann to ask for directions down the stairs. 'Where to? Down here?'

'To the very bottom.'

The stairs opened out into a cavernous space that dripped with cold and time. The Doctor could imagine a team of archaeologists getting very excited down here. Once they'd swept the machines and bottles of wine out of the way.

'So this would be the cellar, would it?' Cellar? More like a catacomb.

The Doctor carried on talking while his mind got on with important things. He was, for instance, dying to have a look at that computer. On the one hand, of course, it was a terribly advanced piece of engineering for its time. On the other, it was an antiquated piece of junk. And the Doctor had always been terribly fond of antiquated pieces of junk. He asked Hermann where the plug was.

Hermann had finally had enough. 'Doctor, your conversation does not interest me.'

The Doctor pouted. 'Really? Oscar used to find me most amusing.'

'Oscar?' asked Romana. She was feeling left out. She knew the Doctor was up to something. She was trying to work out exactly what. This was, she thought, somewhat hard at gunpoint. Guns annoyed Romana. They did tend to go off at the wrong moment, just when things were getting interesting.

As far as she could tell, at a rough glance, the cellar was 20.3 metres below sea level and stretched out 17.4 metres from where she currently stood. Although the computer bank took up only about eight per cent of the volume of the chamber they stood in, it did rather seem to dominate. A very curious design. Anyway, there'd be time enough to work that out in a moment. When the man with the gun locked them up, got knocked out, or simply went away of his own accord. She rather hoped he would wander off as she found guns, on the whole, rather a chore.

The Doctor was sharing her fascination with the computer.

'Oscar?' she repeated.

'Wilde.'

'Was he?'

'In some of his habits.' The Doctor strolled casually over to the equipment next to the computer. 'Good heavens, and a laboratory!' He wheeled on Hermann so quickly that the butler nearly shot him. 'Hermann, are you locking us in a laboratory?'

That would, thought Romana, be a massive mistake. Especially if you didn't want the Doctor accidentally blowing up your house.

Hermann was no fool. He gestured to a small, dank recess under the stairs with a sturdy-looking door. 'In there,' he growled.

The Doctor, Romana and Duggan trooped through into what was best described as a storeroom. The number of chains hammered into the brickwork suggested it had had many uses before. Currently it was somewhere where the owners of the Château left empty packing cases, and heaps of foul-smelling straw that squeaked and rustled.

A small table sat amongst the rubble. In an antique shop it would have had pride of place, possibly its own little pedestal. A grubby oil lamp and a box of matches sat on it, spent matches burnt into the exquisite marquetry.

'There's a light if you want it,' said Hermann dryly.

'How long will that last us?' asked Romana dubiously.

'Two hours. Maybe three.'

'But what happens after that?'

'I don't really think you'll be needing much light after that,' smiled Hermann and left. He locked the door and went up the stairs. He didn't cackle, which was a relief. Romana couldn't stand a cackler. She listened to the muffled sounds of the computer. In as much as a 1979 computer could be said to have a processor, the computer's processor was clearly going full tilt. Interesting. Probably trying to work out how to boil an egg.

She looked around the storeroom. Apart from some light seeping through a grille in the door, they were in complete gloom. Romana, very slowly and steadily, started to pace the cell.

Duggan rounded on the Doctor, and looked as though he was going to hit him.

'What do you think you're playing at, Doctor?' he demanded furiously. He felt betrayed and confused and very angry.

'Be quiet, light the lamp,' the Doctor hissed. Gone was any trace of the children's party entertainer, the amiable

116

bohemian or even the prattling fool. Instead the Doctor was deadly serious. He needed Duggan to light the lamp because his brain had quite a lot of thinking to do.

The Doctor handed the box of matches to Duggan. There was only one inside.

'And get it right,' snapped the Doctor.

'You tell *me* to get it right?' thundered Duggan. 'We could have escaped twice just now if you hadn't—'

Boring boring boring humans.

'Exactly.' With an effort, the Doctor adopted a reasonable tone. 'What's the point of coming all the way here just to escape immediately? First we let them think they've got us safe. Now we can start to escape. Light the lamp.' He clicked his fingers impatiently, pointing at the lamp.

Feeling utterly dismissed and rather miserable, Duggan lit it. He noticed that Romana was watching him severely as she paced up and down. He nearly fumbled it and only managed to get the wick to catch as the match was burning down to his fingers. Duggan had been trained, rather successfully, to endure a large amount of pain, but he really hated being burned by matches. The fish-oil lamp gave off a bout of choking black smoke before filling the room with meagre light and the smell of haddock.

The Doctor had pulled a novelty silver pen out of his pocket and was waving it delicately around the door. If he'd intended doing something eccentric just to annoy Duggan, then he'd accomplished his goal. Duggan scowled as the Doctor held the device over the ancient iron lock. It emitted an undulating whine.

'Sonic screwdriver,' put in Romana helpfully, retracing her steps.

Duggan, never having heard of a sonic screwdriver before, was puzzled. Was it a new kind of lock-pick? It didn't seem to be doing much. 'Well?' he asked impatiently.

The Doctor just grunted. Clearly, whatever he was trying to do to the lock wasn't working. The sonic screwdriver's piercing whine had settled into an accusing bleat.

'Wretched thing doesn't work,' the Doctor admitted, confirming Duggan's worst suspicions.

'You and your clever ideas,' he snapped, grabbing it from the Doctor's hand. That was the problem with fancy lock-picks. Never worked. The thing buzzed resentfully in Duggan's hand as he jammed it into the lock. If only he could get it to bear against the catch and get some leverage there was a slim chance. He twisted it, feeling it bend back like one of Uri Geller's spoons. Rubbish.

'Don't!' howled the Doctor, swatting him away, and cradling his sonic screwdriver like an injured pet.

'Well,' sneered Duggan, 'it wasn't much use for anything else, was it?'

'It was,' said the Doctor protectively, 'very useful against the Daleks.' He held it up to his cheek as though about to add, 'Weren't you, my little darling?'

'Daleks? What?' He was clearly spouting gibberish.

'The Planet Skaro. You wouldn't know it.'

This is all I need, locked in a cellar, no way out, and a couple of lunatic saucer people for company.

The Doctor blew at his sonic screwdriver, dislodged a bit of dust and switched it on gingerly. It emitted a confident whirr.

'Oh, it works now.' The Doctor beamed with delight. 'Been meaning to fix it myself. Thank you, Duggan.' He waved it over the lock. It conked out again. The Doctor, without a moment's hesitation, thumped it furiously against the wall. It sprang angrily back into life and the door flew open.

Delighted, the Doctor swept an arm around Duggan's shoulder. 'I say, would you like to stay on with us as our scientific adviser?'

'Uh?'

The Doctor made to leave the cell, but Romana was blocking his way, firmly.

'Doctor, the horizontal length of the stairs is about 5.48 metres, isn't it?'

'I suppose so. Why, are you thinking of re-carpeting them?'

'Well, the storeroom is alongside the stairs and only 2.49 metres in length.'

'Fascinating,' muttered the Doctor, trying to get past her. Out there was a laboratory and a computer. And he was keen to get his scarf away from that lamp, otherwise every planet they landed on for weeks would smell of fish. Romana continued to block his way. 'Can I go and look at that lab now?' he begged.

Romana stepped aside. He strode purposefully past. 'Come on K-9,' he said, and Duggan trotted obediently behind him.

Romana stood in the cell a moment longer, looking thoughtfully at the walls.

Freed at last, Duggan was itching to escape.

'Right then, straight up the stairs and out of here,' he announced, balling a fist into his palm.

'No. There are bound to be a couple of guards posted at the top,' cautioned the Doctor, a word of friendly advice. After all, he knew his guards like he knew his cells.

'Exactly!' For the first time all day, Duggan looked happy. 'I'm about ready to thump somebody.'

'No,' sighed the Doctor. 'I want to look around the lab first.' Lab. Computer. Then maybe, if nothing else interesting presented itself, escape.

'What use is a lab?' It was such a stupid thing to say even Romana heard it and she was carefully occupied in collecting test tubes. As she strode back into the stockroom, she gave Duggan the kind of withering look his mother gave queue-jumpers at the Post Office.

The Doctor jammed his hands in his pockets and leant back against a bench, trying to concentrate on Duggan and not on the gloriously complicated tangle of wires sitting invitingly on the bench behind him.

'Duggan. In the last few hours I have been thumped, threatened, abducted and imprisoned. I have found a piece of equipment that is not a product of current Earth technology.' Hang on. Not of what? The Doctor guessed his thought and nodded. 'Yes. I think this lab might have something to do with it.'

'Look,' Duggan growled. 'Just cut that stuff out, will you? Leave off and forget it. What about the Mona Lisa?'

'What about it?' the Doctor was sorting through the cables. He hadn't been able to resist.

'You reckon the Count and Countess are out to steal it?'

'Yes.' Fibre-optic cable, sub-etheric beaming wire, headphone lead. Glorious.

The Doctor's single, absent-minded remark was all that Duggan needed. The greatest painting in the world was under threat. The thing about fighting crime was that it was all a matter of getting your priorities right. 'Look, you do what you like. I'm going to stop them.'

The Doctor checked his watch. Ah, what a pity, the little bookshop by the Sacré-Cœur he'd quite fancied popping into would be shut. 'Listen Duggan, they're not going to steal it at six o'clock in the afternoon, are they? Whilst we're here, let's find out how they're going to steal it. And why. Shall we? Hmm? Or are you just in it for the thumping?'

Romana strode past, very carefully holding a large bottle of acid and quite deliberately ignoring the two arguing men.

Duggan, handed a high horse, climbed on. 'I am in this

job partly to protect the interests of the art dealers who have employed me—'

'But mostly for the thumping. Yes, I know.' The Doctor patted him gently on a sleeve and leaned in confidentially. 'Listen, what do you think Romana's up to?'

'I don't know.'

'Nor do I.' The Doctor grinned with delight. 'It looks terribly intriguing, don't you think?'

Duggan pushed the Doctor away and made for the stairs. 'I don't care. I'm going.'

At that moment the door at the top of the stairs opened and a figure started to make its way sluggishly down.

Professor Nikolai Kerensky awoke refreshed from his slumber. No, that was a lie. He awoke surprised. Surprised to find he had been asleep, stunned to find it was actually in the small bedroom he'd been allocated but rarely got to visit. How had he got here? He stumbled around the room, cast a wistful glance through the bars of his window at a café where people appeared to be having quite a good time near some food, and then went over to the sink where he splashed some brackish water over his face and tried not to notice how miserable his reflection was in the cracked mirror.

The Count was not a monster, he told himself. He was just a driven man with money, and that was an unusual combination. There are plenty of driven men and there are plenty of men with money. But it was very rare to find the two combined in a way that's utterly focused on changing the human race. Kerensky sat despondently on the bed, hearing each of the springs creak, and thought about his situation. He was very lucky, all things considered. The Count wasn't someone with a foundation who spoke airily about Progress as though it were a museum he fancied visiting some day, sooner or later, eventually, once he'd fixed that shelf and gone down the shops. No, the Count had a definite idea of changing the world and was running it to quite a ruthless timetable. Perhaps a bit too ruthless. For some people's tastes. Not Kerensky's. No. Not at all. He liked to be driven.

He'd been working so hard down in the lab. Two tests in a day.

Forget exhaustion. He'd gone through that. Exhaustion was like a fondly remembered seaside resort. He was now trapped in some hideous concrete new town of tiredness, stuck in its endless one-way system and roundabouts. It was all so grey and desolate and the road signs to places that were much nicer had all been taken away. Actually, maybe he would have just a few moments more sleep. Since no one was banging down the door.

What Professor Kerensky did not realise was that Hermann had carried the Professor up to his room as he wanted him out of the way for a bit. The Count had things on that were more important, and so, for a few minutes, the Professor could quite happily slip his mind.

Kerensky, however, took this slight as a sign of great benevolence. One that must be rewarded. No. No more sleep for him. He had a vocation. He stood up, ignoring the sad sigh from the bed and, wobbling only a little, made himself head out of the door, and back down to the basement.

The human race had to be saved, and he, Professor Nikolai Kerensky was going to do it.

As he walked down into his laboratory Kerensky had the momentary, and quite absurd, notion that he was being watched. He looked around. Had he heard something? Or was it simply weeks of sleep deprivation finally catching up with him? He would be hearing voices in his head next.

Something was different about the lab. A few small,

irritating changes. The mirror he used to shave was broken. Hermann had promised him that the housemaids would not come down here but he knew that occasionally they did. Things would be cleaned, straightened or generally tidied. Kerensky did not disapprove of the theory of tidiness, he just believed that it was a glorious thing to do only once one had absolutely and finally finished a piece of work. Like lighting the candles on a cake. He enjoyed disarray. Many of his finest ideas, he had once lectured the Count (who had made every show of listening while demolishing a plate of madeleines), many of Nikolai Kerensky's finest ideas were nestled between one scrap of paper and the other. Mess was an excellent incubator.

Talking of which, he crossed over to an actual incubator and tenderly took from it a fertilised egg. He wandered over to a tarpaulin, whisked it aside like a shambolic conjuror, and stood back, taking a moment to admire his work.

He had built this. To a detached observer (of which there were three) it looked like a giant, three-legged metal spider lying on its back. A dome rested on the floor. Three crooked legs rose two metres up from it, ending in sharp blue points, all aimed squarely at a small platform on top of the dome.

Had you ever seen a Jagaroth spaceship before, you would have thought, 'Well, that looks familiar. If a trifle upside-down.'

If you hadn't seen a Jagaroth spaceship before, you would have thought that putting a chicken's egg into the heart of such a magnificently formidable contraption seemed utterly pointless.

The Doctor, who was watching from behind a desk, thought it looked vaguely familiar. But then his entire life was spent thinking things looked vaguely familiar. Normally it was just crazy robots. One day, he rather feared, it would be wives.

Romana, peeping through a wine rack, congratulated herself on her earlier, rather facetious theory about what the bank of computer processors were calculating. She was right. Eggs were involved.

Duggan, lurking behind the storeroom door, was simply nodding happily to himself. A weak little man. Finally, someone to hit.

Still unaware that he wasn't imagining things, and that he definitely was being watched with three quite separate kinds of furious intensity, Kerensky placed the egg on the platform. Then he opened a small flap inside the machine's spherical base, flicked a switch and stood well back.

Waves of very expensive blue energy surged from the tripod, and a bubble slowly formed above the sphere, completely enveloping the egg. Behind Kerensky the world's most advanced computer got to work on the egg, and a few miles away, at an electrical generating substation in the suburbs, the lights dimmed as the digits on a metre began to blur.

In his garret, the artist Bourget was desperately trying not to draw a clock on the face of his latest portrait. He failed, snapping the stick of charcoal in disgust and throwing the pieces into a corner.

Inside the bubble, the egg cracked. Slowly, gently, a newly hatched life pecked its way out with its beak and staggered to its feet for the very first time. Had the chick's eyes been working properly, their first sight would have been of a small shrivelled man clapping delightedly.

Kerensky stared at the chick with joy. The Kerensky Process had successfully accelerated the time period of the hatching process by a factor of 17 Kerenskys. It was quite an achievement.

Kerensky was utterly absorbed in the hesitant footsteps of the hatchling. So absorbed, he failed to notice the large man in a tatty trench coat advancing on him, a fist joyously pounding his hand. He failed to notice the remarkably pretty woman in a schoolgirl's uniform frantically waving at the bovine man to stop. He also didn't notice the eccentric figure who was standing behind him, idly polishing a beaker with the end of his scarf.

Well, not until the man coughed politely and tapped him on his shoulder.

Professor Kerensky stared at the baffling sight of a complete stranger standing behind him. Who was this? What was he doing here? Was this a lost party guest? An artist, perhaps? There was intelligence behind those pale blue eyes. He was also flashing a broad, happy grin. Kerensky suddenly realised it had been a long time since he had seen a genuine smile. The grin broadened into an actual beam of joy at the world.

'Which came first,' the man declaimed in a rich voice, 'the chicken or the egg?'

'Who are you?' Kerensky thought that was a safe question to ask.

'Me?' The man pointed to himself as though he'd never been asked that question before in his life and that, actually, even if he had, it really didn't matter.

'Yes, who are you and what are you doing here?' Kerensky felt a stab of suspicion.

'Me? I'm the Doctor.' As though that answered everything.

The Doctor pointed at the vaguely absurd sight of the most expensive piece of equipment the world had ever seen throwing all its power at a tiny, slightly baffled chicken.

'Very interesting what you're doing here,' he told the Professor. 'But you've got it all wrong.'

*

125

The Château ballroom had been neglected for nearly a century. The silver mirrors had long ago mottled and dulled. The plaster angels had fallen from grace. The exquisite trompe l'oeil ceiling depicting an idyllic forest now flourished with moss. Dust sheet ghosts wrapped around the skeletons of furniture. Sad decay lingered in the air like the last notes of a long-stilled quartet.

Count Scarlioni had come here to put on a show. In almost every sense of the word. Hermann was carefully rolling up the remnants of an Ottoman rug. The Countess was sat on a chaise, one leg tucked under the other, watching her husband closely. She'd already asked him twice if he was all right.

She thinks I'm cracking up, thought Count Scarlioni. If only she knew. If only I knew.

No one ever asked Count Scarlioni how he was feeling. His ever-present smile told the whole world that the Count was having a very good time, usually at their expense. There was no man more confident, more certain of himself.

And yet, right now, on the most important night of his life, Count Scarlioni was feeling suddenly less than certain of himself. Who was he? The Count had always dismissed people who used words like 'literally' and 'actually', but who, literally, actually was he? Most rational people, if they suddenly discovered that underneath their face was another face entirely, would have gone insane. Especially when discovering that the face was so absolutely appallingly horrible, belonging only to an ancient nightmare. And yet, the Count had stared at that tangle of green twitching flesh and thought, 'Oh, that seems about right.'

Which had surprised even him. The new information struck him as positively delightful and explained so much. The reason why he regarded life as such a joke. The sense of knowing exactly what he was put on this Earth to do.

Why, no matter how hard he thought about it, he couldn't remember his childhood. Count Scarlioni was coming to terms with not being real. And yet, he'd never felt more alive.

Suddenly the flute of champagne tasted even more amazing, the pâté even richer, and the cigar smelled even more intense. Life felt glorious.

He'd briefly considered confiding in the Countess. 'My darling, I've discovered the most amazing thing. Look. My face falls off. I know! Extraordinary, isn't it? Shall we have a tug at yours and see if it does the same?'

But no. He knew right now that he was utterly alone in the world, the universe. The only one of his kind. And yet, somehow, not. He'd spent his entire life (he wondered how long that was) knowing that he was carrying out a higher purpose. Sometimes subconsciously, sometimes very consciously. His only regret a feeling that he wasn't entirely complete. That more still had to be revealed to him. But that it was getting so close.

He also knew that confiding his remarkable discovery to the Countess would be a disaster. He knew why she loved him. He was under no illusions about that. He did not particularly wish to complicate things. Not tonight. There was still so much to be done.

But at least he knew now what it was all for. Why he was letting Kerensky fiddle with chickens in the cellar. And why he was really stealing the Mona Lisa.

His footsteps echoing across the sprung wooden floor of the ballroom, Hermann finished his preparations. With the tiniest of flourishes, he swung open the double doors, and admitted the cat burglars. Hermann had recruited them personally. Both were highly skilled and well-paid, and their bodies would never be found. They stared around the ballroom with a mixture of intrigue and alarm.

The Count made his smile twenty-three per cent more welcoming, and handed them drinks personally. They took them gratefully and made a terrible attempt at looking at ease in the room. Nervously, they drank in thirsty gulps. It was clearly a waste of good champagne. But then, very soon, everything would seem such a terrible waste, wouldn't it?

The Count sipped his own glass a little regretfully. He tasted the magnificent bubbles bursting against his tongue and wondered for a second 'how does the mask do that?'. And yet it did. It had fitted itself back together, clinging around his head. For a moment it had felt stifling. How do the eyes work? Why tonight, of all nights? How does it not itch? Actually, I'm sure it is itching. It is. I shall never stop feeling it again. And then the sensation suddenly stopped and the Count got on with enjoying life.

He raised his glass in a toast, not only to the two thieves, but also to Hermann, to the Countess and to the small black metal cube. It was nestling innocuously between an ashtray and a copy of *Paris Match* on a card table which had come from the palace at Versailles.

'The box is a truly remarkable piece of equipment, I think you will all agree,' the Count declaimed as though he was giving a toast. He tapped the metal cube, which purred unctuously. 'This device makes the impossible possible. Perhaps the Professor should see it.' A little extra familiarity crept into the smile for Hermann and the Countess. 'I should like him to know that, whilst he is without doubt a genius, the man...' He stumbled here. The Countess frowned slightly. 'The man he works for is someone altogether more clever.'

Hermann bowed. 'Shall I go and fetch the Professor, your Excellency?'

'Yes!' smiled the Count, condemning the Doctor, Romana and Duggan to instant death.

Hermann went to the door.

'No, actually, no! I would not interrupt him. Besides which, I think our Professor would not approve.' He laughed. It was the laugh of a man who knows exactly what is coming next.

The Countess laughed automatically too.

'Is the machine ready?' the Count asked.

'Yes, your Excellency,' confirmed Hermann. Of course it was.

The Count placed the bracelet onto the top of the cube. The metal glowed with a light that spilled out, casting shadows which danced around the ballroom.

'Then let us begin.'

Unaware they'd just been condemned and reprieved, Romana and Duggan were watching the Doctor from the shadows of the cellars. Romana had seen the Doctor charm a fair number of scientists. It normally started out well and then ended badly.

Ask any scientist and they will tell you that they love being challenged. Only thus is true progress made. But they will be gritting their teeth just slightly.

'Wrong?' Kerensky was yelling and gesticulating, 'Wrong? What are you talking about?'

The Doctor pointed quite casually to the Kerensky Bubble, as though it wasn't the most remarkable achievement mankind had ever made. 'Well, you're tinkering with time, and that's always a bad idea unless you know what you're doing.'

Spare me from the idle curiosity of fools who have read half a magazine article and declared themselves an instant expert. 'I know what I'm doing! I, Professor Nikolai Kerensky am the foremost authority on temporal theory in the whole world.'

'The whole world?' The Doctor emitted a tiny puff of air. 'That's a very small place. When you consider the size of the universe.' Kerensky? He'd heard of a Professor Kerensky who'd done work on quantum bubbles. But surely this must be his older, thinner brother?

Inside the bubble, the now adult chicken observed them both with the quiet patience and wisdom of a chicken.

'Ah, but who can consider all creation?' Kerensky humoured him. At any moment Hermann would turn up and escort this man back to whatever party he'd wandered in from. Clearly one of the Count's artist friends used to hearing the sound of his own voice in salons. 'Who can really consider the size of the universe?'

'Some can. And if you can't, then you shouldn't be tinkering with time.'

Outrageous! 'But you saw it work! The greatest achievement of the human race. A cellular accelerator. You saw it!' Kerensky wondered if he was sounding perhaps a little petulant. The Doctor clucked consolingly as he continued. 'An egg developed into a chicken in thirty seconds. With a larger machine I can turn a calf into a cow in even less time. It will be the end of famine in the world!'

Surely the fool could see that?

'It'll be the end of you.' The Doctor's tone was grim. 'Not to mention the poor cow. Look.'

Kerensky had got so hot under the collar that he had quite neglected his chicken. He turned to look back at the bubble. Inside it the chicken was tottering feebly, its feathers scattering as its skin shrivelled. It tapped its beak feebly against the surface of the bubble and then sank to the surface of the device, at first a heap of bones and then dust.

Kerensky regarded the end result sadly. 'Hmmm. There are a few technical problems,' he conceded philosophically.

'Technical problems!' the Doctor ranted.

Here comes the steamroller, thought Romana. She retreated quietly to the recesses of the storeroom, leaving Duggan to watch the confrontation.

'The whole principle you're working on is wrong,' thundered the Doctor. 'You can stretch time backwards or forwards within that bubble but you can't break into it or out of it. You've set up a different time continuum, but it's totally incompatible with ours.'

Was this shouting man really an artist, marvelled Kerensky? He seemed to have a rather chilling grip on the problems the Kerensky Process was facing. The Professor knew that, true, right now, it was a challenge to reach into the bubble and get the chicken out. But surely not an impossible one. With work, and time and money, he was confident he could breach the fabric of Kerensky Space. Just a little more time. He would find a way. He had to.

'Anyway,' said the Doctor, striding over to the machine as though it was an underused washing machine, 'have you tried this?' He casually flicked a couple of settings with a fingernail.

The pile of dust twitched, sprouting bones and feathers which pulled themselves up and together, tottering to flapping skeletal life. A chicken carcase strutted around inside the bubble, flesh wrapping itself together, shed feathers flying back up into place, eyes and tendons filling themselves out. The chicken appeared to be walking backwards, becoming healthier and more alive and then smaller and younger and fluffier and finally crawling back into an egg and shutting up shop.

The egg lay there silently.

'Now, that!' declared the Doctor, 'That's rather more of an interesting effect, don't you think? Did you know you could build something that could do that as well?'

'Well, no,' admitted Kerensky, suddenly quite fancying a sit down. 'What did you do?'

'What did you think I did?' Hoping that Romana wasn't watching, the Doctor risked rolling his eyes. She had told him not to. 'I simply reversed the polarity.' He uttered that as though it answered everything. He patted the Kerensky Accelerator almost fondly. 'This is all very expensive equipment, isn't it?'

Why was the man asking him this? Was he a journalist? What? Kerensky narrowed his eyes suspiciously and, oddly, when he spoke the plain truth, it sounded coy and evasive. 'The Count is very generous. A true philanthropist. I... I do not ask too many questions.'

'A scientist's job is to ask questions,' snapped the Doctor. 'Like, for instance, what's that?'

Inside the bubble, the egg had gone. Time had continued to flow backwards over it and eventually it had found somewhere else to be. But the flow of energy had continued. Back, back and back at an ever-accelerating rate.

For a very brief instant, a face flickered into being inside the bubble. A face that was a mass of tentacles surrounding a single eye.

Kerensky stared at the sight in disgust. The Doctor thought the creature looked vaguely familiar.

Then the face and the bubble vanished and the machine turned itself off.

There was a moment of pure, stunned silence.

And then Duggan hit the Professor on the head with a spanner.

Professor Nikolai Kerensky, the world's foremost authority on temporal theory, slid to the floor. Completely unconscious for the second time in a day, which was something of a record.

The Doctor boggled at the space the Professor had recently vacated with utter horror.

Duggan was more sanguine. 'Right, then.' He dusted his hands together. 'Can we stop worrying about conjuring tricks with hens and start getting out of this place?'

The Doctor was still staring dead ahead. 'Duggan,' he said evenly. When he used this tone, invasion fleets tended to start backing away nervously. 'If it moves, hit it, is that your philosophy?'

The Doctor bent down to examine Kerensky, running a tender hand over the Professor's world-renowned head. He stood up, relieved. 'Well, he'll be all right.' The Doctor rounded on Duggan, jabbing the air furiously. Despite himself, Duggan flinched. 'But, if you do that sort of thing once more I shall…' The Doctor petered out. He realised he was becoming just as aggressive as this belligerent fool. He scowled. 'I shall have to take very firm measures.'

'Like what?' Duggan growled.

'I shall ask you not to.' The Doctor wagged a finger. Sternly.

Romana, surely more by luck than very precise timing, chose that moment to come skipping out of the storeroom. She also chose to ignore the unconscious scientist on the floor and the Doctor and Duggan squaring up to each other like prize fighters.

'Doctor! I was right!' she called.

'What?' The Doctor never really liked it when someone else in the room was right. 'What about?'

'The room measurements!' persisted Romana.

Oh, that.

'There's another room behind the storeroom wall.'

Really? Romana's sudden fascination with the real estate possibilities of the Château rather disappointed the Doctor.

It was one thing to get locked up. It was quite another to start redecorating.

'I think there's a room bricked up beyond it,' she announced excitedly.

'Is that important?' Duggan sounded thoroughly bored.

That made up the Doctor's mind. 'There's only one way to find out isn't there? Let's go have a gander.'

Chapter Eight
Unique Plurals

The Louvre at night is a remarkable place with a magic all of its own. If you can ignore the patrolling security guards, the gentle buzzing of the alarm systems, and the distant roar of truly dreadful plumbing, if you can ignore all that, then it's a place where the faces of generations stare at each other. The Venus de Milo flirts with an Egyptian scribe, and shipwrecked sailors call for help from the Emperor Napoleon. It is a firmly egalitarian court, presided over by a woman who wasn't even French. That's probably why she's smiling.

The Count walked up to the case which had been erected around the Mona Lisa. 'So, there is the problem.'

There had been many attempts to steal the Mona Lisa. The Count was aware of several, some of which he had had a hand in preventing. The least successful schemes had been foolishly elaborate, and some of the most successful had been carried out by fools, such as when an Italian handyman simply walked out of the Louvre with the Mona Lisa hidden under his coat.

The Count had not been unduly worried by such attempts. After all, a little notoriety had vastly increased the painting's value. However, the surprisingly small, sweet portrait also had become the centre of an entire industry aimed at thwarting theft, acid attack and over-affectionate tourists. The Mona Lisa was protected by the strongest security systems in any art gallery on Earth. There was, however, a way around everything.

'The painting is encased within a box constructed of steel and plate glass. But that –' the Count waved at it – 'is merely a physical barrier to protect the painting from attack.'

He nodded. Hermann's cat burglars crept forward, holding suction pads.

The Count stayed them with a tut. 'No. First, we use an ultrasonic knife to disintegrate the alarm circuits.'

Hermann produced a device, not unlike a large fat Montblanc pen. Indeed, the Doctor would have stared at the ultrasonic knife with surprise and admiration. Hermann swept it with the slow, steady hand of a surgeon, going around the borders of the case. As the machine's whine crept up, the cat burglars eased the suction cups gently, so gently onto the glass. Too early and they would trigger the alarms. Too late and the glass would fall and shatter.

An alarm dinged. Just once. No one breathed. Hermann stopped, holding the sonic knife perfectly still. The alarm's single chime faded away, showing no signs of turning into a trill. Hermann resumed cutting.

The Countess checked her watch. Perfectly according to plan.

With the most delicate of steps, the cat burglars lifted the plate glass out of the way like a mime act.

The painting sat there, exposed and yet still smiling placidly. Bring it on, she seemed to say. If she'd had eyebrows, she would have raised them. One of the burglars couldn't resist reaching out to touch her. The Count swept him aside. 'Wait! Now we come to the second, and far more interesting line of defence. The laser beams.'

The Count clicked his fingers and a criss-cross grille of red light appeared over the painting.

'Interrupt these beams,' the Count's lecture continued, 'and every alarm in France will go off instantly.' A slight exaggeration. But let them feel afraid. 'To get through these beams we must change the refractive index of the very air itself.'

He nodded to Hermann. Hermann who was always prepared. The butler positioned two small spheres on extendible tripods. He placed them in front of the painting and switched them on. The air seemed to ripple, and the light beams bent and sagged, peeling away from the wall and onto the globes, as though drawn by magnets. There was now a large gap between them.

One of the cat burglars went to lift out the painting, but the Countess was there already, her breath audibly excited. She stepped in with the grace of a trained dancer, leaning into the case, plucking the Mona Lisa delicately off the wall, lifting it from the single, normal nail which held it there, and carrying it, gently, thrillingly, over to her husband.

'Excellent,' smiled the Count.

As she handed the painting to him, the Mona Lisa vanished. Along with the Louvre.

Blinking, they found themselves all back in the ballroom. The Count bent over the cube on the card table, and deactivated it. Its metal sides stopped glowing and became dull. The Count straightened up, looking around with a pleased smile.

The others seemed stunned. The holographic projection had been more real than any of them had been expecting. For a moment, the Countess had felt the texture of the Mona

Lisa under her fingertips, the surface coarse as sandpaper. She could have picked at a priceless dab of paintwork with her fingernail. Now nothing. Except Carlos, who was as placid as if he'd just treated them to an illustrated lecture on butterflies.

Smoothly he plucked the bracelet from the top of the box and handed it to the Countess.

'A useful little device, I think you'll agree,' he said. 'Wear it always.'

The Countess slipped the bracelet back on, feeling its familiar tingle as it closed around her wrist. 'My dear,' she breathed, 'you must be a genius.'

Her husband shrugged at the compliment. Fair enough. 'Shall we say I come from a family of geniuses?'

He bent forward to kiss her on the lips. She craned her neck up, excited.

Then, at the last moment, the Count seemed to remember Hermann and his two thieves standing watching them. He turned to them, clapping his hands. 'Tonight! We have had enough of rehearsals. Tonight, the real thing!'

Then he turned back to his wife. With delicate formality, he bowed forward to kiss her hand, his lips brushing, just a little against the bracelet.

Romana sat cross-legged on the floor, surrounded by an impressive pick 'n' mix of acids, spatulas, reagents and scientific etcetera, all collected from Kerensky's laboratory. Using her straw boater as a makeshift mask, she was pouring a noxious solution down a funnel into a small hole in the wall. The mortar was fizzing and smoking.

The Doctor surveyed the lethal cloud spilling from the wall with alarm, yanking his scarf out of the way. 'Your geometry is remarkable, yes. But your chemistry leaves something to be desired.'

The smoke began to clear. A disappointingly precise hole had appeared in the masonry and the already filthy air of the storeroom now smelt of fish oil and vinegar, reminding the Doctor of a chip shop on the Old Kent Road.

He picked up the disreputable lamp and held it up to the crack, trying to see into the room beyond. Nothing except that intangible feeling of cold, ancient air seeping slowly out.

Romana tapped one of the stones. It shifted as little as a wonky milk tooth. But still, it shifted.

'This brick work is very old,' she remarked.

'Four or five hundred years,' mused the Doctor.

Duggan didn't like it. Not one bit. There was something about that hole. There was something about that wall. Duggan liked his walls to be solid. He liked certainties. He liked hitting bad people. That was how you knew who the good people were.

Upstairs, some bad people were going to steal a nice thing and ruin his reasonable career and reliable pension. Yet here he was, in a cellar in a weird cave. Next door was a man who played with chickens. And here were two ludicrously-dressed people making him stare at a hole in a very old wall. Something about that hole made him feel uncomfortable.

He reached into the cupboard of his emotions, felt around for 'Fear', couldn't quite find it, but had no trouble locating 'Anger'.

'Five hundred years?' he sneered. 'In which case it can wait an hour or two more whilst we go and sort these Johnnies out.'

Well of course, thought the Doctor sadly, Duggan would call all foreigners Johnnies. 'In my view,' he cajoled, 'a room that's been bricked up for nearly five hundred years is urgently overdue for attention. It certainly gets my vote.'

He stuck his hand in the air. Romana enthusiastically added hers. Two against one.

A true Englishman, Duggan had never really been that impressed by democracy. 'Come on,' he said firmly. 'Let's get out of here. We've got the Mona Lisa to worry about.'

It was Romana who halted him in his tracks. She was pointing towards the dark hole in the wall, from which air, so very stale, so very cold, was gently drifting. Had the hole grown in size a little?

Very quietly, Romana spoke. 'You can't cope with what we might find, can you?'

The Count and Countess had waved many people off from the gates of the Château. Royalty, the *chic*, everyone from the *Ancien Régime* to the *Nouveau Riche*. But tonight, as they stood at the rear gates of the Château, they watched the two cat burglars clamber into the back of a small Renault van driven by Hermann. The van was dingy, unremarkable, the number plates rubbed down with mud. No one would notice it drive through the streets of Paris, parking up between an old flower kiosk and the catering entrance to the Louvre. The path to the gallery had been carefully mapped out. A fair number of bribes had been paid. An elaborate diversion had been arranged involving a blocked-up sewer flooding a nearby Metro station. When the Metro line had been constructed seventy years previously, there had been a lot of concerns that it went too near the sewer. These had been waved aside by someone.

The crime of the century had been meticulously planned for a very long time. And it was finally happening.

As Hermann's little van drove out through the gates, neither the Count nor the Countess could resist waving it off. As it went round the corner and the gates closed behind it, both sighed. The Countess felt nervous. The Count felt a curious sense of anti-climax. But, being who they were, they did not confide this in each other.

'I'm going to change into something more comfortable,' she said.

'Not a bad idea,' he agreed, smiling at her. It was a curious smile. He rubbed his hands together. 'And then, perhaps, I should go and check on our guests.'

He walked away.

The Countess, left alone, looked out through the gates at Paris. People were hurrying home, going about their dull, ordinary lives. You people have no idea, she thought, no idea what it means to be alive.

Down in the cellar, the Doctor was chipping away at the wall. Romana had located a lump hammer and a chisel used to prise open packing cases. It was doing good, slow work on the masonry. When the Doctor wasn't hitting his thumb.

Behind them Duggan paced like a caged lion. Romana had learned that you could sense a lot from the reactions of primitive beasts. Cows lay down when it was going to rain. Dogs barked before thunder. And Duggan started muttering.

'What's all the equipment in the laboratory for, Doctor?' she asked brightly. Let's keep it light. Let's carry on solving mysteries. Because, in Romana's head, this was all somehow connected.

'Eh?' The Doctor paused, bashed his thumb, and sucked it elaborately. 'Well, the Count seems to be financing some dangerous experiment with time. The Professor thinks he's breeding chickens.'

'Stealing the Mona Lisa to pay for chickens?' Duggan piped up. He thought he'd heard them all.

'Yes,' said the Doctor sourly.

'But who would want to buy the Mona Lisa?' reasoned Romana. 'You can hardly show it off to anybody if it's known to be stolen.' This is where, she thought, computer painting came into its own. There was no original, therefore there was no value in the physical painting itself, only in the artwork, thus preventing this whole tangled mess. How typical of the Earth. No wonder the Doctor liked the planet so much. Needlessly complicated. Things were so much simpler on Gallifrey, she thought, not for the first time that day.

Duggan glanced at Romana as though she'd said something stupid. She felt insulted. 'There are seven people in my little address book who would pay millions for the Mona Lisa just for their private collection,' he informed her smugly.

'But no one could even know they'd got it!'

'Yes, it'd be an expensive gloat. But they'd buy it.' On this one thing, Duggan was rigorously accurate. He'd spent the last eighteen months studying the circles in which the Count moved. When rumours of an attempt to steal the Mona Lisa had surfaced, he'd been not at all surprised to learn that the people most likely to want to own it all moved in the same circles as the Count. A shipping magnate in Crete. A banker in Tokyo. A playboy in New York. The list went on. All seven of them fabulously rich, but also fabulously shady. The kind of people who, if the Mona Lisa fell into their hands, would never mention it to anyone ever again. There were, careful checking had shown, precisely seven of these people. Seven people who were rich enough and who could be relied upon not to brag about it after dinner. These seven people were all, curiously enough, utterly ruthless and intensely private. Duggan had told his Chief his theory. 'You know what? If the Mona Lisa is stolen and one of the Seven buys it, it's going to be quite the bidding war. I wouldn't be surprised if it gets nasty.' He was sure the Count had taken steps to make sure that it was an anonymous auction. But it wouldn't be enough. They'd find out. They'd start killing each other. The world would be no worse off.

The Doctor lifted a large stone out of the wall, waddling away with it and dropping it to the ground. The space was now large enough to show off a little of the room beyond. It seemed to be empty. Duggan found that a relief. Just some old cupboard or other. Big fuss over nothing. Like those chickens.

Romana surveyed the wall with a huff. 'How are we going to move this last bit?' The chiselling had taken quite a while. Were they really going to have to carry on? At the present rate that would take them approximately 7.4 hours. They had enough oil left in the lamp for two.

'I think I'll need some machinery, heavy lifting equipment,' said the Doctor. He doubted his thumbs could take much more.

Duggan decided to be helpful. The sooner they got this wild goose chase over with, the better. 'I've got all the machinery we'll need,' he announced. 'Stand back.'

And then, with the solid bluntness that had just about kept him employed, he shoulder-charged the wall. When Duggan had been at school, he'd been feared in the rugby scrum.

Had it been up to Romana she would have preferred a rather more careful excavation of the wall. But she had to admit, watching him barge through the wall, he was certainly efficient. Resolute French masonry met British beef and, just this once, gave in.

Romana waited for the dust to settle, just a little, then picked up the lamp and went through. The room beyond was precisely as small as she'd expected. Beyond a scrap of a candle and the skeleton of a mouse, there was nothing in it.

Apart from the wall at the end. At first glance the wall was panelled with wood.

Then she realised. The wall was divided into six shallow wooden cabinets.

'What are they, Doctor?'

'I don't know.' The Doctor shrugged, running a thumb cautiously down one of the doors. It came away thick with dust. 'But whatever they are, they've been undisturbed since this room was bricked up centuries ago.'

Cupboards? They'd been to all this trouble for cupboards? Duggan had reached the end of his not very long tether. 'All right,' he groaned, rubbing his bruised shoulder. 'Have a look. Let's get on with it.'

The Doctor chose the top-left cabinet. He had a little difficulty with the catch. Time had rusted it shut, but he was able finally to prise it open.

'Oh.'

Romana and Duggan tried to see, but for a few seconds the contents of the cupboard were shadowed by the door. Then the Doctor swung it fully open and stepped back.

Duggan shook the oil lamp, as though it was malfunctioning.

Inside the shallow cupboard was a painting. Seventy-seven centimetres long. Fifty-three centimetres wide.

'It's the Mona Lisa,' breathed the Doctor.

The Mona Lisa smiled benevolently at everyone in the room, quietly and calmly. Do go on, she seemed to be saying.

Romana stared at it. She mentally computed pi to a few of her more favourite places, then her less favourite ones. And then stopped thinking entirely and just gawped.

'Well,' said Duggan and then ground to a halt for a few seconds. His brain needed a moment to get a breath of fresh air and find something stupid to say. 'It must be a fake.'

'Really?' The Doctor was peering at the painting. 'It's

been here for centuries. Like the brickwork. Five hundred years.'

'Then the painting in the Louvre…' began Romana. Obviously, the one in the museum was a fake. Had been all along. That made a lot of sense. If you'd only ever been displaying the fake, then it was, as far as you knew, genuine. Again, computer painting would sidestep this logic problem beautifully.

The Doctor shook his head. 'The painting in the Louvre is well authenticated.'

Duggan's brain made a noise. Was the Doctor saying there were two Mona Lisas?

The Doctor tapped the painting very, very gently. 'Well, I don't know what's in the Louvre, but this is the genuine article.'

'So is this one,' announced Romana.

She had opened the next cabinet. It also contained the Mona Lisa.

Duggan, slack-jawed and drooling just a little, opened the third cabinet. Another Mona Lisa.

They opened all of the cabinets very quickly after that.

Hidden away for five hundred years, and now finally revealed, their smiles leaping in the flames of Duggan's lamp, were six Mona Lisas.

Chapter Nine
Count
Down

Very few things in the universe shut the Doctor up. But six Mona Lisas did the trick.

Duggan was blissfully catatonic.

It was rather nice. It gave Romana a moment or two to think. Just her, alone in a room with six smiling women. Romana looked again at the expression on the woman's face. 'You'll work it out,' she seemed to be saying.

'I do hope so,' Romana thought.

For a start, these six paintings had to be genuine. You wouldn't go to the trouble of bricking up six colour prints for half a millennia. Logic got her to this point and then had to have a sit down and a cup of tea. Why would you paint six Mona Lisas and then brick them up? These hadn't been left in cupboards and forgotten about. They had been deliberately placed here and sealed away. In a cave deep below the ground. Quite impervious to bomb blast. They'd survived a few tremors and floods. Bricked up so tightly that the Château above could burn down and these paintings would still be here. Smiling away to themselves.

Actually, thought Romana, I wish they'd stop smiling right about now. Another thing about computer paintings. You could change the expressions.

The Doctor had begun moving. In Romana's experience this usually meant some noise would be starting up soon. He was tenderly stroking one of the paintings. 'The brushwork's Leonardo's.'

Duggan nodded in glum agreement.

'How can you tell?' asked Romana.

'It's as individual as a signature.' Leonardo had been a pioneer in many things, including the materials he worked with. An earlier version of the Mona Lisa had been painted on canvas, but, for the final work, just for the hell of it, he'd switched to a thin poplar board, painting in oils of his own devising, using a carefully blended brushstroke he'd come up with, so that the overall painting glowed like a photograph. This haphazard whirligig of invention accidentally made the painting almost impossible to forge. The Doctor's fingertips danced delicately over the surface of the board. 'The pigments are his, too.'

'Is that true of all of them?'

'Every last one,' the Doctor sighed.

They went quiet again.

'What I can't understand is…' muttered the Doctor and then petered out. He chewed the end of his scarf thoughtfully for a while. 'Why does a man who already appears to have six Mona Lisas want to go to all the bother of stealing another one?'

Duggan knew why. This was a surprise to everyone in the room. 'Oh, pull your head together, Doctor,' he growled impatiently.

The Doctor stared at Duggan. Clearly he thought he had the answer. But the Doctor couldn't see it for the life of him.

'I just told you,' Duggan sounded exasperated. Did no one ever listen to him? 'There are seven people in the world who would buy the picture in secret. But none of them are going to buy a Mona Lisa while it's still hanging in the Louvre.'

'Of course,' exclaimed Romana. 'They would each have to think they were buying the stolen one.'

That made perfect sense, Duggan thought for a moment, before his head spun round again. Seven buyers. Exactly seven buyers. Exactly seven pictures. How could that possibly happen? That was such a massive coincidence.

Such a massive coincidence that Romana was already calculating it in her head and getting the sorts of numbers that required chewing carefully before swallowing.

'Seven Mona Lisas… Seven buyers…' The Doctor shook his head ruefully. 'I wouldn't make a very good criminal, would I?'

'No, Doctor,' announced the Count. 'Good criminals don't get caught.'

The Count was lounging in the doorway to the chamber. He was wearing a fabulously expensive dressing gown and covering them with a rather lovely gun. He smiled his most amused smile. He did not look the least bit surprised to see them there. His entire appearance was that of a genial host who finds his house guests helping themselves to the biscuit barrel.

'I see you have found some of my pictures,' he waved at them casually with his gun. 'Rather good, don't you think?' He smiled graciously, then counted the paintings with the gun. 'Five… Six. And after tonight I will have a seventh. The operation is already in hand. Any questions?'

The Doctor suddenly found he rather missed being the most bizarre thing in the room. A trifle dejectedly, he pointed a sad finger at the paintings. 'Can I ask you where you got these from?'

'No,' beamed the Count.

'I see. Or how you knew they were here?'

'No.'

'They've been bricked up for centuries.'

'Yes.'

'I do like concise answers,' sighed the Doctor.

'Good.' The Count's smile dwindled like a merry firework. 'You know, I came down here to talk to Kerensky.'

'Oh?'

'But he doesn't seem to be able to speak to me.'

'Oh.'

'Can you cast any light on the matter, Doctor?'

'No.'

'But I can,' said Duggan, hurling the lamp at Count Scarlioni's head. The Count's gun fired, miraculously hitting neither the lamp nor any of the paintings. Dazed by the sound of the gun, Romana and the Doctor stumbled backwards while Duggan lunged forward, picked up a brick, and drove it into the Count's head.

Count Scarlioni dropped without a word.

Romana checked the body anxiously. Still breathing but dead to the world.

The Doctor shook the buzzing out of his head and surveyed the Count furiously. 'Duggan, why is it that every time I start talking to someone you knock them unconscious?'

Duggan rubbed at the back of his neck, a trifle sheepish. 'Well, I didn't expect him to go down that easily.'

'Perhaps,' the Doctor offered, 'if you don't understand heads you shouldn't go around hitting them?'

'Well, what would you suggest I did?' snarled Duggan. He felt that the Doctor was being a touch ungrateful.

'Duggan!' roared the Doctor and then stopped. For a moment, just a moment, he had forgotten that they were standing next to six Mona Lisas. Lowering his voice respectfully he continued. 'I thought you had a job to do. Stop the Count's men stealing the Mona Lisa.' He stopped, chewing the air. 'The other Mona Lisa. Come on.'

Getting out of the Château wasn't that easy. Romana knew precisely the way they'd come, but the Doctor refused to believe her. Soon they were hopelessly lost in the huge and echoing hallways. In places damp had got in. Paintings that had once been carefully hung now sagged from the walls. Rugs squelched underfoot. Mould and moss flowed through beautiful frescoes. A lot of the paintings in this area had been left to rot. Once prized, the names of their painters were long forgotten, the paint itself starting to seep and flow into the wall. These works had been left to die because they no longer mattered.

Hearing footsteps, they ducked into a chapel. The seats were dusty from neglect, but the air still smelt of incense. An entire corner of the chapel was given over to a reliquary where the purported bones of long-dead, long-forgotten saints all sat in a jumbled heap. Someone still came in here to light candles occasionally. Duggan thought he caught a whiff of the Countess's perfume.

They moved through into another chamber. It had once been a vast drawing room, built up around a central mosaic of a one-eyed Medusa. The mirrors were all splintered. The wallpaper bubbled as insects crawled underneath it. A warped and legless harpsichord splayed forgotten on the floor.

The whole Château had been falling down for centuries.

Romana recognised a Constable. The Doctor wasn't convinced – they all looked alike to him. But Romana was quite firm. Turn left at the Constable she insisted, right at the second Matisse, and down through the corridor of gloomy Dutchmen and they'd be back into the main rooms of the Château.

Which is where the Count's men found them.

The fight was brief and bloody and mostly up to Duggan. There were six of them. They all had guns. Using his fists like a Whirling Dervish being thrown out of a nightclub, Duggan accounted for five. The Doctor, when he was entirely certain that no one was watching, knocked the sixth unconscious with a snatched-up picture frame, finishing off a once-priceless canvas that the maggots had been at.

Duggan surveyed the heap of bodies and chose the nicest gun. 'Amateurs,' he sneered.

Romana examined the bullet holes in the wall. At a glance she could see the many different layers of paint and decoration which had taken place over time. Like the rings on a tree, taking her all the way back to lathe and plaster. And, beneath that, stale air and the distant scrabbling of vermin.

Duggan, happy to have a gun in his hand again, led them towards the main door. He'd get them out. He'd see them through. Just a few more steps and then freedom, and the glory of bringing down the Scarlioni Gang for ever.

A spray of bullets sent them all diving for cover as chips of plaster and shredded pot plants spun up into the air.

Coughing, the Doctor looked up carefully, hat clasped protectively to his head.

The Countess was standing at the end of the corridor, blocking their path. She was holding a mini-Gatling gun and tutting theatrically.

Well, this had not been part of the plan.

The Countess, grinning sweetly, strolled towards Duggan. She could afford to take her time over this. She blew him a kiss and tightened her finger on the trigger.

She had made the terrible mistake of ignoring Romana. As the Countess passed the alcove she was pressed into,

Romana snatched up a vase and brought it down on the Countess's head. She went down like a sack of turnips.

Romana was slightly surprised at herself. She frowned.

'Not you as well.' The Doctor was staring at the Countess's prostrate figure.

'You know, I rather enjoyed that.' Romana was biting her lip.

'Well, I should hope so.' The Doctor sadly picked up a few shards of the vase. 'That was late Ming Dynasty and absolutely priceless.'

Duggan propped the Countess up against a wall. Even unconscious she looked quite beautiful.

Seconds later they were out on the street. All around them, Paris got on with being rather splendid by night. Couples ran down a nearby boulevard laughing. Cars swerved and hooted at each other in curiously endearing ways. A nearby café spilled out onto the street. And, because it was night time, the Eiffel Tower was lit up. Of course it was.

Just for a moment, the giddy fun of that afternoon (really, had it only been this afternoon?) came flooding back to Romana. Yes, there were dangerous time experiments and impossible paintings to contend with. But there was also Paris. A whole city to go out and enjoy. Perhaps they could just… She looked across at the Doctor and could see the grin forming on his face. He was thinking the same.

It was Duggan's single-mindedness which saved them. 'Come on,' he growled. 'We've got to get to the Louvre.' He started off towards the museum.

For a moment the Doctor looked disappointed. Then he strode off in a different direction entirely. 'No Duggan. You have to go to the Louvre.'

What, thought Romana? Were they really bunking off and leaving Duggan to it?

'Romana, you stay with Duggan, look after him, stop each other hitting people.' The Doctor continued to walk off into the night.

Romana was stunned.

'Where are you going?' she demanded.

'I'm going to see a middle-aged Italian,' the Doctor called out. 'Well, late Middle Aged. Renaissance in fact.' The Doctor's laugh echoed as he was swallowed up into the night

The singing finally finished. Harrison Mandel felt as though his head had been filled with chalk scraped from a blackboard by fingernails.

The nightclub audience broke into enthusiastic applause.

'But that was dreadful,' he groaned.

Elena looked at him and tutted. 'It was, darling, it absolutely was. But we mustn't say so.' She stood up. 'Brava!' she called. 'Brava!' She hastily sat down again. 'Don't think I could stand another encore.' She laid a hand upon his leg. 'No. The art of these things is to express oneself while not expressing oneself.'

The applause died and the audience started to make a hurried exit. Harrison stood reluctantly, sad to give up Elena's hand on his knee. 'You see, one does not say that that was dreadful wailing by a singer who can't sing, *mon cheri*, although, undoubtedly, that is exactly what it was. That is not done.' The spilled out into the bar, where there was an audible air of relief. 'One says that it was a bravura voyage into atonalism.'

'One does?' Harrison echoed uncertainly.

'One absolutely does.' Elena paused, clearly expecting him to say something.

'Well,' began Harrison haltingly, 'I did like her dress.'

Elena very clearly didn't show her disappointment. 'Out there in Paris is something beautiful, waiting just for you.

And when you see it, you will find the words.' She took his arm. 'Come, let's go and do something fun.'

The Louvre was not the only art gallery broken into that night. About ten minutes' walk from the Eiffel Tower is a street full of galleries, the kind that sells cheap fakes to expensive tourists.

Skilled hands saw to a lock and deactivated both alarms in seconds. M. Bertrand's gallery was crammed full of absurd things at absurd prices. Thieves can tell a lot about a Paris gallery by the number of alarms it has. Two systems says that there's nothing really worth stealing and you may as well not bother picking the lock. In this case, M. Bertrand was playing the thieves at their own game. There was actually a fabulously valuable Barbara Hepworth sculpture at the back, but as he'd had to get permission from the council to take a wall down to fit it in, he wasn't that worried about thieves stealing it.

The intruder did pause to admire the Hepworth. He even stroked it gently. He was perhaps the only person in Paris who could have removed it without knocking a wall down. But no.

Instead he worked his way carefully through the gallery, torch playing over various paintings. Some watches melting in deserts were clearly derivative. Several early impressionist works were clearly fakes. And some of the string-and-twine sculptures screamed 'bought from a bric-a-brac stall'. The thing that drew the thief was the new exhibit.

M. Bertrand had failed to notice the new exhibit. If he had he would have screamed in surprise while hastily scribbling out a price ticket. The truth was that M. Bertrand's long lunch yesterday had been so long it had lasted until the following morning. He'd crawled in so late he'd barely had time to drink an espresso and shrug before heading out for lunch again. Because of this, M. Bertrand had entirely missed his remarkable new exhibit.

The intruder did not. He was only mildly distracted by the need to return and admire the Hepworth again. Other than that, he more or less made a beeline for the new exhibit.

It was a blue box, well over two metres high by about a metre wide. M. Bertrand would have been delighted by it, partly because it was such an unusual thing. When he'd been in London in the 1960s, they were everywhere. Police boxes were a convenient way for policemen to phone the station, while giving them somewhere handy to have their sandwiches and store their criminals (so long as the criminals didn't eat their lunch). With the rise of the radio and the sandwich bar, the police box had gradually been phased out. Which was a shame, as there was something about the sheer boxiness and the blueness of it and the words 'Police Box' that made the box really so very reassuring. Plus the fact that it hummed to itself.

Not that every police box hummed to itself. Just this one. It was a happy little 'all's well with the world' hum which sometimes, it had to be said, seemed very much at odds with the things going on around it. But anyway, hum it did. It was all part of how reassuring the box was. 'I'm perfectly content to be here,' the box seemed to be saying, 'so that's not a problem for you either is it?'

Even the sign on the front of the humming blue box was reassuring, if misleading:

POLICE TELEPHONE
FREE FOR USE OF PUBLIC
ADVICE AND ASSISTANCE OBTAINABLE
IMMEDIATELY
OFFICERS & CARS RESPOND TO URGENT CALLS
PULL TO OPEN

The intruder went up to the reassuring door of the reassuring box and fitted a key to it. It opened and, with only a short pause to hoik his scarf out of the way, he strode inside and the door closed again.

Things stayed that way for a minute or two.

And then the hum got a little louder, as though the box was thinking about something very hard. Then, as if this had been the plan all along, the box went elsewhere loudly.

The Doctor had vanished.

Impossible man. Romana found a small iron bollard and kicked it soundly.

One minute he'd been there, ordering them to go and save the Mona Lisa, the next he'd vanished into the night and literally off the face of the Earth. The penny had dropped a second too late. She'd hurried after him, and found herself standing in a street full of geraniums and absurdly empty of Doctor.

The Doctor really was surprisingly good at making himself scarce when he wanted to. When some trigger-happy guard with a staser pistol was firing at him, or when Romana wanted to know what the Moog Drone Clamp was doing in the kettle. These were just normal, boring everyday disappearing acts. But this was it. This time he'd pulled the big one.

He'd done it. He'd gone and abandoned her on Earth. He'd raced back to the TARDIS, full of confidence. Quick trip off into time and then back. The terrible truth was that the Doctor could end up anywhere. He was hopeless at piloting the TARDIS. Really, truly utterly hopeless. He was best off sticking to the Randomiser. But no, the Doctor was so absolutely delighted at how much better he'd got at flying it recently that he'd completely failed to notice the remarkable coincidence of Romana's arrival. She'd quickly mastered the art of leaning over the controls to tell him how marvellous he was while subtly tweaking the Mandril Condensors before he landed them inside a sun.

And tonight he'd wandered off. So full of idiotic *joie de vivre*. Romana looked around, at the warmly lit bars, at the crowds of happy people wandering down the street, at the man squeezing a box until it begged musically for mercy. Paris. That was it. The Doctor was so idiotically full of the joys of Paris that he'd gone gambolling off. Without her, he was doomed. He could end up absolutely anywhere in time and space. Or a sun. Again. Serve him jolly well right.

But what about her? Romana looked around herself. At Duggan, glaring at her with a kind of slack-jawed expectancy. Well. She could team up and have adventures with him, she supposed. She thought about that for a bit.

'What are you laughing at?' said Duggan.

'Oh, nothing,' Romana set off. 'Come on. Let's go and save the Mona Lisa.'

The Doctor stood inside the TARDIS and wondered about things. He was helped in this quest by his robot dog. K-9 had wandered across to greet him eagerly.

'Hello, K-9,' he'd beamed. 'How are you?'

K-9 had begun a lengthy diagnostic report, complete with a list of complaints about malfunctioning servo units which had yet to be replaced despite frequent requests, a fluctuating diode in his vocal circuits, and a disappointing charge in his new battery. Thank heavens K-9 had not yet discovered how to fill in complaint forms.

The Doctor loved having a robot dog. Unlike humans, K-9 asked relatively few questions, nearly always provided answers, and didn't go wandering off and then have to be rescued from the Ogrons. However, the Doctor had very deliberately left him out of the trip to Paris. He'd made the quite reasonable argument that K-9 would find it difficult gliding across the cobbled streets, but really, really, he rather thought that K-9 would miss the point of Paris entirely. He would just not enjoy himself. There was no poetry in K-9's soul.

'Good boy, K-9,' said the Doctor, cutting across the dog's list of grievances. He applied himself to the task of setting the coordinates.

Tricky. The TARDIS had shown a remarkable improvement in her behaviour recently. He wondered if fitting the Randomiser had helped. Relieved of the pressure of constantly being asked to land somewhere specific and then missing, the TARDIS instead could arrive anywhere and anywhen in total confidence that she wasn't disappointing. This meant that, on the rare occasions when the Doctor asked her to do something specific, such as, say, hop 500 years that-a-way and a few countries to the right, well, things went better than ever before.

Although, all of a sudden, staring at the array of slightly alarmed dials and big red buttons, the Doctor suffered a rare pang of self-doubt. That time when they'd been aiming for the Horsehead Nebula and, quite remarkably, hit it? Hadn't Romana been standing at his side? And also, when they'd arrived at the Medusa Cascade, hadn't Romana been standing just opposite, her hands idly close to the drift compensators? Funny how that kept happening. Curious.

The Doctor dismissed the idea as ridiculous, paranoid fantasy. It was all down to how much better the TARDIS was behaving these days. They'd learned to respect each other. Just plug in the date which one did simply by... well, a bit like that, wasn't it, K-9, no quiet I'm thinking, ah yes, splendid, and then nudge the location over there by... now, were we talking miles or kilometres? When did the French go metric, that might well be important. Or not, as the case may be.

The Doctor crossed his fingers, ignored an urgent warning from K-9 and pulled a lever. Here goes nothing, he thought.

'Oh,' said the Doctor later as the thumbscrews approached. Funny the difference a syllable makes. Take 'Leonardo', for example. One of the most romantic names in any language. 'Leonard', not so much. It lacked that certain... *je ne sais quoi*, that was it. What a lovely French expression. How silly of him not to have used it while he was in France. Rather than...

Brilliant Italian Renaissance sunshine poured through the windows of the studio. It had that smug quality of light that said, 'You will paint something wonderful about me, won't you?' And the man who lived in the studio (not owned, he didn't own anything, really) had certainly made every effort to paint that sunshine very hard indeed.

Easels and paints were everywhere. Intricate designs hung from the walls, and elaborate drawings spilled over the tables and spread out across the floor. Somewhere underneath all that sea of thought was quite a nice carpet. But all you would notice at a glance was a profusion of artistic disarray.

This was a room crammed full to bursting with genius. Otherwise it was completely deserted.

Right up until the moment that, with a whoop, a large blue box appeared hurriedly in a corner, shooing a lot of air molecules elsewhere. The door opened and the Doctor stuck his head out, eyes tight shut. He opened them cautiously, looked around in amazed delight, leapt outside, shut the door and patted the blue box fondly. Hadn't they done well?

TARDIS, by the way stood quite often for Time And

Relative Dimensions In Space. Sometimes the Doctor also said it was Time And Relative Dimension In Space. Which was actually even more meaningless. Rather like the machine itself, the TARDIS's name made sense only so long as you didn't think too hard about it.

Right now, the Doctor was busy being simply delighted. Here he was. Leonardo da Vinci's studio. Even parked in the same spot as last time.

'Leonardo? Leonardo!' he called. No sign of him. Ah well. He'd be along in a moment. Probably off buying baguettes. People in the Mediterranean were always doing that.

He pottered around the studio, looking at this, marvelling at that, happily swapping gossip with Leonardo's songbirds. The weather had, apparently, been rather glorious recently, and the Doctor couldn't disagree.

'Ah that Renaissance sunshine!' he enthused, basking in it. The Doctor rarely got an opportunity to bask in anything other than his own cleverness, so he enjoyed the lazy smoky sunshine. It was one of his favourite things about this period. And he liked a lot about the Renaissance. He continued to rifle through Leonardo's studio, chuckling at the paintings. No, the old fellow still hadn't really finished anything. He never really did. A constant fiddler, a fellow who just couldn't leave well alone. A meddler. Imagine that. What a pity.

'Leonardo!' he called out again. 'It's me, the Doctor,' he put in reassuringly. Perhaps Leonardo was hiding somewhere, afraid his visitor was a debt collector, or a patron demanding to know why his wife's portrait was another decade overdue. 'Leonardo? Are you there? Hello?' He checked behind a curtain and peeped under a table. 'The paintings went down very well,' he continued coaxingly. 'Everyone loved them. So many people have said how good they thought they were. The Last Supper, remember that one?' The Doctor had spent ages trying to sneak into it. 'The Mona Lisa?' he asked hopefully. No response. And yet, he was now convinced he wasn't alone. 'I said the Mona Lisa, remember? That dreadful woman with no eyebrows who wouldn't sit still, eh? Leo…?'

He picked up a model, buzzed it around the room and then smiled. 'Still, your idea for a helicopter took a little longer to catch on, but as I said, these things take time.' That was a footstep outside. Definitely a footstep. Playing hide-and-seek with one of the greatest geniuses the world has ever known? There were worse ways to spend an afternoon.

Any second now, Leonardo would pop out from behind the arras. That was it. He twitched it to one side.

'You!' the rapier landed on the Doctor's shoulder and he blinked.

He found himself facing a hog-faced guard whose armour smelt of onions.

'You! What are you doing here?'

'Me?' The Doctor was all innocence. He really wished the guard would give him a chance to clean that rapier before stabbing him with it. It looked filthy. Rather like the guard. Did he sleep in that armour?

The guard screwed up his face with suspicion, causing what the Doctor hoped was a lump of dirt to fall off of it. 'Who are you? What are you doing here?'

Isn't that obvious? 'Well, I just popped in to see Leonardo, actually. Is he about?'

The Doctor had known that tourists, debt collectors and angry clients were a bit of a problem for Da Vinci, but had it really got so bad that Leo had hired a bouncer?

The rapier jabbed the Doctor's coat. 'No one is allowed to see Leonardo.'

'Is that so?' The Doctor felt a sudden nagging worry.

'He is engaged on important work –' the suspicious, feral

face narrowed even further – 'for Captain Tancredi.'

'Captain Tancredi!' gasped the Doctor.

'You know him?'

'Nope.'

'He will want to question you.' The guard nodded, in a you'll-get-yours way.

This might not be altogether good, thought the Doctor. The Renaissance was charming, what with that lazy smoky sunshine. But quite a lot of that smoke was caused by burning heretics, thinkers and the eccentrically dressed. Oh dear.

'He'll want to question me? Well, I expect I will want to question him.' The Doctor, sensing a sticky wicket, realised he was being forced to his knees, and picked a nice clean spot of rug to kneel on. He might not, necessarily, have the upper hand here, but he might as well be comfortable. 'We can have a pleasant little chat, can't we?'

The soldier leaned close to the Doctor and, much to his horror, breathed over him. 'He will be here instantly,' he announced smugly.

Footsteps came clipping up the steps, and the door to the study flew open. A figure stood there, taking in the scene, perfectly silhouetted by that Renaissance sunshine. The man strode into the room as though he owned it. Which, in fact, he did.

Advancing on the Doctor was a perfectly handsome man, wearing the lavish costume of a captain in the private army of an Italian duke. In order to stop things looking too severe, his armour was bedecked with ostrich feathers and fitted over a blouse. The flourishes did nothing to offset the air of lethal menace with which the figure advanced on the Doctor.

This then was Captain Tancredi.

Only…

'You!' The Doctor's tone was grim. 'What are you doing here?'

The figure nodded, as though this was a fair point. If he was surprised, his face didn't show it. Instead Captain Tancredi was smiling. 'I think that is exactly the question I ought to be asking you.' The smile broadened. 'Doctor.'

Captain Tancredi looked exactly like Count Carlos Scarlioni.

PART THREE

'Qu'est-ce que l'histoire? Sinon une fable sur laquelle tout le monde est d'accord.'
('What is history? It's a fairy tale we can all agree on.')

Napoleon Bonaparte

CHAPTER TEN
RENAISSANCE MAN

Getting into the Louvre was easier than Romana had expected. They'd just walked in. No one challenged them, no one called after them, no one shot at them, and no alarms went off. It was all rather refreshing.

They wandered the corridors, Duggan's flashlight playing cautiously across the statues. A lot of them seemed bothersomely incomplete. Romana noticed they'd placed these to one side, clearly while they went off hunting for the missing bits. A headless winged angel, for instance, was popped out of the way up a staircase. It all seemed so terribly careless. Humans were very bad at looking after things.

She noticed Duggan's body language was becoming increasingly tense.

'I thought the Louvre was meant to be well guarded,' she said.

'It is.' Duggan's tone was grim. He ran a gloved hand over a box on the wall. It had once been a motion sensor. 'It looks as though every single alarm in the place has been immobilised. A fantastic feat.' He sounded grudgingly impressed.

'The Count seems to have some clever technology here as well,' said Romana, peering at the burned-out circuitry. Had it been knocked out by a targeted electromagnetic pulse? Fascinating.

They wandered into the Mona Lisa gallery and Romana stepped in something. She lowered her torch and gasped. She'd trodden in the body of a security guard.

'There's another alarm been immobilised,' growled Duggan.

That was too much for Romana. 'You have a pretty cynical attitude to life don't you, Duggan?'

'Well…' Unapologetic, Duggan gave her a decidedly non-Gallic shrug. 'When you've been around as long as I have… Actually, how old are you?'

'A hundred and twenty-five.'

'What?'

Romana didn't bother elaborating. She'd wandered over to the Mona Lisa herself. Or rather, the space where the Mona Lisa had once been. The case had been neatly – very neatly – broken into and the painting removed. All that remained was a lattice of laser beams, exactly taking up the dimensions of the painting. The overall effect was striking and not a little sad.

'She's gone,' Romana said.

Duggan knew they shouldn't have wasted time fooling around in cellars. He buried his anger in a low growl. Part of him just couldn't believe that the painting had actually been stolen. 'That system around it, those beams, they should be absolutely impregnable. It can't be turned off.'

'Well they seem to have managed it somehow.' Romana peered at the beams. 'Maybe by distorting the refractive index of the air.'

'Umm, yes,' Duggan muttered doubtfully. 'But to get at that painting you'd have to pass through the beams, like this…'

He stuck his hands between the lasers. If his hunch was right, the alarms wouldn't go off.

His hunch was not right.

A lot of alarms went off.

'Hell's bells,' screamed Duggan, clapping his hands to his ears.

'That's what it sounds like,' Romana agreed, shouting over the clamour. 'What do we do now?' She could hear shouts. She could hear dogs. That was not good.

'Split up,' Duggan yelled over the din. 'We'll meet back at the café.'

'Really? How do you suggest we get out?'

'See that window?' laughed Duggan. He pointed at a very nice stained-glass window at the end of the gallery. It had once belonged to a cathedral.

'Yes.'

Duggan threw himself at the window. There was the sound of breaking glass, a thud, and then more alarms went off, and the distant dogs got very excited indeed.

Left alone in the Louvre, Romana put her hands on her hips.

'All this fuss over a painting,' she sighed.

Professor Nikolai Kerensky woke up. He had conflicting thoughts about this. Two periods of sleep in twenty-four hours had been a literally undreamt of luxury, and he was rather regretting that it was over. Yet, here he was, lying on the cold stone floor and his head hurt quite a lot. Someone had broken in… that man with the scarf? And someone had hit him. On the other hand, the chicken experiment had been most satisfying. More or less.

He hoisted himself up, holding on to the edge of a bench until the room settled down a little. He felt the lump that was forming on his skull tenderly and then examined the blood congealing on his hands.

'Academic life,' he sighed.

He shook his head. It hurt.

'Chickens,' he muttered, looking at the Kerensky Accelerator. That was intact, at least. And hopefully his head was as well. If industrial saboteurs had smashed the device and injured his brain then he might not be able to build another one. He worried about that. A great loss to the world. A grave disappointment to the Count.

Tenderly inching his way towards the stairs he realised he had to summon the Count. He would like to know there were intruders in his laboratory. He pulled the bell rope. No answer. On his way to the stairs he had realised the storeroom door was open and a strange light was coming from it. How puzzling.

He noticed a hole in the storeroom wall. What had the intruders been up to? Curious, he edged inside and stopped in amazement when he saw what was on the wall of the hidden room.

'Mona Lisas?'

The good thing about Duggan, Romana thought, was… well, she was sure it would come to her eventually. When she had a chance to draw breath, maybe. With the Doctor, even when he was being outrageously annoying, he would then go and do something brilliant or charming and she would remember he was the most extraordinary person she had ever met.

Duggan was different. He was built so solidly that perhaps they'd forgotten to put any higher functions in. Brains are soft things, after all, and Duggan seemed terribly hard. Maybe he preferred to have his emotions displayed on cushions. On a previous visit to Earth, Romana had been intrigued to notice a shop selling small pillows with the names of feelings embroidered on them. The Doctor assured her that humans liked to buy these to place on their chairs. Romana was dubious. She tried to imagine Duggan sat on a chaise longue, surrounded by cushions saying 'Love', 'Happy' and 'Hugs'. She wondered if they sold ones that read 'Angry', 'Grumpy' and 'Fighting'.

Right now, the two of them were fleeing through Paris, and Duggan was a puzzle that she completely forgot when they turned a corner and found themselves on the banks of the Seine, chains of lights swinging away from the black iron street lamps in endless glowing ropes that reflected perfectly on the calm waters of the night river. It was absolutely beautiful. For a hearts-stopping moment it felt as though the city belonged just to her and it was magical. It was a sensation you certainly couldn't crochet onto a cushion.

Romana knew then what it was to be alive and exactly why the Doctor cared so much about these funny humans and their wonky planet. It was because, even when you being chased through a city at night by men with dogs, it could offer you up a tiny moment of surprise and wonder. She nodded to Paris.

Duggan grabbed her arm. 'What are you dawdling for?' he growled, steering her by the elbow. 'You can send yourself a picture postcard later.'

That wasn't even funny, thought Romana as he shoved her into an alley behind some bins and then darted off, drawing their pursuers away.

Kerensky scrambled through the rough opening and trod awkwardly up to the six paintings smiling at him.

'But… Mona Lisas,' he murmured, baffled and despairing.

He spent a few moments wondering if he'd be better off asleep, and then he noticed the body on the floor.

It was Count Scarlioni.

Kerensky knelt down, arguing with himself. If the Count was dead, was that it, the end of his work? He'd never be paid, but did that mean he was free? Facing unemployment but freedom? He checked the Count for a pulse. He was still breathing. But even so. Kerensky could risk it. No one had come down looking for him or the Count. People were always looking for the Count. Ergo no one was around. He could do it. He could escape.

Kerensky edged out back into the laboratory and glanced up to the top of the cavern's steps. Freedom, possibly. Even if he was stopped, he could claim he was looking for assistance for the Count. But he suspected, he very much suspected, he wouldn't be stopped. He could do this.

He put his foot on the first step. And then thought about it some more.

The work, the Count's work was important. Someone had tried to kill him for it, they had tried to dissuade Kerensky from taking part in it. The Count was a strange man, yes, but he was a great benefactor to all humanity. And, if Kerensky left the basement and the Count died after all, then that would be on his conscience. Also there might never be a Kerensky Accelerator.

Slumped, Kerensky trooped reluctantly back into the hidden room, and bent over the Count. He felt the Count's forehead, testing it for lumps. He stopped, concerned. The Count's head felt wrongly spongey. Had he been more badly hurt than it appeared? Even in his sleep, the Count was smiling slightly.

At Kerensky's touch the Count stirred, his voice little more than an urbane croak.

'Doctor, would you care to explain to me how you come to be in Paris 1979?'

'Doctor, would you care to explain to me how you come to be in Florence 1505?'

Captain Tancredi was proving how easy it was to lounge in thick leather armour. He placed his elaborately feathered helmet on a table, drumming his gauntleted fingers on the surface. 'I am waiting, Doctor.'

It was curious the way he said it. Both as though he was impatient and as though waiting was all he really did in life Well, that would make sense. A lot of things made sense. Obvious really. If you're a long-lived species, simply get Leonardo to paint seven Mona Lisas and then wait 500 years until they became really, really fashionable and there were exactly seven people willing to buy one.

No. That was nonsense, wasn't it. Exactly seven buyers? And how would you know that you'd backed the right horse? You could have got Signorelli to knock up half a dozen Nude Youths and be left with nothing but a cupboard full of biceps and disappointment.

Also, and this was the really good point, how on Earth did Captain Tancredi know he'd met him before later? Oh dear. Tenses were going to prove a problem here. How awkward. Unless Scarlioni was another time traveller or simply living his life backwards. There was a third possibility, one so nonsensical that the Doctor pocketed it to use on a future occasion. Actually, now would do nicely.

'Ah well…' He looked up at the Captain with complete candour. 'You want to know how I come to be here? Well, the truth is, I tend to flit about a bit. Here and there.'

'Through time?' offered the Captain.

'Well, yes, I suppose so,' the Doctor agreed gratefully. Have I thought this through? Yes, yes. Pretty watertight.

'How, precisely?'

'I don't know.' Oh dear. Well, at least that much was just about the truth. The Doctor filled in a bit of time by saying 'ah', 'well', 'oh' and 'hum'. Always fooled Romana. 'It just happens.' He shrugged around the Guard's rapier resting lightly on his shoulders. 'You see, there I am peacefully walking along minding my own business and suddenly *pop!* there I am in a different time, or even a different planet. I had a very traumatic childhood.' The dolorous touch at the end was good.

Tancredi said nothing. He just regarded him slowly and longly, as if he were a glass of lemonade on a hot day.

'So…' The Doctor hated a silence. 'Enough about my problems. What are you doing here, old chap?'

'Being.' Captain Tancredi paused for a moment, and then nodded, presumably to himself. He paced the room, selecting the most ornate chair in the room and settling in it. Still on his knees, the Doctor shuffled across to him. The guard let him go. The Doctor had long ago mastered the art of humiliating people from a position of unimportance.

Tancredi waved a hand magnanimously, and the Doctor settled himself cross-legged on the rug, like a child ready for story time.

'I will tell you,' began the Captain. 'The knowledge will be of little use to you since you will shortly die.'

'Is that so?' The Doctor took the announcement casually. 'I did wonder when that would happen.'

Tancredi almost didn't seem to be listening. 'I am the last of the Jagaroth. I am also the saviour of the Jagaroth,' he announced grandly.

'Well, if you're the last of them, then there can't be that many about to save…' the Doctor began helpfully, and then frowned. 'Wait a minute, the Jagaroth?'

'You've heard of us?' Tancredi smiled suspiciously.

'Well,' said the Doctor as vaguely as possible. 'On one of my odd little trips. You all killed yourselves with a massive war, oh, way back when…' Now when was it? It would come to him in a soned.

'I think four hundred million years is the figure you are looking for, Doctor.'

Ah yes. 'Is it really? How time flies.' Did that mean that Tancredi was 400 million years old? You'd need quite a cake to fit the candles on that. No wonder he looked so uninterested by life. 'So what are you doing here?'

'Surviving,' Tancredi admitted candidly. He seemed different to Scarlioni. More serious. Less louche. 'Survival is the prime motive of all species. We were not all destroyed in the war. A few escaped in a crippled spaceship and made planetfall on this world in its primeval time. We found it uninhabitable.'

'Four hundred million years ago?' consoled the Doctor. 'Yes, the place would have been a bit of a shambles. No life yet to clean it up.' A terrible thought struck the Doctor. 'No life?' he muttered under his breath.

'We tried to leave, but the ship blew up,' Tancredi announced simply. He was urbane, yes, but beneath that there was almost no emotion. 'I was fractured. Splinters of my being are scattered in time. All identical, none… complete.'

Extraordinary, thought the Doctor. You'd need a pretty unique blend of collapsing warp bubble, unstable gravity and atmospheric pressure to cause that. How odd. So there were bits of Jagaroth all over time. Nonsense, which made a lot of sense. Presumably the different fragments were all able to communicate sporadically, with different levels of self-awareness. Otherwise Scarlioni would have recognised him instantly, wouldn't he? Did that ring true? Oh, it was all so tricky. This was going to require a serious amount of thinking.

The Doctor suddenly realised the Count was staring at him. Severely. The guard flashed him a grin, barely looking up from polishing his rapier with spit and a grubby cloth.

'Doctor.' Tancredi's tone was that of a tolerant headmaster. 'I'm afraid I am not satisfied with your explanation.'

'Well, as I told you…' began the Doctor. Perhaps he should suggest that, see, there'd been an explosion in his spacecraft and he'd just found himself scattered across time. He'd heard that recently somewhere, hadn't he?

Tancredi suddenly noticed the large blue box in the corner. He found it strangely reassuring. How curious. He gave it a leisurely thwack with his sword. 'What is that box?'

'That?' The Doctor sounded surprised. 'I don't know. Do you think it might have been following me?'

Tancredi suddenly sprang to his feet, furious. 'I want the truth, Doctor!'

The Doctor sprang to his feet as well. 'Don't we all.'

For a moment the two stared at each other, eye to eye. There was something about the Jagaroth and the number of their eyes wasn't there? The Doctor scratched his brain and tried to remember.

Captain Tancredi carried on looking at the Doctor, his smile barely flickering. Maybe this one did the planning and the Count did the smiling? Idly, the Doctor stepped away from the Captain, and whipped a cloth from a nearby easel, revealing the Mona Lisa.

'Ah,' said the Doctor, sounding completely unsurprised. 'The original, I presume. Completed in 1503. It's now, what, 1505? And you're getting the old boy to knock you up another six of them, yes?'

Captain Tancredi's face tried to do startled. It succeeded a little. 'Doctor,' he hissed warningly.

But there was no stopping the Doctor. All those little cogs and gears in his mind, even the wonky ones, were now spinning at full pelt. 'Another six Mona Lisas, which you then brick up in a cellar in Paris for Scarlioni to find. In four hundred and seventy-four years' time. What a very nice little piece of capital investment.'

He smiled, to himself, the Mona Lisa, Captain Tancredi and even the guard. Only the Mona Lisa smiled back.

'Doctor…' Tancredi loomed over him. 'I can see that you are a dangerously clever man. I think it is time we conducted this conversation somewhat more formally.'

'Oh.' Fair enough. The Doctor straightened the lapels of his coat and brushed away a scrap of dust.

Tancredi turned to the guard. 'Hold the Doctor here whilst I fetch the instruments of torture. If he wags his tongue, confiscate it.' He made for the door.

The Doctor felt rather dismissed. 'How will I be able to talk if you—'

'You can write, can't you?'

'Well, yes.' The Doctor's mouth fell open. Seeing the gleam in the guard's eye, he shut it hastily.

Tancredi favoured the Doctor with as much of a smile as he could muster, and left the room.

The guard moved over to the Doctor, holding his sword to his throat.

The Doctor swallowed, which he found surprisingly difficult. 'Mad, isn't he?' He spoke with a whisper, covering his mouth with his hand. Just in case of any sudden movements. He managed to perfectly conjure the kind of whisper that suggested that it should be patently clear to both of them that Tancredi was something out of a cuckoo clock. If such a thing had been invented yet.

The guard ignored the Doctor. The only thing he was giving away was a smell.

The Doctor had won harder battles. 'Tough job humouring him, I bet. Ha ha.'

The sword at the Doctor's throat didn't waver by a millimetre.

'You, ah, don't believe all that nonsense then, do you?' The Doctor risked waggling a finger towards the door the Captain had gone through.

'What?' said the guard. Finally!

'Well, you know, I mean...' The same finger tapped the side of his head. 'Jagaroth, spaceships, and so on. It's all a bit much, well, isn't it?' The Doctor rolled his eyes.

'I am paid simply to fight,' the guard said.

'Yes, but quite honestly, when you think about all that... Jagaroth spaceships,' the Doctor repeated. The phrase stuck in his mind.

The guard shrugged, neatly bringing the point of his sword to rest against the Doctor's Adam's apple. 'When you've worked for the Borgias, you'll believe anything.'

'The Borgias?' Oh dear. 'Yes, I do see your point.'

With a casual flick of his scarf, the Doctor knocked an easel over onto the guard. The Doctor's plan, such as he had one, had been to distract the guard for long enough to leap into the TARDIS and get out of here. The guard rather disappointed the Doctor by being a highly skilled fighter. He kicked the easel to one side, knocked the Doctor to the floor, and stood over him, the tip of his rapier pushed rather uncomfortably into his throat.

'As I said,' sneered the guard, pressing down just a little, 'I am paid to fight.'

'And as I said,' croaked the Doctor, 'I do see your point.'

The soldier was standing on the Doctor's scarf. The Doctor gave it an experimental tug. Nothing apart from a nasty smile and a little more pressure on his windpipe. 'I'm sorry,' he said, 'but standing on a fellow's scarf is a bit thick.'

A slow smile spread over the Doctor's face. He fished around in his pocket and produced a Polaroid camera which he may, or may not, have once borrowed from a Japanese tourist to see how it worked.

'What do you think of this, then?' he asked the guard.

The guard frowned. He had absolutely never seen anything like it in his life. Almost absently, his blade nicked the Doctor's flesh.

'It's all right, it's all right,' the Doctor whispered reassuringly to them both. He pointed the camera up at the guard. 'Come on, now,' he coaxed. 'Smile! You can do it!'

To the Doctor's surprise the guard produced a rather beautiful smile that reeked of radishes.

The Doctor pressed a button and the flash went off, causing the guard to screw his eyes up and let out a whimper of terror.

'Haha!' said the Doctor, climbing to his feet as the blinded soldier staggered around. 'Wait a tick,' he shushed the guard, who was advancing on him menacingly. 'Hold on…' The camera whirred to itself and spat out a Polaroid print. He held the photograph up to the guard, who stared, stunned as his own screwed-up, startled face appeared back at him. He glanced around the room, at the painstaking paintings and then at this. The most perfect, naturalistic reproduction of anyone the world had ever seen. Him.

He would probably have collapsed anyway, but the Doctor helped him down with the tiniest jab of Venusian karate. The guard sank dazed into a chair, and the Doctor made for the TARDIS. And then stopped. A rather clever idea had come over him.

Glancing at the guard, he checked that he was still doing a remarkable impression of an expiring haddock. Excellent. The Doctor strode over to six painstakingly prepared poplar boards, all of them roughly four by three. He could guess what those were. Poor Leonardo. He so hated deadlines.

The Doctor pulled a marker pen from his pocket and

scribbled something on each of them, grinning away to himself.

Then he darted over to Leonardo's desk. He glanced at a mirror. Actually, he could probably manage Leonardo's mirror writing by himself. This is what he scribbled on some parchment:

Dear Leo,
Sorry to have missed you. Hope you are well. Sorry about the mess on the boards, just paint over, there's a good chap. See you earlier, love,
The Doctor

Dear Leo,
Sorry to have missed you. Hope you are well. Sorry about the mess on the boards, just paint over, there's a good chap. See you earlier, love,
The Doctor

Very pleased with himself the Doctor stepped back. Onto the point of Captain Tancredi's sword.

'Oh,' said the Doctor.

'Oh, indeed,' echoed the Captain. 'Just going to pop off through time again, Doctor?' An eyebrow arched and he tutted. 'How discourteous when I've just gone to the trouble of fetching you some thumbscrews.'

Meanwhile in 1979, Count Scarlioni was suddenly waking up to a lot of things.

He was pleased to wake up somewhere dark. He was less pleased to see Kerensky crouching over him. He looked worried. Still, at least the fool could answer a very important question.

'Kerensky? Where am I?'

'In Paris, of course.' The Professor looked exceedingly worried.

'Paris?'

'Yes.'

'Paris.' The Count licked his lips and was pleasantly surprised to find he had lips. 'So it was a dream. Perhaps just a dream.' He dismissed all the thoughts that were crowding out his head. Spaceships. Time travel. The Doctor. All merely a dream. He could get on with being, with being…

'But who are you?' Keresnky asked exactly the question that was occupying the Count.

'I am who I am.' The Count stood up, brushing ancient dust from his dressing gown and tried not to notice the six Mona Lisas staring at him. His tone hardened. Distract Kerensky with a threat. 'I am the one who pays you to work.' He gestured towards the laboratory. 'Now, to it! Time is short.'

Kerensky didn't move. He was pointing at the Count in clear terror. 'But your face!' he wailed.

What? The Count's hands went to his face. It felt… baggy. Loose. Out of place. All things which a face shouldn't feel. Horror crept into the Count's soul. What if he hadn't dreamt it? What if it was all real? 'Do you want to pick a quarrel with my face, Professor?' he snarled. His hands were, of all things, smoothing and patting his face down. Pulling the nose back into the centre, tugging the hairline down and evening out the ears. Easing everything back into place as though there was something terrible underneath. His hands were working with instinctive skill. How many times had this happened? 'Beware… I do not choose to pick a quarrel with *your* face, Kerensky. I might use implements sharper than words.'

Suddenly his face felt fine and the Count relaxed. It had all been a dream. He knew exactly who he was. He was Count Scarlioni, the most audacious art thief the world had ever know. Just that. And that wasn't a bad thing to be at all.

For once, Kerensky didn't seem intimidated by the Count's threats. 'But Count, who are the Jagaroth?'

Oh god.

The Count staggered back against six paintings which he had been very successfully ignoring. So. No dream. It was all true. He touched his face again, feeling both overwhelmed and terribly sad. Also, he'd clearly been talking in his sleep. Bad dreams.

'The Jagaroth?' He ran his tongue over the words while knowing that he had no tongue. 'You serve the Jagaroth. Now work!' He shoved the Professor towards the laboratory, suddenly quite desperate to be alone.

Kerensky barely moved, riveted by his employer cradling his head in his hands. He spoke with the halting voice of a man trying to reassure himself of the world. 'It's the Jagaroth who need all the chickens, is it?'

This was too much. Count Carlos Scarlioni started to laugh. He very nearly didn't stop.

'Chickens?' He rounded on the Professor, his smile flickering into life once more. 'You never cease to amaze me, Professor. How such a giant intellect can live in such a tiny mind.' He tapped the Professor's head. It felt wrong. So solid and firm. He had the urge to tap it some more. Until it cracked like one of Kerensky's precious eggs. But then a voice stopped him.

'*Scaroth!*'

It was his own voice. His real voice. Shouting into his brain. Clearing away all the thoughts he was trying to put in its path. There was no denying this voice.

'I must think,' the Count wailed. 'I must have time to think.'

Kerensky was proving irritatingly tenacious. Like the Black Death. 'But then what have you been making me work for? I thought we were working to feed the human race…' He tailed off, miserably.

'The human race? Ha!' More thoughts crashed into the Count's brain. He could barely cope with them, yet there was a tidal wave more on the way. He rounded on the Professor, terrifying and magnificent. He clasped the Professor's shoulder, the clasp swiftly turning into a grip. 'We are working for a far greater purpose, on a scale you could not possibly conceive. The fate of the Jagaroth lies in my hands. And you will work for my purpose. Willingly or unwillingly.'

Chapter Eleven
Follies

'Split up, meet back at the café' had been Duggan's instruction. Easier said than done.

For once in her life, Romana was well and truly lost.

She had, after all, been bundled away from the café in the back of a van. She had only just arrived in Paris, and had only the sketchiest idea of where the café was. It was near a cathedral, on a reasonably busy street bustling with shops. It was on the corner and it looked sort of beige with red canvas blinds.

Romana very quickly discovered that nearly every street was near a cathedral, and nearly every corner had a sort of beige café with red canvas blinds. Also, in the middle of the night, all the shops were shut and the streets looked completely different. Paris was empty. It really was just her and some distant barking dogs that she hoped were just being chatty rather than hunting her.

It really didn't help that every street had three different signs, each one contradicting the other. It was as though

Paris just didn't want to be tied down. Romana ran across a bridge which only served to confirm her suspicions – it was covered in padlocks, as though the people were trying to stop it from wandering off somewhere else. This city was utterly baffling.

Romana walked on, pretending very hard that she was getting her bearings. She suddenly found herself standing on the edge of an eight-lane motorway. Ho-hum. They definitely hadn't come this way. Which meant…

She ran on some more. Now, ah yes, this was the square where she and the Doctor had laughed at the statues. And behind the square that led through to…

Romana was almost convinced she'd been in this square before. Only the fountains had been turned on then. Or maybe it was a completely different square. Now, then, had they been here just before heading to the café? Perhaps they'd come through here from the Louvre. How many metres had that been? Well, for once, Romana wasn't certain. She'd just been through a crack in time.

She concentrated on finding the Louvre and then, remembering that the Louvre was now concentrating quite hard on finding her, she gave up on that plan and sat down on a bench.

If Romana had been the sort to have a damn good cry, she would have had a damn good cry. She was lost and very much alone, stranded on an alien planet with little immediate hope of rescue and she was being hunted for art theft and murder. Not bad for a day that had started out with plans for sightseeing and bouillabaisse.

There was a chill in the night air and Romana suddenly regretted gadding about in a schoolgirl's uniform. It had seemed rather fun a few hours ago. As Romana refused to cry, the sky did it for her, drenching her in a cold rain that sank immediately into her soul. Romana got up from the park bench, thought about kicking it, and then hurried away into the night.

Duggan leapt over the wall and into the path of a snarling police dog.

'Sorry, Fido,' he sighed, punching it in the throat.

The dog stared at him in outrage, whimpered, and then sank to the floor.

A gendarme rushed up to Duggan, no doubt using the French for 'But sir, you appear to have hit my dog!'

Duggan hit him as well, and then carried on running.

This, he thought, was more like it.

Romana discovered herself in an area where she was no longer alone but rather wished that she was. 'Not just right now, thank you,' she said crisply and hurried off, ignoring the wolf whistles and cat calls that followed her. It was annoying, as she'd seemed rather close to the café. Something about the street seemed a little familiar. Was it the poster for that exhibition? Was there something about that cathedral that made it different from all the other cathedrals she'd wandered past?

She found a tourist sign helpfully indicating that she was 1.5 kilometres from the Louvre. Finally, something that was talking her language. She scrolled back through the day and figured that that was just about correct.

That was one good sign. Another was the realisation that she could still read what was written on it, which meant that her telepathic link to the TARDIS translation circuits was still working. So at least the Doctor hadn't flown into a dwarf star. Yet.

Two bits of good news gave Romana a new and positive outlook. If she walked in a circle from here, checking every café along the way, then she'd probably possibly find

Duggan. The closest thing she had to a friend in the whole wide world.

Romana laughed bitterly to herself.

This was it. She was sure of it. She'd been quite sure about two other cafés and, what with that and the rain getting worse, her confidence had taken something of a knock. This, she decided, looking at the beige café with the red canvas blinds, was it. And, if it wasn't, then it would just have to do.

Reaching into her sleeve she pulled out her own sonic screwdriver. She'd made it recently as the Doctor's had struck her as both a neat idea and in need of improvement. Rather like the Doctor.

She waved her sonic screwdriver along the glass door, and felt satisfaction as the stainless-steel lock pinged back on itself. Good.

She stepped into the café, closed the door to keep out the rain and congratulated herself on her stealth. With a bit of luck, no one would ever know she'd been there.

A window pane smashed and a hand came grasping through the side door as Duggan fought his way in.

'I thought these places were meant to be open all night,' he growled.

'You should go into partnership with a glazier,' said Romana, quite pleased to see him. 'You'd have a particularly symbiotic working relationship.' She brushed some broken glass from his sleeve, not entirely sure why she was bothering as there'd only be some more along in a minute.

'What?' grunted Duggan.

'I'm just pointing out that you break a lot of glass.'

'You can't make an omelette without breaking eggs,' Duggan announced as though it was the wisest thing in the world. He picked up a bottle of wine and cracked it open against the counter. He poured them two glasses.

Thoughtfully, Romana picked up the broken top of the bottle and slowly unscrewed the metal cap. 'If you wanted an omelette I would expect to find a pile of smashed crockery, a cooker in flames and an unconscious chef.'

'Listen.' Duggan was bullishly defensive. Just as he was bullishly happy and bullishly bullish in general. 'I get results.'

'Really? The Count's got the Mona Lisa.' Romana couldn't resist that.

Duggan said nothing. He fished around under the counter and brought out a basket of only slightly stale bread, bringing it over to a table. He slumped heavily into a chair, not meeting her eye.

Deciding to be placating, Romana sat down opposite him, nibbling a bit of bread and sipping the wine. It was actually not too horrible. Red and sharp, it cut neatly through her mood and the rain.

Duggan emptied his glass and poured himself another. 'Yeah. He's got seven of them. Seven! You know what I don't understand?'

'I expect so.'

'There are exactly seven potential buyers and exactly seven Mona Lisas.'

'Yes.' Romana had been wondering about this.

'But, six of them have been sitting bricked up for centuries.'

'Buyers?'

'No, Mona Lisas,' Duggan chided her, glad to have the upper hand for once. 'Where did they come from? How did the Count know they were there?'

'Taxes the mind, doesn't it?' Actually, these were pretty decent questions, Romana reflected. Basic, but fundamental.

Duggan's brow creased. Then more of his face creased. It took Romana a while to realise this was worry.

'There is one answer,' he said very slowly and carefully. 'But...'

'But what?'

'No.' Duggan shook his head. 'You'll think I've gone mad and no, it's crazy, my brain's too tired. Forget it.'

'No.' This might be when Duggan did his best thinking. Or his only thinking. 'Do tell me.'

'You'll only laugh.'

'You're man enough to take that, aren't you?'

'True,' Duggan conceded. 'Well, I was thinking of all that weird equipment in the Count's lab. I mean, one answer to this whole business would be that somebody had... er...' He screwed his eyes shut and sneaked the words out while he wasn't looking. 'Er... discovered time travel.'

'Don't be silly.' Romana stifled a giggle.

'Yeah.' Duggan mimed punching himself in the head. 'Forget it. I'll think of something more sensible in a bit.' He took a swig from the broken wine bottle and suddenly spluttered, sitting bolt upright.

'What's the matter?'

'Oh nothing,' Duggan moaned indistinctly. 'Just cut my lip.'

The long night took its time passing.

Duggan was all for racing back to the Château, even after Romana pointed out that they'd probably die. 'Yes, but I'll take a fair few of them down with me,' he growled.

'Enough to save the world?'

'So what do you suggest we do?'

'Wait,' sighed Romana. She took another sip of her wine. It was proving, in its own way, quite pleasant. She couldn't imagine herself drinking more than a glass of it. But in its haphazardly garden-sheddish muddle of alcohols, esters and norisoprenoids, wine was rather interesting. She was surprised the Doctor hadn't drunk any. Yes, they'd wait here till the Doctor deigned to grace them with his presence. Do what the universe does and give the Doctor the benefit of the doubt. She sadly noticed she'd finished her glass. Duggan was dabbing mournfully away at his cut lip.

'We wait for the Doctor till morning,' said Romana.

'Don't you sleep?' asked Duggan, a little thickly.

'Not often.'

'Oh.' Duggan settled himself into the wooden chair and closed his eyes.

Romana looked at her empty glass. 'It's a pity,' she sighed, 'that everything is shut.'

Duggan opened his eyes. 'Lady, that's where you're wrong,' he said, brightening. 'This is the City That Never Sleeps.'

'I'm fairly sure that's New York.'

'You've never travelled.'

'I assure you I have.'

Duggan stood up, shaking off his tiredness as a dog shakes off water. 'You've not travelled,' he repeated firmly, offering Romana his hand. 'Come on. Let's hit the town.'

Much to Romana's surprise, Duggan managed not to knock anyone unconscious. The city which had seemed empty turned out to be, just a few streets away, crammed full of life.

They went a little way up the hill to a crowded basement with red walls. It was so full of smoke Romana assumed it was about to explode. It was filled with staggeringly loud noise which the people seemed to be trying to escape from in an alarming series of leaps and shudders.

'What's that?' she hollered above the din.

'It's called Le Disco,' said Duggan.

They went somewhere else.

'Oh, I do like the outfits,' Romana enthused, applauding wildly.

Tomorrow, yes tomorrow, definitely and absolutely, when the TARDIS came back, which it definitely would, she would see if the Wardrobe Room had one of those outfits. It looked tremendous fun.

The figures swung themselves across the stage in a series of high-leg kicks. Romana had never dreamed that you could make a dress entirely from sequins and feathers, but it was clearly highly manoeuvrable. Very practical. So long as the next planet they landed on wasn't cold.

'You want to go out dressed like that?' Duggan boggled briefly. Then remembered what Romana was currently wearing. And smiled. *C'est la vie.* It was about the only bit of French he knew.

'I say,' said Romana, tapping her glass. 'Is there any more of this wine?'

Duggan was showing Romana some fresh air very quickly.

'Hrnk,' she said.

'Have you really never drunk before?'

'Of course I've drunk,' Romana concentrated, very studiously, on the two Eiffel Towers and wondered if she was falling through another crack in time. 'Mostly water,' she said with thick dignity.

'Wait a second, you've NEVER drunk wine?' Duggan was incredulous. 'How old did you say you were?'

'One hundred and twenty-five.'

'Yeah, twenty-five,' he nodded. 'And you've never got drunk? What did you do with your evenings?'

'A lot of reading and, lately, a whole lot of running.'

Romana was performing Graves's Three Tests for imminent dimensional collapse and the initial results did not look promising.

Duggan walked her to the riverbank, which, so long as the wind was going in the right direction, didn't smell too badly of drains. The view, when it wasn't jumping up and down, was breathtakingly lovely.

'We have to save this city,' Romana told Duggan very, very seriously. 'Its waveform is collapsing.'

'Yeah, yeah,' he said, helping her to sit down on a bench. 'How's that?'

'Better, but still bad.' Romana smiled at him, holding up a hand. 'You see, I am unusually susceptible…' She lingered over the word. 'Susceptible… to the tracks of time. And something is very wrong with Paris.'

There was one Latin phrase which every Frenchman knew. They would repeat it to each other late at night, in cafés, bars and nightclubs, saying it with a stern waggle of a finger or a sly wink. The phrase was *In Vino Veritas.* In Wine, Truth.

People were looking at them. A nearby couple were, in that very French way, trying to talk about the beauty of the riverbank rather than each other. Duggan realised they were in the way. People in the way got noticed, and they were, he remembered, currently suspected of stealing the Mona Lisa.

Duggan briefly suggested they go back to his hotel and try and find Romana a room. It wasn't much of a hotel and he doubted it would be much of a room, but it would be better than nothing. The plan stalled when he asked Romana her surname.

'Smith,' she announced eventually.

No. Duggan doubted that, even in Paris, he could get away with an expenses claim for a room for a woman called Smith.

So they went back to the café, smashed another window, and dozed awkwardly on chairs that were designed purely for dinner and gossip.

Chapter Twelve
Déjà
Vu

So. Not dead then.

Scaroth lay on the ground, expecting to see burning debris everywhere.

Nothing. Just some shaggy, grunting creatures. They were waggling bones and staring at him in fascination. One of them, with no idea what to do about this unexpected appearance, threw a stone at him. It missed, and no more followed.

This was all rather unexpected. The planet was supposed to be uninhabited. Could they not even get that bit right?

Actually, where was he? This couldn't even be the same planet, could it? Gone were the desolate rocks and thin red atmosphere. Instead he was lying in a lush valley under a warm blue sky. And again, those creatures, watching him.

He stood up warily. What if they rushed him? Those bones had the look of clubs. And of course he had no weapons on him. Nothing.

He was taller than they were. They looked so very

different. They were hairy and their flesh was an unsettling shade of pink. They grunted.

One, he guessed, the leader, broke free and lurched towards him, waving the bone above its head. It was a threat. They were clearly used to preying on creatures larger than themselves, which was disappointing. On the other hand, the leader did not appear entirely happy about approaching Scaroth. One of the creatures nudged it forward. It looked at Scaroth. While he couldn't translate the grunts their meaning was clear. 'Look, sorry about this, but anyway, got to keep one's end up…'

Scaroth snapped its neck with ease. The slight hesitation had been fatal. The reaction amongst the group was pleasing. They seemed very upset and also afraid. Good. He could use both of these things.

By the evening they had taken him to their cave and started to worship him. This suited Scaroth well as he needed time to think. To think and to dwell on the voices in his head. He was slowly realising that he was not quite as alone as he had first thought, and that, worse, this made his situation really very complicated.

At first the voices came to him like the names of things forgotten. Then they formed in his head as ideas. It was very hard to explain. He was trying to remember the shape of his ship. Initially, nothing came to him. Nothing at all. Which was… which was…

He stalled, searching for words he was lacking to describe a thing he was missing. Two came to him eventually. It was Absurd. It was Frightening. The concepts arrived eager and out-of-breath, as though they had been running from a long way away. Shortly afterwards, the shape of his ship popped into his head, equally breathless. You wouldn't believe where I've come from, the ship seemed to be saying.

Really? It was absurd, it was frightening. Why was his brain working so slowly? Was it shock? More ideas turned up, all of them absurdly frightening.

As the tribe watched, their new god started muttering to itself, shaking its terrible head, and wailing. This made the tribe gather together and wonder about whether they'd made the right decision in worshipping it and wouldn't be better off throwing things at it again.

The muttering of God subsided. The evening drew in.

Scaroth was starting to realise that, although his body was complete, although his brain was functioning, his soul was not. If he wanted an idea or a memory, he had to reach out and fetch it. Fetch it through time. At some level, this was, ah, exhilarating. At another it was, hmm, horrifying. As far as he could tell, he was the earliest of himselves. The first fragment. The earliest by a long way. The others... eleven of them... were scattered through a long corridor of time, each of them only vaguely aware of the situation and of Scaroth. As the years moved on, the links became ever more tenuous, the delays in thoughts reaching back to him ever longer.

Scaroth was momentarily very pleased there was no one of equivalent intelligence around to talk to, as it would all be so terribly hard to explain. Then he realised how alone he was.

Scaroth shivered. The cave was very cold. Cold and dark. Why did no one light a fire? He glanced around at the tribe. They looked back at him in awe. And still no one lit a fire. Scaroth finally realised why not. Oh. This was going to take a lot of time.

Scaroth sat in the cave, now illuminated by fire. The tribe stared at him, delighted that they had not killed their new god after all, and waiting for the next revelation.

It had been a whole day since he had invented something. Surely he would stop muttering to himself soon. Stop muttering and show them something else wonderful. Maybe they should sacrifice something to him? What did he like? Would bison do?

Scaroth was thinking very hard and talking to the fragments of himself as best as he could. Eventually an analogy formed itself. It was like when he was back in the warp control, at the top of the ship. Hearing other voices reporting back to him, shouted numbers and problems and statuses echoing through the pathways of the ship. A cacophony that had only one thing in common. All of them expected Scaroth to do something.

He had thought a lot about that. What to do now? An idea started to form. It was absurd and frightening, and would require all of them to unite. From this very first fragment of himself all the way across time to his twelfth fragment. Obviously, this final fragment had the least idea about itself. Because it was so very far away from him. He could imbue it with purpose. That was all. Which was disappointing because that was the one that had the most to do. The final fragment. The one that lived at the very end of time itself. Beyond it was nothing.

It was late in the laboratory and Kerensky felt tired again. The final fragment of Scaroth was drawing like a man possessed. Circuit diagrams, equations and algorithms poured out of him, filling sheets of graph paper, notebooks, and spilling onto napkins. Kerensky stood by him, trying to keep up.

'But...' he offered at intervals.

The Count ignored him and carried on drawing.

Kerensky stood and watched, feeling tired and hungry and sorry for himself. Had the Count really meant those threats? Was he really that sort of person? He couldn't possibly be. It was hard to associate the urbane cruelty of the man he'd known with this strange, snarling figure. Who appeared to be rewriting temporal physics while working his way through a bottle of champagne.

Which had arrived on a tray with just the one glass.

With a flourish and a swagger the Count pushed the papers across to Kerensky.

Kerensky, finally afforded a proper look, leafed through them. He was prepared for the nonsense scribblings of a drunk madman. What he got was much worse.

He stared, aghast. The Count shook his head, tutted, and swigged at his champagne.

Kerensky had another look.

'But…' he said eventually.

Not at all discouraged, the Count poured himself another glass of champagne, holding it up to the light. He tapped the papers. 'Now Professor, see the true results of your labours. This is what you will produce for me.' The Count smiled his most encouraging smile.

Kerensky picked the papers up listlessly and gazed at them again. They slipped from his fingers.

'Look at it!' snarled the Count.

Kerensky flinched.

The Count tapped the paper courteously.

Kerensky held the papers once more. The diagrams had failed to rewrite themselves. He made a play of going over them again. Maybe he had missed something. The numbers were nonsense, the equations silly, and the circuit diagrams were so farcical they were practically hiding behind a curtain from the vicar.

But, put together, they formed something that was pure black comedy.

The Count helped himself to a plate of pâté, watching

him keenly. Kerensky tried to ignore him smearing it thickly onto the soft white discs of baguette. Tried to ignore the crumbs falling across the diagrams. Kerensky tried to concentrate on the papers before him, and find the good in them.

'But Count…' he began, carefully. 'This is… this machine is precisely the reverse of what we…' He faltered, and a final bit of ego flickered one last time. '… what I have been working on.'

The Count nodded, accepting this. Magnanimously, he pushed the plate towards Kerensky, who helped himself gratefully to a chunk of pâté.

While the Professor chewed, the Count leaned forward, smiling at him with the benevolence of a snake. 'You will agree that the research you have done under my guidance points equally well in either direction.' To illustrate his point he crossed his arms over. Pâté went one way, champagne sloshed the other.

'Yes, yes it does do that,' Kerensky agreed reluctantly, finishing the slice of bread and wishing there was more. More was not offered. 'But to do this means increasing the very effect I was trying to eliminate.'

'Precisely.' The Count drained his glass and filled it again. He waved back to the papers. Go on. Have another try.

Kerensky read on. Then stopped. If the numbers had been laughing at each other before, now they were definitely laughing at him.

'But the scale of this is fantastic,' he expostulated. Fatigue, hunger and confusion shook his voice. 'What are you trying to do, Count? This is monstrous beyond imagining.'

'Monstrous!' For some reason, that last phrase clearly tickled the Count. It was the widest smile he'd ever seen. Any wider and surely the face would split open. The Count leaned over Kerensky, so much taller and so much more dominant. He leaned in so close, Nikolai could hear the bubbles popping in the champagne. The Count's tone was intimate, amiable, coaxing. 'But you will do it for me, Professor, won't you?'

'No,' whispered Kerensky, terrified. 'A thousand times no.' A thought struck him. He didn't want to seem too defiant. 'But, even if I wanted to, I could not.'

'Oh?' The Count leaned back, an eyebrow arched. He was not cross. He was amused.

Kerensky jabbed at the last diagram. 'Equipment on this scale... power on this scale... It would cost millions and millions.' He warmed to his theme. The world had limits. The Count had to understand his place in the scheme of things. 'Even you, Count, could not afford such things.'

Scarlioni nodded, clearly taking the point on board. He even shrugged. Ah well, you have me there, he smiled.

At that moment, Hermann came running down the stairs, holding a parcel wrapped in brown paper. He was waving it around and looked, for once, overcome with joy. Kerensky felt a sinking sensation.

'Sir!' Hermann bellowed delightedly. He hadn't made even the tiniest bow. 'The Mona Lisa is no longer in the Louvre!' He shook the parcel.

What? thought Kerensky and sat down heavily.

'Excellent Hermann, excellent,' the Count purred. He shot the stunned Professor a little smirk of triumph. 'See? There's always a way.'

The normally staid butler was almost quivering with excitement. 'The moment the news breaks, sir, each of our seven buyers will be ready.'

The Count slapped the Professor heartily on the back. He raised his glass of champagne to Hermann. 'To the fools!' he toasted. 'The poor simple fools.'

Herman bowed.

'How much money will that bring us in, Hermann?' The Count gestured in a Tell-the-Professor way.

Hermann made much of pretending to calculate the sum. 'About a hundred million dollars, Excellency.'

The Count nodded at Kerensky. See? his triumphant smile said.

The processor in Kerensky's brain was working overtime. He stared miserably at the plans for the Kerensky Accelerator. There was no excuse for not building it now. Because everything he'd refused to believe about the Count was true. He was a criminal, he was ruthless, he wasn't working for the good of humanity at all. He was a monster. He glumly looked at Hermann and the Count. What had they been doing all this time?

Hermann had handed the painting over to the Count, who tore the wrappings apart with Christmas-morning vigour. He held it aloft, shaking it with triumph.

Being this close to the most famous painting in the world should have had some joyous effect on Kerensky. But he had seen it several times before. The painting smiled at him quietly, little caring that she had just struck him dumb with horror.

Seven Mona Lisas. How had the Count known about the other six Mona Lisas? They clearly weren't a surprise to him. Or Hermann. Kerensky sneaked another glance at the plans for the Count's device. He felt a pain in his stomach that for once wasn't hunger.

He looked up. The Count was smiling at him. 'Continue with your work, Professor,' he beamed amiably. 'And enjoy it. Or you will die.'

CHAPTER THIRTEEN
THE FATHER
OF INVENTION

Thumbscrews are strange things. They work on pretty much the same principle as the flower press, which is a delightful invention capable of preserving flowers. A thumbscrew is nowhere near as jolly. It is a large adjustable vice which slowly squeezes, crushes and flattens whatever is placed inside it. To make sure of its agony, the bit that does the squeezing and the crushing and the flattening has a lot of pins in it, just to help out. Like most torture implements, these thumbscrews came in a solid shade of black. That hadn't prevented this particular set from picking up a few stains along the way.

The Doctor stared at the thumbscrews fastened to his hands and winced.

'Already?' Captain Tancredi clucked. 'I haven't even started yet.'

'I know. It's just that your hands are cold.' The Doctor looked up at the guard in mute appeal. The guard pushed the rapier firmly into its familiar place at the Doctor's neck.

A notch was now forming.

The Captain stepped back from fastening the thumbscrews. The Doctor was sat at a table. Leonardo's *Medusa* had been painted at this table. Wonderful positive things had happened here. And soon the Doctor would forever remember it as the reason he found tying his shoelaces bothersome.

The Captain was all smiles now. Whereas Count Scarlioni had a whole range of smiles, the Captain had just the one. It was cruel.

There was an air of distinct menace about this situation. The Doctor knew it all too well. Bad things were about to happen. Probably to him. It was going to get distinctly unpleasant and, at best, he'd end up craving a change of shirt. The real knack was remembering to sound insouciant. It was easy enough under mild duress, but it took effort to scream insouciantly.

The thing he hated about medieval torture devices was that they were so definite. Mind probes and so on you could edge away from, getting on with composing Argolin haikus while your body obliged with the yelling. The grander methods of torture normally had that kind of flaw. The Doctor lived to hear a slightly annoyed rasp of 'Increase the power!' It normally meant that he was winning, more or less. They'd brought out the biggest bit of their arsenal of agony and he was off and away finding synonyms for 'sand' and 'sunset'. How terribly embarrassing for his tormentors.

But thumbscrews? It never failed to amaze him that tiny bits of your body, boring, slightly silly bits could be used to cause so much pain. It was a deliberate act of humiliation. 'We are going to hurt a part of you that you don't think about at all.' And then, of course, you're going to have to learn to do without it.

Poor old thumbs. That little bit of evolution that allowed

tools to be made, swords and ploughshares to be hefted and now meant that he'd spend the rest of this life finding jam jars tricksy. Ah well, best get on with it. The Doctor winced again.

'So sensitive?' cooed the Captain. 'I think we're in for a little treat.'

'All this is totally unnecessary, you know.' On balance, the Doctor preferred the Count to the Captain. There seemed more of a chance for a natter and a cup of tea.

'You make it necessary, Doctor,' chided Captain Tancredi, winking at the guard. 'You will not tell me the truth.'

The guard smirked as the Captain bent over the thumbscrews. The guard liked this bit. The screaming was fun. The results were always extraordinary. But put you off a nice lump of sausage for a fortnight.

The thumbscrews began to turn. First the one on the left.

'Ah!' the Doctor exclaimed. 'Well, do you know, I've changed my mind.' He looked bashful. 'If there's one thing I can't bear it's being tortured by someone with cold hands.' He leant back in his chair candidly. 'What do you want to know?'

'Excellent Doctor,' smiled the Captain as he gave the thumbscrews the tiniest, most playful of tweaks. 'I want to know how you travel in time.'

'Simple.' The Doctor tried shrugging, which, when you're wearing thumbscrews is next-to-impossible. 'I'm a Time Lord.'

Captain Tancredi did something remarkable at this point. There were a whole range of reactions to being told you're sitting in the same room as a Time Lord. The most simple one was 'What's a Time Lord?' but the Doctor also got a fair few hisses of 'Ah, the Ancient Enemy!', some rather embarrassing attempts at worship, and letters of complaint from historians.

When the Doctor told Captain Tancredi he was a Time Lord, the Captain simply responded, 'And the girl?'

The Doctor was alarmed by this sudden turn in the conversation. A time-jumping wobbler like Scaroth, he could deal with. The Doctor, despite all appearances, knew what he was doing. But Romana was barely more than a Time Tot. Oh yes, very clever, snappy dresser, rather *chic*, great company if you were sharing a cell, but still just a little wet around the ears. He'd never tell her to her face, of course. Because he was rather afraid that she'd then do something impossibly clever just to spite him. But still, there was just the tiniest chance that Romana would fall into the clutches of this pan-temporal popinjay back in 1979. And then the Count could do two abominable things to her. He could threaten her, or, worse, he'd charm her. Romana's great weakness was charm. After all, that's why she stuck around with him.

Aware that the Doctor's thoughts had wandered away, the Captain gave the thumbscrews another gentle tap. 'The girl. The truth, Doctor?'

'What girl?'

That really wouldn't wash any more. The Count grasped both screws and looked the Doctor right in the eye. 'Time is running out, Doctor.'

'What are you talking about? This is only 1505, you know.'

The Doctor had overdone the flippancy. The Captain got ready to give the thumbscrews a vicious twist.

Finally, thought the guard. The juicy bit.

'All right, all right!' the Doctor got in quickly. 'I'll tell you.' Must stall for time. Must find a way to get out of this. Must not drop Romana in it. Ah. Genuine curiosity. Works wonders. 'One thing I'd like to know first. How do you communicate across time with the other splinters of yourself?'

'Doctor,' scowled the Captain. 'I am asking the questions.'

Yes, admitted the Doctor to himself. But it's a good question, isn't it?

The Count strode through the Château laughing. He was in a genuinely good mood. He could feel things moving inside his mind. Long-lost pieces of jigsaw clicking into place. He'd done it. The challenge he'd been set long ago, so long ago, finally neared completion. He saw that now. It really was just a matter of dotting the 'i's and crossing the 't's.

Which, he realised, as he paused in front of one of Turner's boiling skies, included building the most complicated time machine this world had ever seen. Would ever see.

His smile flickered and then fell. It should be fine. Kerensky, for all his annoyances, would do it. He was a brilliant mind. Scarlioni had made quite sure of this. He would carry out the new plans. Scarlioni had watched the Professor as he worked, and had thought, 'I know what this is.'

Sometimes children repeat classes. It happens. You move them from one school to another. They sit down in an unfamiliar room, surrounded by new and worrying classmates, and then the teacher begins to explain the lesson. At first the child feels utter incomprehension. Then the realisation dawns: 'I know all this. I have done this.' Then the child sneaks a glance around at his classmates, no longer terrifying and strange. 'These poor fools. They know nothing.' By the end of the lesson, boredom has set in and the child is flicking pens and setting fire to the desks.

In much the same way, Count Carlos Scarlioni had realised that he was, at first, following Kerensky's work, and then instinctively correcting it. He had felt no alarm at this. It was what he was supposed to do. And now the Patron had overtaken the Professor.

It was all part of the plan. The plan was working perfectly. There were seven Mona Lisas. There were seven buyers. Equipment would be bought, power would be allocated, government officials would be bribed, power station employees would be paid not to go on strike. Everything would go marvellously to plan and eventually the world would never be the same again.

He realised Hermann was now standing by his side and asked him to bring yet more champagne to the library. They'd never get through all of it, he thought sadly.

A nagging doubt wandered into his mind. Something was wrong. Oddly not here and now. No, something was wrong five centuries ago. That Doctor, that prattling fool. Something to do with him. The uncertainty grew in Scarlioni's mind. Had he dreamt it? Was that it?

Hermann watched the Count stride away.

Hermann was puzzled. This should be the happiest night of the Count's life. And yet, for once, his master did not seem happy.

The Countess noticed the change in her husband.

Carlos swept into the room and barely acknowledged her. She had placed the ice pack theatrically on her forehead, and was managing her bravest wince. Carlos would glide to her, falling to his knees by her chaise, kiss the tender bruise in her forehead and promise her, oh so valiantly, that it did not mar her beauty. 'And anyway, *ma chérie*,' he would purr. 'Real beauty is what's inside.'

Occasionally, Heidi indulged herself in such romances. It often seemed that she was living inside one. You could live in Switzerland, surrounded by money, but feel no romance. And yet, here she was, with a fabulous palace, a beautiful, dashing, clever husband. They were the stars of

Parisian society and also pulling off the greatest crime the world had ever known.

It was, she thought, all gloriously romantic. But Carlos sometimes behaved as though it was just a part he was playing. What was really going on inside his head? She sometimes wanted to ask him, but then her bracelet itched and she would think about something else.

Hermann brought them champagne on a silver platter that a Crusader had pillaged from Jerusalem. Carlos smiled wryly as he and his wife compared notes on the escape of Duggan and his associates. Clearly, amazingly, that English idiot had done the best thing a fool could do – find some clever friends. So what, though? They didn't matter. Hermann assured them the finest corrupt policeman in Paris were combing the city for them. Their quarry would soon be back here, grovelling, screaming and making a mess of the carpet.

Facetiously, the Countess even suggested presenting the flamboyant one with a bill. What was he called, again? The Doctor, wasn't it? The Count had smiled at that and then repeated the name, at first with a laugh and then with a far graver tone. What was troubling him? Déjà vu, or some forgotten memory?

The Countess ordered him not to worry. After all, the hard bit, the audacious bit, had just happened. The Mona Lisa had practically stolen itself. The finest cat burglars in France were even now bobbing down a storm drain into the Seine. It was all going wonderfully to plan.

To plan? Carlos had nodded. He'd been staring out of the window, looking at the twinkling lights of the wonderful city. In Paris's long history, things very rarely went to plan unless you were ruthlessly determined. For a plan to work, it had to be extraordinarily thorough. They had left nothing to chance. The Count scratched at an itch above his right eye and then wandered over to the mirror. He stared at his face in the mirror and tried to work out what was wrong with it. Something was missing. Its absence was clear, and was obviously disconcerting the Countess. Hermann had looked at him strangely as well. The Count searched his reflection and he could not see what it was. Two eyes, sharp nose, a mouth, ears, hair. But something was out of place. Oh that was it. Somewhere along the way, he'd lost his smile.

Try as he might, it would not come back.

'Why do you still worry, my dear?' The Countess appeared, draping an arm across his shoulder, puffing away at her cigarette holder. Her eyes were gleaming like jewels. 'We have the Mona Lisa! We've done it! Think of the wealth that will be ours.'

'The wealth is not everything.' She really was such a petty creature, Carlos found himself thinking.

The Countess took the dismissal in good stead. Of course, how bourgeois to talk about cash at a time like this. 'The achievement,' she breathed. 'Oh, I know, the achievement!' She tapped him on the chin fondly.

Gently, he lifted her hand away and turned to her. 'Achievement?' He stared beyond her, attention fixed on the Paris skyline. 'You talk to me of achievement because I steal the Mona Lisa?'

He laughed then, and something in that laugh chilled her. It had been a long time since Heidi had been made to feel stupid.

'Can you imagine how a man might feel if he had caused the pyramids to be built? The heavens to be mapped? Accounted for the movement of the planets? Created the first wheel! Showed the true use of fire.' The Count gazed out at Paris and found it, after all, nothing. 'To have brought up a whole race from nothing. To save his own race.'

The Countess was baffled. Carlos was behaving oddly. She'd been expecting him to perhaps feel a little anti-climax, but this was something else. Gone was the dryness, the suave calm. Instead he was shaking with zeal. She felt a sudden thrill. Perhaps this vast crime was simply a way to open a door to something more shocking, even more daring. But she was also puzzled. 'What are you talking about my dear? No one can achieve everything!'

'I do not ask for everything.' Carlos didn't seem to be listening. His tone struck her as so odd. Both magnanimous and yet humble. Like the rich man bargaining with death. That was it. They had a picture of that somewhere. Of course they did. Several. 'All I ask for is but a single life… and the life of my people.'

His people? What was all this? Was he trying to tell her something, something about the real origins of his family? Could that be it? The obsession with wealth, the recovery of hidden artworks. Spouting nonsense that sounded like the myth of the Wandering Jew. Really? Was that really what he was trying to tell her? Why even bother keeping something like that a secret? Like she would care. Surely there could be no secrets between them. She adopted a coaxing tone. 'Are you feeling all right, my dear?'

'Yes.' The Count was years away. The room was fading around him. Little hooks were tugging away at the corners of his brain. Connections were forming. This strange body, this terrible face, this whole stupid world was a trifle.

Heidi watched Carlos in concern. This wasn't the first time he'd been like this. She'd once found him lying on the floor of a hotel room in Geneva, shaking off all attempts at assistance. The hotel doctor had called it the *petit mal* and told her not to be concerned. He was right. It had passed with no ill effects. Such things happened to great men. She should have seen it coming – the concussion caused by that idiot Duggan was just the sort of thing to set this off. She should have recognised the signs. This strange euphoria was the last of the tide rushing out before the big wave came crashing down. The vacancy and the shaking, the raving. At times like this, he seemed so small, so human. She needed to be with him always and yet, right now, it was as if she wasn't there at all.

The Count could hear only one word. One word burning across every pathway in his brain.

'*Scaroth.*'

He mastered himself with an effort. 'Don't worry. I am feeling quite well. Please leave us.'

'Us?' The Countess was startled.

'Me!' he thundered, desperately. 'Please leave me!'

He knew she was rushing to his side, wanting to comfort and hold him. There was an ice pack. There was champagne. There was a chaise. She would fuss around him as though he were a spoilt pet dog. Why wouldn't she just go?

'Leave me!' he snapped, and then, with a ghastly attempt at a grin, softened his tone. 'I will join you in a minute.'

The last thing she wanted to do was leave him in this state. Not now. 'Are you sure there's nothing I can do?'

'Go!' he screamed, jerking a hand towards the door. He wouldn't turn around, wouldn't even face her. His voice was little more than a croak. 'Go.'

She tried not to be, but she was hurt. It was annoying that she wasn't allowed to be sympathetic. To show her kinder, truer feelings. If it was a romance, then he would have let her nurse him. But no. The Count always kept her at a distance. Always.

Plucking up her glass, Heidi swept from the room, making sure the door slammed behind her.

Carlos didn't hear it. The lights of Paris had gone now.

214

Everything had gone except for eternity. It was all rushing together into one single beautiful word that made complete sense of everything.

'*Scaroth.*'

Five centuries earlier, Captain Tancredi was transfixed by the same word, by the stream of thoughts pouring through his head. The connection was forming, but just now it was quite inconvenient. What had earlier been the odd little trickle of thoughts now became a flood, facts racing through him between the beginning of history and its very end.

Tancredi could sense himself starting to shake. His hand flew to his face, feeling for once how unreal, how unnecessary it was. Oh, to tear it off and show these fools what he truly was.

'I say, are you all right?' That was the Doctor, still prattling away. He must not show his weakness to him.

Tancredi, swaying only slightly, cleared his throat and looked around for the Doctor. For a moment he was blind, and when his vision cleared there was no sign of him. Tancredi realised he'd somehow turned himself around, staring at a painted Medusa. He shivered. How long had he been in the trance? Seconds, hopefully.

'*Scaroth!*'

No. He focused on the Doctor, still sat there, smiling away, waggling the thumbscrews at him in a friendly wave. Tancredi advanced on him. What had they been talking about?

'Continue Doctor,' he began, his mouth dry. Safe opening. Right. Yes. The Doctor had been speculating on how exactly his various fragments communicated. And now this happened. As if he could see it coming. How was that possible? Even for a race as old and cruel as the

Time Lords? 'You were saying the interfaces of the time continuum were unstable. I know that!' Tancredi groaned bitterly. The guard was looking at him in concern. Tancredi waved him away. He needed neither help nor burning as a demon. Not just now. He pounded his fists desperately on the table. 'Tell me something useful, Doctor!'

He leant forward to twist the screws, and that voice called again, jerking him up in puppet twitches.

'*Scaroth!*'

'Wait,' he pleaded with himself. Just a few more moments with the Doctor and he would have something of real value to tell them. He was interrogating a Time Lord! 'Wait,' he begged.

'Righty-oh,' said the Doctor.

'Not you! Continue talking, Doctor.'

'*Scaroth!*' the summons came again.

'A moment,' he whimpered. The Doctor was a Time Lord, a race as ancient as the Jagaroth. But so little was known about them – they were a race of unneighbourly observers, keeping themselves to themselves. How did they travel through time? It was all a mystery. One he could solve right now with the thumbscrews.

He staggered furiously to the table, and stood over the Doctor, wavering. He licked his lips, or tried to. Something went wrong. Where was his tongue? At the edge of his blurring vision, he saw the guard flinch. The fellow had seen too much and would have to die.

'I say,' hissed the Doctor to the guard. 'Is he always like this?'

'It's not my business to notice,' the guard hissed back, barely hiding his alarm.

'Ah,' the Doctor sympathised.

Tancredi steadied himself against the desk, motioning to the guard. 'Hold him!'

The guard, with a hint of an apologetic shrug, brought his rapier to bear.

The Doctor had once, for reasons that were really very complicated, been banned from the Adventure Playground at Whipsnade Zoo. However, the skills he'd learned on the rope slide came in handy as he whipped the thumbscrews off the desk and plunged them onto the point of the sword. With dexterity that amazed the Doctor most of all, he'd threaded the thumbscrews onto the rapier without losing even a single digit. He now slid the thumbscrews down to the pommel. As the puzzled guard tried to tug away, the sword shattered with a satisfying snap. Always, the Doctor thought, use your enemy's own strength against him. And pay the extra sixpence for a flake on your Mr Whippy. Those were two good rules to live by.

The guard stood there, waggling the swordless handle around, piggy face crumpling with childish misery. He rushed at the Doctor. The Doctor bowed, smiled, and tripped him with the flat of the sword blade. The guard fell against Captain Tancredi, who didn't even seem to notice.

The Doctor moved quickly. With an unwieldy shrug, the blade fell to the floor. Meanwhile, the Doctor twisted open the thumbscrews with his teeth and, with what he hoped was a practised stumble, fell against the door of the TARDIS.

The guard was close behind him, and, on occasions like this, the TARDIS key just wouldn't be found. Holding up one hand to stop the guard, the Doctor hastily patted down his pockets. Breast pocket, outside left, inside left, outside right, inside right, trouser right, trouser right, back pockets, oh dear –

The door sprang open. 'Good dog, K-9,' the Doctor breathed, falling in and slamming it shut behind him.

The guard beat against the TARDIS door with the hilt.

And then stopped. There was something about the box that was oddly reassuring.

'Captain!' he called.

But Tancredi barely seemed to notice. The Captain's face was twisted in misery and something worse. It was all askew. 'Leave us!'

'Us?' The guard looked around hopelessly.

'Me,' Tancredi scowled, his whole forehead crumpling. 'Leave me!'

The guard, smartly sensing he'd rather be anywhere else, saluted neatly, turned on his heel and didn't stop until he reached Padua.

'*Scaroth!*'

Captain Tancredi fell into himself. At first it was a random jumble of thoughts zipping backwards and forwards, a frantic inrush of faces and identities.

In the Vatican, a Pope dropped his chalice to the floor, and turned away from his Cardinals. He was speaking in tongues again.

A crusader paused in ransacking Jerusalem.

In Ireland an abomination screamed at the stake as the flames rose around it.

At the Senate of Byzantium, friends rushed a senator hurriedly from the chamber.

In a Venetian palazzo, a slumbering English nobleman talked in his sleep.

In a house outside Athens, slaves ignored the cries of their master.

In Egypt, a labour gang stopped work on the Great Pyramid of Cheops. The awful figure of the architect stood atop the pyramid screaming at the sky.

In Babylon, an astronomer fell forward across his star charts.

On the banks of the Euphrates, the first wheel tumbled from its inventor's hand.

In a cave, the first firemaker spoke to the fire and the fire spoke back to him. The tribe watched in awe.

It was like the first day of sunshine after an endless winter. All those thoughts crowding in, extra dimensions looping and tangling. Questions answering themselves. Let there be so much light.

The Scaroth had a litany of sorts. It was recited as they arrived and drew sense from it. Some of the splinters knew exactly who they were and what their part was in the great purpose. Others were lost in their own identities and found the process a shock. One could only ever enter the gestalt in dreams. And yet, he too worked for the purpose. Seeing it to its final completion.

> *Scaroth. We are here.*
> *Together we are Scaroth.*
> *I am Scaroth. Many together in one.*
> *The Jagaroth shall live through me.*
> *Together we have pushed this puny race,*
> *These humans, shaped their paltry destiny*
> *To meet our ends.*
> *Soon we shall be.*
> *The centuries that divide me shall be undone.*
> *The centuries that divide me shall be undone.*
> *The centuries that divide me shall be undone.*

Inside the TARDIS, the Doctor and K-9 looked at Tancredi's figure babbling that last line over and over, staggering around Da Vinci's studio, hurling chairs, scattering tables and smashing priceless models into matchsticks. Clearly the interface wasn't the only thing that was unstable.

The Doctor sucked his thumb tenderly, and stroked K-9. Well, maybe he'd not got to meet Leonardo, but he had still learned a thing of two. And caused mischief.

'Mission accomplished,' he chuckled. Feeling very pleased with himself, he activated the Fast Return Switch and sent the time machine plunging towards twentieth-century France. Hopefully.

Only when he was falling through the Time Vortex did the Doctor realise what he should have done. He should have gone back outside the TARDIS and reasoned with Tancredi. Told him that the Time Lords were on to Scaroth and he needed to abandon his plan pronto before they came down on him with all their pomp and might. Well, mostly pomp.

Instead of which, the Doctor now realised he'd left Scaroth with the impression that he and Romana were just wandering dilettantes. Which may well have been true, but was terribly unhelpful.

No, he should definitely have gone back and said something. Naturally the French had a phrase for it. The art of coming up with a pithy comeback just a bit too late. L'esprit d'escalier. One thing the Daleks had no sense of.

Tancredi flailed miserably into the manifestation, trying to sort out the tangle of his thoughts. He had been so close, so close to giving them the secrets of time travel, pulled from a very Time Lord. And he'd failed.

He was snatched momentarily out of the gestalt by a large blue box saying 'Boo!' It had hollered at him and then hurtled out of existence. The universe sighed with relief. Tancredi gaped in amazement, and then plunged back into the abyss.

Five centuries later, Count Carlos Scarlioni emerged from

the gestalt, to find himself standing in his library. He knew so much. Some of it would fade, but this time, oh yes, this time, there was something he had to cling on to.

'The Doctor,' he murmured. 'So the Doctor has the secret.'

His smile was wide and hungry.

'The Doctor. And the girl.'

Chapter Fourteen
Material Witness

The exhibits in M. Bertrand's art gallery had passed a relatively peaceful night. Now, as dawn rose over Paris, the gallery's newest and loudest exhibit returned with a happy thud.

Peering out through the door, the Doctor found himself exactly where he wanted to be. It was worse than he'd thought. For the TARDIS to end up exactly where the Doctor had asked it to go meant that something was very badly wrong with the space-time continuum.

The interfaces between the twelve segments of Scaroth were forming a causal link through planet Earth's history. This meant two things. One, time travel was going to be a doddle so long as the Doctor didn't mind meeting a lot of ranting lunatics in wigs. And two, Scaroth's plans were drawing to their conclusion.

'The centuries that divide me shall be undone?' he muttered to K-9. 'I don't like the sound of that at all.'

*

223

Outside M. Bertrand's gallery, he pulled the door shut behind him. He reached up to the alarm above the door, found the wires severed by the sonic screwdriver and twisted them back together, all the while looking like a child who definitely hasn't done anything wrong, certainly didn't break anything and has been very well behaved all afternoon.

'The centuries that divide me?' he muttered again, wiping his fingerprints off the door handle.

He set off into Paris at his most worried saunter.

The Doctor was still worried as he crossed in front of the Notre-Dame cathedral. He reached a corner, stood outside a café, and sucked the air. To the left the Louvre, to the right the Château. He wondered about barging in to confront the Count, teeth blazing and hope something brilliant sprang to mind. Or, he could just make sure that the Mona Lisa wasn't still happily sitting smirking exactly where she was supposed to be. Perhaps that would be an idea.

Slightly sadly, the Doctor decided to do the sensible thing first. Feeling he was forgetting something, he set off, away from the café.

Inside the café, Romana's eyes opened to find someone had placed a fresh cup of coffee on her table. She looked up blearily, wondered why the world hurt so much, and then noticed le Patron placidly moving between the tables, sweeping up the mounds of broken glass. She smiled at the old man. He gave her the merest of unconcerned shrugs and carried on sweeping.

She sipped her coffee tenderly and wondered if Paris did such a thing as a bacon sandwich. No sign of the Doctor. On the one hand, it would be nice to know she wasn't stranded here for ever. On the other hand, she wasn't sure she could survive his booming tones just now.

She looked over at Duggan, sprawled fast asleep at the next table. He was snoring. For once he looked almost at peace. Romana caught herself smiling fondly at him. Duggan wasn't a bad man, she supposed, in his own blunt way. No. Stop that. You're getting as bad as the Doctor. Next you'll be asking if we can keep him.

She stepped over to the snoring detective. She noticed le Patron had also placed a cup of coffee on his table.

'Wake up,' she whispered. 'Your coffee will get cold.'

No response.

She tapped Duggan gently on the shoulder. He leapt up, pulling his gun from his pocket, sending the coffee cup smashing to the ground.

Romana winced. Everything was rather louder than it needed to be today.

'What?' snarled Duggan, whirling around himself in a fighting posture.

Le Patron immaculately swept the coffee cup up from around his feet.

Romana handed Duggan her cup. 'Here. Have some coffee.'

Duggan slugged it back, wiped his mouth with the back of his hand, and then slumped back down at the table, dejected as a bloodhound. 'That's it. I'm washed up.'

He remembered the Chief had once told him scathingly, 'Duggan, you're the kind of chap who can't fall out of his chair without missing the floor.' Duggan had always thought that a little unfair, and yet, here he was. 'I'm sent to Paris just to check if anything odd is happening in the art world. And what happens? The Mona Lisa gets pinched from under my nose. Odd isn't in it.'

Duggan took another slurp of Romana's coffee. He put the cup down. She reached for it hopefully. It was annoyingly empty.

'Well,' she said crisply. 'When you've quite finished with that coffee we'd better go and get the Mona Lisa back, hadn't we?'

'Which one?' growled Duggan, a trifle too loudly for Romana's taste. 'I've seen seven!' His fist started to pound the table rhythmically. She wished he wouldn't do that. 'Seven! Mona! Lisas!' Oh, he was going to do that. 'What are we going to see today? A couple of dozen Eiffel Towers lying about?'

'The real Mona Lisa,' Romana muttered through gritted teeth. 'We'll go and find the original one.'

'But how do you account for the others?' Duggan was starting to whine.

Romana shut her eyes and thought about regenerating. Maybe that would make the pain behind her eyelids go away. Was this what it was like for the Doctor, always being followed around and constantly being nagged with obvious questions? Well, was it? What do we do now, Romana? What does it all mean, Romana? How do we save the planet, Romana? She counted quickly to ten million and then answered. 'Oh, I expect Scarlioni located his seven buyers, popped back in time, had a chat to Leonardo, got him to rustle up another six, bricked them up in his cellar to age properly, stole the one from the Louvre and now sells the whole lot for enormous profit. Sound reasonable?'

Yeah right. Duggan made a sour face. 'I used to do divorce investigations,' he muttered glumly. 'It was never like this.'

Le Patron shuffled over and brought Romana a fresh cup of coffee. Heaven.

'As far as I can see,' Romana continued, thinking aloud, 'there's only one flaw in my line of reasoning.'

'Go on, surprise me.'

Duggan reached for Romana's coffee. She swatted him away.

'That equipment of Kerensky's wouldn't work effectively as a time machine.'

'Keep on surprising me.'

'Well…' Romana held up two sugar cubes. 'You can have two adjacent time continua running at different rates, but without a field interface stabiliser you can't cross from one to the other.'

'A what? You can't?'

She bumped the two sugar cubes together. They remained, like Duggan, obstinately solid. Then she dropped them into the coffee and swirled a spoon around in it until the sugar lumps were firmly dissolved. 'Something like that, I guess.' She sipped her coffee. 'Come on, let's get along to the Château, where at least you can thump somebody.'

While Romana and Duggan were making their way towards the Château, the Doctor was crossing a busy stretch of road on the other side of the Seine. Two tourists asked him to take their picture. He obliged, and then made his way past the Pont Neuf at a run.

Although museums are decidedly boastful about the things they do have, they are reticent to the point of shyness about the things they are lacking. The theft of the Mona Lisa was about to become the biggest news story across the world but, from the outside, the Louvre looked pretty much as normal. Perhaps a few more badly parked police cars than usual. On the inside, the Mona Lisa gallery simply read 'fermé' without further explanation. Someone had placed an easel nearby with a placard advertising some simply lovely Dutch paintings of rotten fruit that disappointed tourists might care to have a look at. On the whole, they did not.

*

Harrison Mandel had been feeling rather intimidated by Elena.

Like most Parisians, she didn't seem to really have a job, or, if she did, it appeared to involve going into an office, pecking some people on the cheek, and then going out for coffee. She had a wearyingly endless amount of time to drag him to art in the hopes that he would be enraptured by it.

Most of it had seemed nice enough, but he could really take it or leave it.

He'd frankly been dreading the Louvre. It seemed so big. So many things that Elena would say lots of clever things about and then wait for him to say something vaguely coherent. He'd only try his best, mutter awkwardly, and then be dragged on to the next thing. Somewhere inside the Louvre was going to be what Elena had taken to calling 'that perfect moment of beauty in Paris that would change his life for ever'. And he had the nasty suspicion they weren't going to stop until he found it. Actually, thought Harrison, I rather like things the way they are.

As they approached the Louvre, he couldn't help but notice all the police cars parked up.

'Oh, that's probably the police on strike,' Elena said, as though this were a usual occurrence.

As they got closer, he noticed a lot of worried people muttering outside.

'Oh, that's probably just the museum staff on strike,' Elena said, as though these things happened.

As they got closer, Harrison saw a reporter standing with a camera crew.

'Oh, that's probably just the Mona Lisa being stolen again,' Elena said, as though this was one less thing to worry about.

As the Doctor ran up, he noticed the police cars drawn

up outside. A shrugging match was going on between the police and a traffic warden. The Doctor strolled past, overhearing 'The Mona Lisa... stolen' and hurried into the museum.

As Madame Henriette would later tell her cats, she had had little to do that day. Sadly few people were interested in taking her exclusive, deluxe and select tours of the Treasures Of The Louvre (Excepting the Mona Lisa). She patiently explained to her furry darlings that this might be the last salmon they would see for a while. 'If the Mona Lisa is not found,' she sighed, 'it will be tinned pilchards for all of us.'

The cats looked at her vaguely and carried on eating the salmon. There would be more salmon. They knew this.

For Madame Henriette, it had been a horrible and strange day, made more so by the sudden reappearance of that terribly odd man with the scarf. 'He terrifies me,' she told the cats. 'You would not like him.'

The cats agreed. He sounded more of a dog person.

Madame Henriette had had little better to do than fuss anxiously around some detectives, trying to extract the smallest morsel of gossip from them. So far they'd been ignoring her birdlike attempts to talk to them. She was alarmed when the Doctor suddenly materialised at her elbow.

'Excuse me,' he bellowed to her in what was a dismal attempt at a whisper.

Madame Henriette let out a hushed shriek.

'Did you notice two people trying to stop the Mona Lisa from being stolen last night?'

'M'sieur?' Madame Henriette gasped.

She noticed a detective turn, suddenly noticing them. This could be disastrous. It was one thing to want to know everything about the theft of the painting. It was quite another for an authorised conductrice of deluxe, exclusive and select tours to be accused of involvement in it. Disastrous.

If this hopeless eccentric had information, she hoped that he would impart it to her subtly. Instead he seemed to be trying to land aircraft. Looking like a portrait by Toulouse Lautrec sprung to life and fallen on hard times, the man clearly had no idea of being anything other than the centre of attention.

'I say,' he boomed, waggling his hands at different heights. 'Have you seen a pretty girl who talks rather a lot and a young man who hits things?'

He mimed hitting. Madame Henriette squeaked. The detective watching them nudged his colleague. They both started looking in their direction, and Madame Henriette's destitution edged a little closer.

'I knew the painting was going to be stolen,' the man informed her and the entire room. 'As soon as I heard the theft was going to take place, I sent my friends along to stop it, which they obviously didn't. I can't rely on anyone.' He pulled a face of dolorous annoyance. 'I say. Did you see where they went?'

Madame Henriette was aware the detectives were nudging their colleagues. They were putting down their coffees and moving closer.

'No, m'sieur,' she ventured quickly. 'But I think, perhaps, you had better speak with the police. They're just over there, I believe…'

'Pah!' The man ignored her, making a dismissive noise that was quite marvellously French. 'No, sorry, no time.' He shook her hand, stepped back and suddenly gave her the most beautiful 'it'll all be all right' smile she had ever seen. 'I'd love to stop and chat, but there's the human race to think about… Bye now!' With a wave, he headed out.

Several detectives watched him go. One swigged the last of his coffee and followed at a run.

Much to her relief, Madame Henriette found herself standing alone in a completely empty gallery, vaguely aware that something much more exciting was happening just outside. For a moment she felt sad. But she had got used to loneliness.

'That man,' said Madame Henriette to her cats later. 'He was in the Louvre yesterday talking about the universe, and today he was worried about the human race.' She stroked a reluctant tail. 'You know, I think secretly he must be a Frenchman.'

The Doctor weaved through the tangled streets of the Marais, unaware that he was being followed. As he marched through the bustling crowds, stopping to take the occasional photograph for a tour party, he little realised that his description (at each repetition a little more outlandish) was being relayed on police car radios.

One detective was sat outside a café watching the world go past over a brandy. He watched the third most wanted man in Paris saunter past and then strode inside to use the telephone.

He had a message for Count Scarlioni. The Doctor was coming.

The Doctor found the café without difficulty. The place was bustling with early-morning customers, some of them slapping each other on the backs in an early-morning *bonne journée* way, some of them smoking in desultory corners, and some of them crowded around a television which, the Doctor completely failed to notice, was relating the story of the theft of the Mona Lisa, accompanied by a picture of the painting herself, and also a very grainy picture of what looked worryingly like Romana and Duggan climbing over a wall.

The Doctor swept up to the bar. 'Patron!' he called. 'Have you seen those two people who I was with yesterday?'

Le Patron stared at the Doctor, his old face completely inscrutable.

'You remember,' the Doctor cajoled. 'We kept on being held up and attacked and smashing things?'

Le Patron shrugged unconcernedly. He picked up the neck of a broken bottle from the table, looked at it significantly for a moment and then slung it in a bin. But that was his entire comment on the matter.

'Ah. I see,' the Doctor pressed on. 'Did you happen to notice which way they went?'

Le Patron shrugged once more, and, with the air of not having heard him at all, shuffled slowly and patiently away to a corner, where he rifled around amongst scraps of paper while puffing air through his teeth. The Doctor was thoroughly dismissed. The Doctor wasn't used to being ignored, ever. And yet Paris was managing that quite well.

'Thank you,' said the Doctor to thin air. 'Thank you very much.'

The Doctor looked around the café. Of course they'd come back here. Romana was sensible. They'd be here at any moment. Probably just doing some shopping.

'They can't have been stupid enough to go back to the Château.'

Le Patron shuffled over, sliding a crumpled scrap of paper across the bar to him. The Doctor read it.

'Dear Doctor, we've gone back to the Cha—' He groaned, crumpled the note into his pocket, waved his thanks, and ran out of the café.

Count Carlos Scarlioni faced Romana and Duggan at

gunpoint across a vast dining table heaped high with French pastries. He sipped his favourite *tisane* and regarded them with benevolent amusement while Hermann gloried in relating the story of their capture.

Their clothing was tattered and they both looked utterly miserable. Hermann had marched them in with their hands up just when the Count had been expecting his three-minute eggs. Still, this was just as enjoyable. He helped himself to another croissant, slathering it with butter before popping it into his mouth.

'... as soon at the alarms sounded, Excellency,' Hermann was saying. For once even he seemed to be amused. 'He was halfway through the window, she was outside.' Romana and Duggan winced at the memory. 'I thought you might wish to speak to them, so I called off the dogs.' A trace of regret. 'They cannot be professionals, Excellency.' Hermann ended his speech with a chiding cluck.

Romana estimated that the croissant, a delicate combination of flour, egg, sugar and fat, would provide a good enough set of complex carbohydrates and protein chains. That should stop her head from trying to leave. She eyed Duggan scathingly. She'd found the low wall, she'd got them over the broken bottles cemented into the top of it, she'd got them safely through the overgrown ornamental jardin, past the peacocks, and she'd even found a small window with a catch that would surrender ideally to her sonic screwdriver. She was just reaching for it when Duggan had smashed the window and it had all gone horribly wrong.

She glanced at the table. Seating for twenty-four, at least 470 years old, bits of it had been revarnished in the last century, one of the legs had been replaced. There were two place settings. At one end of the table, the Count, and at the other, a plate with the remains of a single croissant sliced into neat slivers. The Countess. She was sat ignoring them magnificently.

The Count tore into another croissant, smearing jam onto it and cramming it into his mouth. He was in a delightfully good mood. He licked traces of jam from his fingers, and then drummed them happily on the table top. When he spoke, he addressed Romana with the sweetness of honey.

'My dear, it was not necessary for you to enter my house by, well, one could hardly call it stealth. You only had to knock on the door.' His smile projected seventy-three per cent bonhomie, mixed with the merest hint of social reproof. 'I have been very anxious to renew our acquaintance. Indeed, I was on the point of sending out search parties.'

'Listen Scarlioni,' snapped Duggan.

The Count wiped some crumbs from his velvet smoking jacket. 'I was talking to the young lady.' He smiled dangerously. He stood courteously, bowing Romana to take a place by him.

The Countess, with complete poise, turned the page of her newspaper and loudly ignored the whole room.

Romana sat down, hands still held wearily high.

'Tush,' clucked the Count, motioning that of course she could lower her hands. They were friends, after all.

Romana lowered her hands gratefully.

Duggan did likewise, but a vicious jab from Hermann convinced him that he was not included. Sourly, Duggan raised his hands again.

The Count offered Romana a plate and gestured to the table. Eagerly, she helped herself to the most ridiculous pastry she could find. Spoilt for choice, she eventually settled on what appeared to be a pastry galleon with custard cargo and glazed fruit sails. It was annoyingly wonderful.

The Count leaned forward. The Countess affected magnificently not to notice.

'My dear,' purred the Count confidentially, 'I think you can be very useful to me.'

Do go on, thought Romana. She may be stranded in time having an adventure on her own, but she definitely got a better class of villain than the Doctor. Did Davros wheel out a fruit platter? He did not.

'You better not touch her,' growled Duggan from the wall. More for something to say, than anything else, guessed Romana. Bless.

'Do be quiet,' murmured the Count as one would to an ill-trained dog.

'Thank you,' Romana reassured Duggan. 'But I'll look after myself. I feel safer that way.' He looked hurt, but Romana didn't notice. She'd just discovered a slice of kiwi fruit. Delightful.

The Count was fixing Romana with an attentive gaze and a most welcoming smile. 'Well my dear?'

'Well what?' Romana spoke with her mouth full.

'I do believe you have some highly specialised knowledge that will be of immense service to me.'

'Who me?' Romana looked the picture of total innocence.

The Count leaned even further forward, captivating and hypnotic. His smile was a perfect blend of respect and regret that she would not confide in him. 'I am talking of temporal engineering. You are, I believe, a considerable authority on time travel.'

'Look here, I was only joking about that!' boggled Duggan desperately. 'She knows nothing.'

'Duggan's right. For once I know as little as he does.' Romana reluctantly put down her pastry and firmly pushed away her plate. When she spoke, her voice was cold as sorbet. 'I'm afraid I really don't know where you got that idea from.'

'No no no, that really won't do,' tutted the Count's smile. He paused, with the mild embarrassment of someone about to betray a confidence. 'Your friend the Doctor let it slip.'

'The Doctor!' He was alive. But… 'But he's in…' Well, could be anywhere.

'Sixteenth-century Florence?' The Count finished her sentence smugly. 'Yes. That's where I –' he coughed – 'we met him.'

The Countess pointedly failed to look up from her newspaper. If she was surprised at this turn of events, she somehow neglected to show it.

The Count and Romana gazed at each other across the table. Even though her eyes lacked their usual lustre, he could see that she was working things out frantically, slotting things into place and opening things up. Rather like his Chinese puzzle box earlier. Take your time, my dear, his smile said. We have a lot of work to do together and I should like us to start out understanding each other perfectly.

Duggan made some noise. 'Can anyone join in this conversation or do you need a certificate?'

The Count winced, as though hearing an untuned violin in an orchestra. 'Hermann, if the Englishman interrupts once more, kill him.'

Hermann assented happily. Duggan shut up.

The Count stood, and, with elaborate courtesy, pranced round and drew back Romana's chair. The Countess watched all this without comment. 'Now then, my dear, perhaps you'd care to come downstairs and examine the equipment in more detail.'

Romana stood gracefully. 'And if I refuse?'

The Count hid a yawn. 'Oh, do I really have to make vulgar threats? Let's just say I will destroy Paris if it will help you make up your mind.'

'Am I supposed to believe you can do that?'

'Well,' the Count smiled teasingly, 'you won't know till you've had a look at my equipment, will you?' He swept Romana to the door, and then nodded to Duggan. 'Hermann, bring him.'

Left alone, the Countess surveyed the remains of her croissant, slotted a cigarette into her holder, but did not light it.

For Professor Nikolai Kerensky it was the last straw. A few short months ago, there was a waiting list for his seminars. Now he was being made to stand at the back of his own laboratory while a schoolgirl marked his homework.

The Count had swept in with these two strangers. The man was crumpled and dejected, as though he was having a bad day with the first theory of relativity. The girl looked completely unbothered, as though she was popping in to have a polite look at a reupholstered settee.

Kerensky made to interrupt, but the Count smiled him his most dangerous smile and Nikolai remembered about the gun that Hermann was pointing at the man whose knuckles scraped across the floor.

When the Count had first entered, Kerensky had armed himself with all he had to hand, which was knowledge. He had reasons why he had not yet begun work on the Kerensky Accelerator. Not excuses, but reasons. He had valid questions, he had points of concern, he had issues and he had things that needed discussion. He had got no further than 'But'. The Count had simply pooh-pooed him. That doesn't matter, not now. This young lady is going to have a look at your work and tell me what she thinks of it.

The utter crushing humiliation of it all. Kerensky slunk dejectedly on a stool.

'Can he?' hissed the crumpled ape.

'What?' said the schoolgirl, poking at a compressor.

'Destroy Paris?'

'With this lot?' she snorted.

'Yes.'

'No trouble.' She stood back, her nose wrinkled in disgust.

Destroy Paris? What nonsense. Kerensky really must protest. He got to his feet, but the Count's smile made him sit right back down again. The Kerensky Process, he still validly believed, held the key to the salvation of the human race. Chicken Experiment #1 proved it. Thanks to the Count, things had taken a worrying turn, indeed, but destroy Paris? What a horrific accusation, as though he, Nikolai Kerensky would ever permit such a thing! The girl must be denounced. Surely the Count could see the patent absurdity of her words.

And yet she carried on talking, her air a trifle dejected. 'If he chose, he could blast the whole city through an unstablised time field.'

Well, yes, he supposed she had a point. But you'd have to try very hard. A rebuttal needed to be issued.

The bullish man sneered at her. 'You don't seriously believe all this time-travel nonsense do you?'

'Do you believe wood comes from trees?' the girl snapped.

'What do you mean?'

'It's just a fact of life one's brought up with,' she sighed.

Despite his fury at her, Kerensky warmed to her. Perhaps, just perhaps, once he had entirely refuted her allegations, he might allow her to join his research team.

The Count cut across all of them. 'You see the truth of my words, don't you, my dear?'

The girl turned to him. 'That you can destroy Paris? Yes.'

That was it. He needed, nay demanded, an explanation. 'Why all this talk of destruction? What are you doing with my work?'

The Count coughed, as though covering a minor social embarrassment caused by a child, and then turned his most inviting smile on Kerensky. 'Professor, tell you what, I shall show you. Perhaps you would care to examine the field generator?'

He'd used the exact same tone at their first meeting when he had invited him to examine the list of dessert wines. That seemed so long ago.

The Professor left his stool and walked stiffly over to the field generator using all the dignity he could muster. His work may have been called into question, but he was genuinely puzzled. Despite the crackling air of menace in the room, perhaps, just perhaps, between them, the girl and the Count had uncovered something, some weakness in the field generator that was possibly directly harmful. It was, after all, just possible that he, Nikolai Kerensky had overlooked something. The endless hours of work, the lack of sleep. Well, if there were some flaw, he would shoulder the blame. Some of it.

But no. Nothing wrong. Thought not.

Standing in the heart of the device, he tapped one of the three prongs over his head, just to make sure that there was stasis. Yes. The Kerensky Accelerator was working perfectly.

He straightened up, pleased to find the Count smiling at him.

Then the Count said something that would haunt Kerensky for the rest of his life.

'You will now see how I deal with fools.'

And then the Count had flicked a switch.

'No!' screamed Kerensky desperately, 'Not that sw—'

Itch.

For a moment nothing happened. And then, for many years, nothing happened.

It took Nikolai Kerensky the rest of his life to die.

Standing at the heart of his machine, looking out at those four faces staring in at him. All of them frozen, all of them unmoving. Watching him.

Once a year, one of them would blink. It would happen in turn, like the changing of the seasons. The stupid man, the clever girl, and then Hermann. The Count would never blink. It had taken Kerensky this long to realise that the Count never blinked.

He was a fool not to have noticed. But then again, he had plenty of time now to dwell on his mistakes. His biggest mistake had been never building a field interface stabiliser. The Count had asked him often enough, and he had always nodded and said it was on the list. The truth was that it was tricky and there were so many other things to do. After all, he had argued to himself, why would you need to cross between two time fields while the device was running?

Now here he was, trapped inside the Accelerator while it was running and completely unable to ever leave it. Outside the bubble, his life was racing past in the blink of an eye. He tried to imagine what that must look like, his features blurring, his limbs jerking, his hair growing long, his skin sagging.

But, inside the bubble, life went on at very much the same pace as usual.

Nothing happened.

Ever.

He had a long time to dwell on his mistakes. On the things that he had got wrong. What he could have done better. What he could have said. The irony was that he now had plenty of time to build a field interface stabiliser but no way of doing it. He went through his pockets on that first day. Two pencils. A scrap of paper. He spent ages working out a message, a formula to write on that piece of paper, something that could tell them how to build an interface stabiliser in time to save him. He waved it at them. But he knew, even as he did it, that, although he had managed a remarkable breakthrough in temporal theory all squeezed onto a single side of paper, it was fruitless. The time it would take to read the paper and react to it, the time it would take to talk about it, even to find a screwdriver, in that time he would already be dead.

His time passed so quickly for them. But for Kerensky so slowly.

He was so bored. He memorised the entire contents of the laboratory. He spent days just staring at the Mona Lisa casually propped up against a wall. No one in history ever looked at that painting in the same way that Kerensky did, squinting to perceive every element of the mystical city of domes and valleys in the background. What world was that, what fantasy of rocks?

Kerensky would never know, but he visited it in his mind. He paced the confines of his bubble, retracing childhood walks through the streets of Budapest. He tried to recollect songs, he thought of books. He begged for hunger to kill him. Or thirst.

But nothing did.

For ages, the sound of his last syllable echoed through the air. 'Itch.' A famous last word if ever there was one.

Sometimes he sat down on the platform. Sometimes he slept on it. Then stood up again. Regretfully. Starting another day. An endless day.

For a few years, he watched the girl stretch out her hand, trying to reach through the bubble towards him. Every day her hand got closer. It was something to look at. He knew what the end result would be, of course. Her hand took so long to get so far. And then, one month, it stopped.

No field interface stabiliser, he told her. He knew the exact week, the very day in which the stopping would happen and had prepared a speech. His hand was there, fingertips out to touch hers. Just in case the impossible happened and she broke through.

He then watched the years go by as the hand drew slowly back. Done. Finished, retreating. Leaving him there. Alone for ever.

He looked at his own hand, older now. The skin as frail as parchment. His bones ached. But not enough. There was still a lot of time ahead of him.

He remembered the advice of his doctors. Nikolai, you must eat less of this, you must drink less of that. You don't want to die a young man. He bitterly regretted ever listening to any of them. In the end, it had made little difference.

It was taking so long.

He looked at their faces. He did so a lot. At the face of Hermann, impassive, curious. He had never in his life known exactly what the butler was thinking.

The baffled man, whose name he had never learned, stared at him in puzzlement for a couple of decades.

The young girl, the one who had reached out to him, stared at him, oh so slowly, in terrified horror and awful understanding.

And the Count beamed broadly at the entire room as though the horrible death of Professor Nikolai Kerensky was some wonderful joke. 'You will now see how I deal with fools.'

A fool? Sometimes he argued at the injustice of the verdict, at others he accepted, bitterly, that perhaps he had been a fool after all. He screamed and raved at the Count. He composed epic poems, he wrote them on the other side of the scrap of paper which held Kerensky's Final Equation. In the end he just screamed.

The Count's only response was a surprising one. The

man never blinked, he'd seen that. But, just once, he had winked.

In the end, Professor Nikolai Kerensky died of boredom.

The last thing he saw was the face of Count Scarlioni. And that smile. That dreadful lingering smile.

PART FOUR

Edmond: *J'veux changer d'air. Ma vie n'est pas une existence.*
Raymonde: *Ah ben si tu crois que mon existence c'est une vie.*
(Edmond: *I'd like a change of air. My life is no more than an existence.*
Raymonde: *What, you think my existence is a life?*)

Hôtel du Nord

Chapter Fifteen
The Discreet Charm
of the Bourgeoisie

Romana was appalled. She watched as the Professor blurred and shrivelled away to a skeleton in an instant. She turned furiously on the Count.

Who greeted her with a little, sarcastic bow. 'There you are. The unfortunate effects of an unstabilised time field.' He did a little what-can-you-do shrug, before putting seventeen per cent more menace into his smile. 'And I shall do exactly the same thing to the whole of this city unless you reveal to me the secret of achieving a stabilised time field.'

Romana's headache had come back and she needed a moment to think. A moment she didn't get as Duggan roared, 'You're mad! You're insane! You're inhuman!'

'Quite so.' The Count acknowledged the comment curtly. 'When I compare my race to yours, human, I take the word "inhuman" as a deep compliment.'

Duggan boiled over with fury. The Count risked the tiniest of glances at Hermann, just to see how he was taking

249

it. The Count and Hermann had an understanding. It had always been based on not bringing into the open what could be kept quite happily sealed behind closed doors. Of course, Hermann had an inkling that his employer's origins were somewhat unusual, but he had never seemed to let it bother him. That said, this was the first time the Count had ever addressed the issue in front of him.

The Count was pleased to see Hermann's gun didn't waver from Duggan. Not by a whisker. That was good. One less thing to worry about. Pretty much Hermann's motto. Ah, he would miss Hermann.

Duggan was off again, and of course he was using words to be tiresome. 'You couldn't possibly—'

'Oh, do be quiet,' the Count said, annoyed that he'd ever taught them language in the first place. He put just an extra little hint of threat into his bored smile.

Romana did not miss the hint. She leaned back against the computer and struck up a carefully jaunty air. She'd learnt it from the Doctor and it seemed a rather practical way of demonstrating eternal insouciance. Wave your tentacles at me all you like. I am a Time Lord of Gallifrey. 'Count, you must have realised that I am not from this planet any more than you are. Why should it worry me if you destroy Paris?'

'What?' Duggan gaped like a goldfish. 'What are you talking about?'

Oh, enough, thought the Count, genially jamming his hands into his jacket pockets. 'Hermann, I do think you'd better kill him.'

'No!' shouted Romana without thinking and wished she hadn't.

'Well, I think you've just answered your own question, my dear.' The Count graced her with his finest victory smile. Tut tut. 'Not a very clever bluff.'

Pained, Romana turned to Duggan. 'Just be quiet now,

will you?' she murmured gently. The grown-ups have some talking to do. She smiled at the Count. 'All right. What are you trying to do?'

'You agree to cooperate, then?' The Count extended his victory smile to the whole room.

'Just tell me what you're trying to do and I'll see.'

'Excellent.' Fine, thought the Count, let her have her little illusion of independence. What harm could it do? He nodded to Hermann insouciantly. 'Take the Englishman away and lock him up. I will keep him as an insurance policy since it is unfortunately not possible to kill him twice.'

Duggan scowled at the Count as Hermann shoved him into the storeroom, bolted the door, and then busied himself amongst the wine racks.

Hermann, of course, being Hermann, brought them over a delightful amontillado and some biscotti before retreating upstairs. How thoughtful of him. After all, it did seem a pity to let the sherry go to waste. The Count offered some to Romana but she recoiled from the wine as politely as possible, contenting herself with nibbling on a biscuit and waiting for him to speak. Suddenly the cellar seemed a lot less cluttered. Just the Count and the Time Lady and the device that would free him.

The Count told her his problem. It felt curiously like giving a little speech at a soirée. Put in such bald terms, it sounded ridiculous. A mild embarrassment between friends. 'My problem is very simple. Four hundred million years ago, the spaceship I was piloting exploded whilst trying to take off from the surface of this planet.'

'Ah. That was very clumsy of you.'

'A calculated risk,' conceded the Count. At this distance there seemed little point in getting cross. 'The spaceship was severely damaged. I was in the warp-drive cabin and when the explosion occurred I was flung through the time vortex and –' a delicate cough – 'splintered into twelve different parts which now lead... have led, independent but connected lives in different times of this planet's history.' He tutted as though someone had served white wine with beef. 'Not a very satisfactory mode of existence, I'm sure you'll agree.'

'So you just want to reunite yourself, yes?' Seems fair enough, actually, thought Romana. Let the Doctor have all the 'the universe shall be mine' stuff.

'Well, I'd like to do a little more than that,' expanded the Count, sipping the sherry. He had the casual air of someone asking if he could perhaps have an extra duck egg on his niçoise salad. 'I wish to return to where my ship is... was... and prevent my original self from pressing the button that caused the explosion. I want to save everyone on board. The last of the Jagaroth.'

Practically an errand of mercy, thought Romana, if you ignored the skeleton in the corner. And the rather pathetic jumble of equipment it was held in. 'You were hoping to do that with this lot?' She sounded dubious.

Every now and then, the Count met the mechanic who serviced his Rolls Royce. Judging by her tone, he and Romana would get along fine. But no matter. Let her be rude about his lives' work. She came from an ancient race of privileged time sensitives. He had had somewhat of a standing start. 'Do not underestimate the problem with which I was faced. My twelve separate selves have been working throughout history to push forward this miserably primitive race so that even this –' he waved around at the computer, the banks of equipment, and yes, poor dear Kerensky – 'even this low level of technology could be available to me now.'

'But this won't work.' Romana dismissed it all with a snort. 'Put yourself in that time bubble and you would either regress back to being a baby or go forward to old age.'

'I had…' The Count paused, sadly. 'I had worked out a way. A very difficult way. That I think would have taken rather a long time. But now, with your assistance, I shall be able to return with ease.' He dusted his hands. Perhaps he was brushing away biscuit crumbs. Perhaps he was writing off a complicated plan that had been gestating for millions of years, involving all twelve of his fragments and seven Mona Lisas. Never mind. It had kept him busy. 'Now…' He gestured to Romana. 'Build me a field interface stabiliser.'

Romana hesitated, looking around at the room. Was it possible? the Count wondered. No more tinkering, no more endless experiments, no more expensive, tedious invoices. Would this girl just glance around the room and conjure up a time machine? It seemed too easy. Her eyes returned to him, doubtful.

'Do it.' He smiled encouragingly.

There was a long pause. Maybe it just wasn't possible.

'"The largest doors open to the littlest keys, 'No thank you' and 'If you please'",' Romana intoned neatly.

'Oh, but of course.' The Count pressed his fingertips together in apology. 'Build me a time machine, *please*.'

Romana grinned back. 'All right. I'll help you.'

The masks were the difficult bit. It was easy enough for the first few fragments of Scaroth. Even the one stranded among the Egyptians found itself welcomed with open arms. Apparently strange-headed aliens claiming to be gods were always turning up, and so Scaroth fitted right in. The Egyptians were, on the whole, a talented people. Much could be done with them. They'd once been ruled by a quite remarkable set of aliens who'd abandoned a lot of very useful technology, which was untidy but very helpful. He hunted through their artefacts, hoping to find something as simple as a time corridor, but his life span among the humans was annoyingly short. He blinked out of existence knowing that somewhere, out among the desert, was exactly what he needed. Possibly.

He had, however, learned that aliens did visit this planet, occasionally, and he built up a storehouse of their leftovers. It was the start of his habit of collecting. Sadly, he did not encounter an alien race who could build him a time machine, but he found a lot he could work with.

The masks for example. By Greek times they were useful and by Roman times they were vital. He got the idea watching a play in a Greek amphitheatre. All the actors performed behind masks, becoming the characters they inhabited. In some ways, for such a primitive culture, he felt rather proud of them sometimes. As the people grew more hesitant about his alarming appearance, he retreated behind a simple theatrical mask and gauntlets, claiming injury in battle. That won him respect. It was surprising among the humans that, even though they were achieving really useful things in terms of philosophy and mathematics, if you told them you'd been horridly wounded in combat, they'd be terribly impressed. How very Jagaroth, he thought.

He began work on a more advanced mask. At first he tried fashioning something from canvas around a wooden frame, but the results were repellently crude. He went to see an artist. Sculpture was really finding its feet and he threw money at the brightest and best, until he found one who showed real promise.

He sorted through what other races had abandoned. A force that could control all plastics had recently arrived, realised there was nothing to take control of, and left promising to come back in a few thousand years. They'd left behind a pan-polymeric protoplasm which looked quite promising. He presented it to the dubious sculptor.

'What would you like me to make?' the sculptor asked.

'Oh…' He had enjoyed learning to shrug. It seemed to help with humans far better than sticking knives in them. 'You have a fine face. Make that.'

Phidias did so and did so remarkably. It took a few attempts, but they eventually had a very promising mould and a worthwhile prototype.

'But what is it for, my lord?' the sculptor asked.

When Phidias had met him wearing the mask in the agora a few days later, the sculptor had started screaming in horror. And so that had marked the rather abrupt and bloody end of Scaroth's first experience of being a patron of the arts.

But he'd found it a useful experience. Artists were adept at creating things which survived their little butterfly lives. Their works carried on after them. It amused him, in the far future, to visit galleries and touch the objects he himself had seen carved. They'd maybe lost a bit here, a bit there, but they had endured. He felt strangely proud.

The Roman Empire proved a good base. The transport links were really excellent. The one problem with a far-flung place like Egypt was that it was a long way from anywhere. But Rome spread itself neatly and quickly out across Europe and beyond. It proved useful for ensuring that the Scaroth fragments could swiftly lay their hands on their inheritance.

The Primary Fragment knew where they all were. The original gestalt manifestations allowed him to control and provide for them all. He knew where and when they were and could ensure that the ones with little self-awareness, little more than cries in the night, would swiftly be equipped with at least a mask.

His solution had worked well. Regrettably, he had not been able to save one fragment. Occasionally, echoes of it wandered screaming into the gestalt. The humans had burned it.

But he made sure that never happened again. Once he'd been a Roman Consul, later he was the Holy Roman Emperor. As Pope, he could issue edicts, and control a marvellously unquestioning network of spies and assassins. Confused splinters could be apprehended, looked after and provided with identities.

Others did perfectly well for themselves, displaying an almost natural ability to spring to life, find the mask he'd left for them, and merge into society. As the distance between himself and the fragments grew, this ability evolved.

The final fragment was the most impressive in this regard. For most of the time, it worked quite happily for their greater purpose whilst having little awareness of what it truly was. It entered the manifest only when dreaming, carrying out their goals subconsciously. In some ways this was worrying. In others it was reassuring. This was someone unburdened by a sense of history.

The fate of the Jagaroth lay with Count Carlos Scarlioni. And he was a man who knew he was placed on this planet to get things done.

A maid was sweeping the front steps of the Château.

The Doctor marched up to her and tapped her on the shoulder.

'Good morning,' he said. 'I should like to make an appointment with Count Scarlioni at his earliest convenience.'

She stared at him in astonishment.

The Doctor's hands were held high above his head.

They stayed that way – the Doctor insisted on it – as she led him through the porch, down a hallway, and into an even bigger hallway at the base of a sweeping stone staircase. There they found someone who would point at gun at him.

It was Hermann. The butler bowed, and obligingly pointed a gun at the Doctor.

'Ah good, someone in authority,' smiled the Doctor. He dismissed the maid, who scurried away, relieved. 'Would you please inform the Count that I wait upon him?'

Hermann regarded the Doctor. He was working out if it would be acceptable to just shoot him now. He said nothing.

'Ah, the strong, silent type, eh? Once knew a young chap like you. Never said a word. "Well," I said to him, "No point in talking if you've got nothing to say." Did well in the end, though. Name of Shakespeare. Shows how we can all misjudge people.'

Hermann didn't react. But then, the Doctor was no longer playing to an audience of one. The Countess had come down the grand stone staircase and paused on the landing. She wondered if the Doctor's last remark was addressed to her. He gave her a cheery wave with one of his hoisted hands.

'Good morning! Have you read any Shakespeare, Countess?'

'Ooh, a little.' She smiled. Why not show off, eh?

She descended coolly, taking her time, making her grand entrance. She dismissed Hermann. 'No doubt,' she told him, 'the Count would like to know of his visitor. I will be fine.' Really, she wanted to speak to the Doctor alone. She wanted the chance to learn a little about this Romana. The easiest way to do this was, of course, by impressing him, and the Countess always knew how to be impressive. She steered him towards the library, past a corridor of treasures.

The Doctor lingered over them as they passed. A Botticelli surely consigned to Savonarola's Bonfire of Vanities. Lysippos's bronze of Hercules, last seen before Constantinople fell. An exquisite Bellini thought lost in a fire at the Doge's Palace. As far as he knew, they hadn't been

257

heard of for centuries. And wouldn't be heard of again.

Going well so far. With a swing in her step, the Countess led him into the library. The room was large and neat and soaked in knowledge. The mid-morning sun beat through the windows. She strode over to the grandest bookcase in the library. At a touch of a lever, it slid back to reveal another bookcase behind it. Her lit cigarette and the ungloved fingers she danced across the spines would have made a bookseller flinch. She plucked a thin volume from the shelf, blew the dust from it, and passed it to the Doctor.

'*Hamlet*,' she announced.

She'd wanted the Doctor to be impressed. He leafed through it, nodding. The book was ancient, the paper inexpensive, but filled with a crabbed script that flowed until it filled the page.

'First draft,' she added, gilding the lily.

'This has been lost for centuries,' the Doctor marvelled. He stopped leafing through it and looked at her. This book was impossibly valuable, wonderfully rare, and had been preserved with loving skill. The Count wasn't just a collector, he was a connoisseur. The Doctor almost wished that for once he could sweep aside all the reversing the polarity of the death ray nonsense and just sit down for tea and a natter over macaroons. If it wasn't for the Count being a homicidal maniac, the two of them would get on famously. What a pity.

'I assure you it's quite genuine,' the Countess added. She was enjoying her moment.

'I can see that for myself,' the Doctor nodded, running a thumb along the edge of a page. 'I recognise the handwriting.'

'Shakespeare's,' she nodded back.

'No, mine,' the Doctor said abruptly. 'He'd sprained his wrist playing croquet.'

The Countess glared at the Doctor. Could he take

nothing seriously? Heedless, the buffoon carried on talking, finger rushing along a page. 'Here we are. Tsk, tsk. "Take arms against a sea of troubles." I told him it was a mixed metaphor, but he would insist.' He pulled a regretful *moue*. No mending that now.

Despite herself, the Countess giggled. There was something about this Doctor. He wouldn't let her enjoy a single moment of being impressive. He just wouldn't stop babbling away.

'Doctor, it is quite clear to me that you are perfectly mad.'

'Well, only nor-nor west, nobody's perfect.' The Doctor's grin, as warm as a winter hearth, suddenly died out. 'If you think I'm mad because I say I met Shakespeare, then where do you think your precious Count got this from, eh?' He shook the volume dangerously hard.

'He's a collector.' Obviously. 'He has money and contacts.'

'Personal contacts?' The Doctor made it sound like an insult. 'Just how much do you really know about him? Rather less than you imagine, I think.'

All things considered, the time machine was coming along nicely. The Doctor had once shown Romana a television programme called *Blue Peter*. Like most things the Doctor was inordinately fond of, the appeal of it missed her completely. It mostly featured Boy Scouts collecting milk-bottle tops, and people who should know better making toys out of pipe-cleaners, cardboard and whatever else came to hand. Just when the results looked like a tottering pile of junk, the presenter would sweep it to one side and hastily produce a rather more complete one that had clearly been assembled by an expert. 'Here's one I prepared earlier,' they would then lie shamelessly.

Romana stood in the rather unpromising ruins of the

Kerensky Accelerator, using her sonic screwdriver to conjure a vortex breach trigger out of some valves and a corkscrew. She had vastly increased the memory of the computer to almost a megabyte and the two of them were getting on marvellously. It was terribly interactive and provided an immediate response in seven computer languages and five protocols. She'd accelerated it until it was pretty much the prime computer on the planet. Clever prime, she thought. If it wasn't for her headache and the fact that she kept having to step over the skeleton of the poor Professor, she would have said things were going swimmingly.

Duggan also wasn't helping. Whenever she passed his cell he would growl 'traitor' at her, which struck her as pretty ungrateful. If he was trying to spoil her concentration, he had another thing coming. If she could put up with the Doctor, she could put up with anything. Actually, it was rather nice to have her own project.

Hermann came rushing down into the cellar, wearing a look almost of panic.

The Count was sitting, eating cheese and watching Romana with a smile of approval. Seeing Hermann's expression, he burst out laughing. 'The Doctor!' he snapped jubilantly. 'Here!'

Hermann frowned. 'So I have just discovered.'

'I knew it!' The Count clapped his hands together with glee.

Romana couldn't help but feel a little hurt, like an understudy who had thought they were going down a storm, only to see the star hobbling back into the limelight. All the same, she could do with a second opinion, and possibly cream off a bit of grudging praise for her solution.

Seeing she'd stopped work, the Count wagged a finger at her, then dotted up a stray crumb of gorgonzola. 'Carry on with your work, my dear,' he smiled. 'You're doing terribly well.' He turned back to the butler. 'So, we have a full house, do we? Excellent, Hermann, excellent. Ask him to step down here, would you?' He turned back to Romana with a smile that was both generous and triumphant.

Yes, thought Romana, he'll be very pleased with all we've done. She paused, suddenly uncertain. Won't he?

The Doctor was splayed out in a library chair. He was spreading out across the library in a jumble-sale sprawl. Already he was quite at home, filling all of it with his scarf, piles of discarded books, and his boots propped up against a table which had been designed for better things. He'd only been in the library ten minutes. Imagine the chaos if he had sat there for a day, the Countess thought.

She'd invited him here in the hope of learning something about Romana, but the Doctor seemed determined to bat away all enquiries about her. Every now and then, the Doctor would drum his fingers on the arm of his chair impatiently and then flash the Countess a winning look. He was waiting for something, she thought, but what? He couldn't possibly expect to leave here alive. What did this lunatic have up his sleeves? Blackmail? A weapon? Knowledge? He was definitely playing for time.

She ran through the options and drew a blank. What did the Doctor have? Nothing. But they had the Mona Lisa. There was really nothing they couldn't do. Carlos and her.

'Tell me…' The Doctor seemed to have been suddenly struck by a thought. 'How long have you been married to the Count?'

What a question! 'Long enough,' she replied, refusing to take offence.

'"Long enough"? Oh, I do like that, discretion and charm,' the Doctor beamed at her witticism. 'So civilised. So terribly unhelpful.'

261

'Discretion and charm.' How perfectly he put things. 'I could not survive without them. Especially in matters concerning the Count.' She felt she'd evoked the right level of enigma about her husband. But also, a worry: had she somehow given something away?

'There is such a thing as being discreet.' The Doctor steepled his fingers and rested his chin on them thoughtfully. 'There is also such a thing as being wilfully blind.'

'Blind!' She hooted with laughter. 'I help him steal the Mona Lisa, the greatest crime of the century—'

'The Mona Lisa?' the Doctor muttered. For some puzzling reason, he had underlined the 'the'. Why, what other one was there?

'Exactly!' she retorted. 'And you call me blind?'

'Yes!' The Doctor sat up in his chair, a thundering cascade of movement. 'You see him as a great master criminal, an art collector, an insanely wealthy man. And it suits you to see yourself as his consort. But tell me this…' He paused, lethally. 'What's he doing in the cellar?'

That floored her. She hesitated.

The cellar had long been a bone of contention between the two of them. 'I'll show you when it's ready, my dear' or 'Perhaps tomorrow. Not today,' and 'Hermann says it would be a bad idea to disturb the Professor right now.' Just to underline that Hermann was a frequent visitor, an insider on some project that she was best kept out of. It had always niggled her. But how could the Doctor possibly know that? She shifted in her chair. It suddenly felt uncomfortable. Maybe it was time to have it reupholstered.

'Oh, he's tinkering, that's all.' She wafted the Doctor's question away. 'Every man must have a hobby.'

'Man?' The Doctor was deadly grave. 'Are you quite sure about that?'

'What?' The Countess tried to laugh, but her mouth was dry. 'I...'

The Doctor was on his feet now, striding around the library. Wherever he went, little turrets of books went toppling. 'A man, yes,' he sneered, 'but with one eye and green skin?' He did an absurd mime.

The Countess tried to laugh again. Nothing happened.

The Doctor was in full flow. 'Ransacking the treasures of history to pay for the time machine he hopes will reunite him with his people, the Jagaroth?'

Finally the laugh came. She dismissed him completely.

But the Doctor didn't seem to notice. His tone was scornful. 'And you never noticed a thing? How discreet. How charming.'

That should have pulled her up, and indeed it gave her pause for thought, but really this man was too much. How shriekingly funny.

Hermann entered, coughing politely. 'Excuse me, my Lady, but the Count is very anxious to see the Doctor in the cellar.'

Good, she thought. That would be the last she heard of him.

The Doctor nodded farewell to her. 'Think about it, Countess.' He pointed to an imaginary dot in the centre of his forehead. 'Think about it.' He bowed, and seemed so sad.

Left alone, the Countess continued to laugh. All this, this château, this wealth, this view, this achievement – all of it conjured up by something that you'd pan fry with garlic? What a wonderful world it was to have such madmen in it.

And then, the Countess closed the curtain, stopped laughing and turned away, chewing on the edge of her cigarette holder. She tried to light a cigarette, but her hand was trembling.

Although the Doctor had gone, the room still seemed full of him, somehow.

She crossed to the fireplace where a little blaze was crackling away. She noticed the flowers on the mantelpiece had died. How sad. They'd been so pretty yesterday. She plucked the heads off the roses and dropped them into the fire, one by one. They burned surprisingly well, sending little puffs of smoke up the chimney.

Struck by a thought, the Countess weaved her way through the scattering of books, reaching up to slide back a panel that Carlos didn't think she knew about. But of course she did. She knew everything.

Behind the panel was another ancient book. Only it wasn't a book at all. A hermetically sealed fake. Inside it was a sealed plastic bag. Inside that was an ancient oilcloth parcel. Inside the oilcloth were some scraps of parchment.

One piece of parchment really didn't look that impressive. Well, not until you realised it was the original design sketch for the Great Pyramid of Cheops. Somehow it had survived the sacking of the library of Alexandria. Nestled atop of it was a tourist trinket given by Champollion to the Emperor Napoleon. Aged up to look ancient, but really little more than a tracing of a temple frieze. It depicted Horus, Isis, Ra and, at the end of the frieze, the figure that had somehow struck her as odd when she'd first seen it, so odd she'd felt the bracelet tingle on her arm. It was an image that, for no good reason, her subconscious had never let her forget.

It was the figure of an Egyptian god with one eye and green skin.

The Countess sank into a chair and covered her face with her hands.

Chapter Sixteen
Goodbye,
Not Au Revoir

The Doctor glided into the cellar like a galleon at full sail. Hermann's gun didn't matter; the skeleton in the corner didn't bother him at all. He stopped halfway down the steps, waited until he had everyone's attention, and then swept into the laboratory, waving to everyone. 'Ah, Count, hello. I wonder if you could possibly spare me a moment of your time? Romana! Hello! How are you? I see the Count's roped you in as a lab assistant, eh? What's that then? What are you making for him?'

The Doctor hit pause in his promenade, smiling at her. Expecting a response.

Romana, holding up a triumph of solid-state micro-welding, sucked her lip, and felt oddly guilty. 'Er,' was all she managed.

'Is it perhaps a model railway?' prompted the Doctor. 'Or a Gallifreyan Egg Timer? I do hope you're not making him a time machine because I shall be very angry if you are.'

Romana's confidence stumbled. She looked worried and

started to make very vague placatory noises.

But the Count cut across, every inch the genial host. 'Ah Doctor! How delightful to see you again. Why, it seems only four hundred and sixty years since we last met.'

'Four hundred and seventy four,' the Doctor corrected, convivially. 'Indeed. I always find the weather so much more pleasant in the early part of the sixteenth century, don't you? Where's Duggan?'

'The Englishman?' The Count snorted and jerked a thumb towards the storeroom. 'In there.'

Duggan's face appeared at the grille in the door. He looked as dejected as a lost dog in a cage.

'Hello Duggan!' the Doctor greeted him like an old friend.

'Doctor, get me out of here.'

'I do hope you're behaving yourself. Good, good.' The Doctor dismissed all thoughts of Duggan from his mind. He needed the room. 'Now Count, what I've come here to say is that, if you're by any chance trying to go back in time, you'd better forget it.'

'Oh? Why do you say that?' smiled the Count pleasantly, as though told it might rain.

'Because I'm going to stop you,' the Doctor pronounced gravely.

'On the contrary.' The Count waved this away as jovially as if someone had said they'd better not have another drink. 'You're going to help me.'

'Am I?'

'Oh, indeed you are, Doctor.' The Count treated him to his widest, most celebratory smile. 'And if you do not, it will be very much the worse for you, for this young lady, and for several thousand other people I could mention if I happened to have a Paris telephone directory in front of me.'

Romana looked alarmed, but the Doctor had been down this road so many times he knew which service stations to avoid. 'You know, that sort of blackmail won't work on me, Count, because I know what the consequences would be if you got what you wanted. I'm afraid I can't let you fool around with time.'

'Whatever else do you ever do?' The Count looked hurt.

'Ah, well, yes, but,' began the Doctor, 'I'm a professional. I know what I'm doing.' He considered pausing for effect, and then saw that Romana was about to say something rather unhelpful. 'I also know what *you're* doing, Count. Romana, put down that equipment.'

'Doctor,' chided Romana, 'it's all right. He only wants to get back to his spaceship and reunite himself.'

'PUT IT DOWN!'

Romana winced. The Doctor had never shouted at her before. Irritated with him beyond measure, she slammed the equipment on the desk.

The Count hastily snatched it up, examining it like a rare jewel. His face shone with pure delight. 'Doctor, as entertaining as this is, I think we can dispense both with your help and your interference. Your friend has done her work very well indeed.'

Romana couldn't help smiling. Until she saw the Doctor's face. He was angry. End of the world angry. The Doctor made a clumsy attempt at knocking the device from the Count's hands, but Hermann made a brutally efficient attempt at knocking the Doctor to the floor.

The Count tutted down at the Doctor and waggled Romana's device at him.

'Count.' The Doctor started to pick himself up. 'Don't you realise what will happen if you take yourself back out of human history?' His voice was very grave.

'Yes.' For once, the Count didn't treat it as a joke. He

looked around the cellar, and he may as well have been surveying all eternity. 'Yes I do. And I don't care one jot.' He smiled, but this time there was precisely no humour in the smile. 'Hermann,' he said, pocketing the device, 'lock them up. They shall stay there long enough to watch my departure. After that…'

Hermann bowed curtly and turned to the Doctor with a gleam in his eyes.

'Kill them in whatever way takes your fancy,' the Count announced. He climbed the stairs feeling suddenly weary. 'I must make my farewells to the Countess.' With a wave of his hand, the Count was gone.

It would be unfair to say that the Count had a list. But he took a long route back to the library, saying farewell to a few favourite works of art. Ones that perhaps hadn't found their fans, but that were, in their own way, very dear to him. He'd spent the last day eating some of his favourite meals. He'd drunk some truly exquisite wines, he'd made sizeable inroads into the vintage champagnes, and really, really made the most of his last hours on Earth. Once he'd realised that was what they were.

Now he just had to say goodbye to his wife and have one final glass of that brandy he'd last drunk with Napoleon. Luckily, both the brandy and the Countess were in the same place. Jauntily tossing Romana's device in the air, he strode into the library, his most exuberant smile on his face.

The Countess was pointing a gun at him and had been crying.

Alors. How trying.

'My dear?' he asked, raising an eyebrow.

'Close the door.' Her voice and her grip on the gun were shaking. The Count regarded both with a little alarm. The gun was one of his best inventions. Ironically, considering the position he was now in, he had invented it as an efficient way to shut these creatures up and stop them from bothering him. Ah well, what was it that man had once said? 'Hoist by your own petard.' Yes. Quite.

Weapons came in and out of fashion. The pikestaff, the arrow, the mace, even the petard, all were languishing a little. But the gun really had proved to be the little black dress of weapons. Over the years it hadn't changed that much. It had become faster and more efficient and that was about it.

He could have progressed weapons a bit further. But he'd pretty much stopped at the gun because he had invented something that could kill him with ease. One thing he'd learned about humanity. They could be so terribly ungrateful.

The Count had, of course, been held at gunpoint before. But that had always been fine. He'd greeted it with *sang froid* because he'd believed himself to be immortal, he'd believed himself to be the most important person on the planet, working to change the world for ever. He'd recently learned that all of this was true, but also, well, tricky.

His other fragments were, if you wished, immortal. He was not. He was the very final fragment of the very last of the Jagaroth. He now knew he was impossibly precious and, for once, he felt vulnerable.

Especially when confronted by his wife with a gun. If it had been a hoodlum, a heavy or a thug then that could have been got around. They were probably threatening him because they wanted some pieces of paper or something shiny. But no. The Countess was pointing a gun at him because she was angry. And angry people did very silly, regrettable, messy things.

The Count had never been angry in his life. People got angry because they didn't get their own way. The Count had never had this problem. If people were in his path, he simply removed them. However he had to.

And now he was stood in the doorway, staring in alarm at his wife. He realised he had licked his lips nervously. (How do I do that? he wondered. No, not now.)

'Close the door,' she repeated.

He did so. For once he had to force a smile. So. Just the two of them in the library. This might not end well.

'What are you?' she snapped hoarsely.

'I beg your pardon?' As pithy comebacks went, it really was below par, but he reasoned that, on this one occasion, he could be allowed a handicap.

She came forward, step by step across the carpet. Now he was almost at point-blank range. Well, that was not good.

'What have I been living with all these years?' she shrieked. Her voice was hoarse and dry. Regrettable. So much emotion. He had expected better of her. Especially as, one of the many uses of the bracelet he had given her was to suppress these nagging worries. He had found it terribly helpful over the years. His other fragments had discovered that, unless you were Pope, not being married aroused more questions than was entirely helpful. And so the bracelet had come about. Its low-level hypnotic field induced susceptibility and devotion, without, after a few refinements, making the poor things as docile as cattle. He so liked them to have independence and character. Heidi had delivered both in spades. And now, rather too well. What an alarming turn of events. He rather suspected the Doctor's hand in this.

Heidi was asking more questions. 'Where are you from? What do you want?'

'If you would allow me to take those questions in reverse order, what I want is a drink. Would you care for one?' Smoothly, patiently, he crossed to the drinks cabinet, fully intending to keep his appointment with that exquisite brandy. Be a shame to miss that.

He selected his favourite glass, bowled in at the top in order to enhance, well, everything about the brandy. He was taking a risk, of course he was, but if he showed her how rattled he was, then he was lost.

'Stay away!' she was shouting now. The poor thing was actually terrified of him. How interesting. He could use that.

The Count took no notice of her and picked up the brandy bottle, rubbing a thumb through the patiently acquired dust as he twisted the stopper.

'Put it down!' The bracelet and the gun were rattling together. That thing could go off at any second. So close to his goal.

The Count put the bottle down slowly and turned to face her, his smile at its most *charmant* and empty.

'Who are you?' She looked at him as though seeing him for the first time.

Clearly there was no sense in pussy-footing around this. But he did find it rather difficult to say.

'I…' he began and stopped. His mouth was dry. He really could have done with that brandy. 'I am Scaroth.'

'Scaroth?'

'The last of the Jagaroth,' he smiled, aware of how little that meant to her, but everything to him. 'It has not been difficult to keep secrets from you my dear,' he purred, casually shooting his cuffs. He knew he was about to be deliberately, maliciously cruel. It wasn't perhaps the best tactic, but for some reason he just couldn't stop himself. 'A few fur coats, a few trinkets, a little excitement…' He smiled. Mere nothings for a soul.

If he'd hurt her, she did not show it. There was still some of that admirable cool-headedness about her. 'What are the Jagaroth?'

'The Jagaroth?' Absurdly, he was really rather enjoying being honest with her. 'An infinitely old race. And an infinitely superior one.'

She took this in. The general lack of alarm and screaming told him that yes, he really had made an excellent choice in her. What a shame it was ending like this. Perhaps it wasn't too late. But no. In for a penny…

'Allow me, my dear, to show you what you want to know.'

The Count showed her his smile for the very last time. Then, starting above his right eye, he tore his face apart in slow, steady strips, the flesh forming little mounds on the floor.

He heard her gasp, but the gun did not go off. Which was a relief. She had probably gone into shock. That happened.

For the first time in their marriage, the Count and Countess stood face to face.

She had broken. He could see that. Somewhere inside her eyes. He knew now that she would not fire the gun. He was the strong one.

'I am Scaroth,' he told her. 'Through me my people shall live again.'

She just stood there. Quivering like those apes had so long ago.

What would happen next? Scarlioni just didn't know.

Well then, best get on with it. In case she suddenly found her trigger finger.

He coughed delicately.

'I am glad to see that you are still wearing the bracelet I designed for you, my dear. It is, as I said, a useful device.'

The Countess had dropped the gun, her hand going to the bracelet as it started to emit a piercing noise. Her fingers were scrabbling at that awkward fiddly catch. Maybe she'd undo it in time. Maybe she wouldn't. How interesting.

The Count stroked his signet ring, and the Countess

started to scream in agony as the bracelet discharged its power pack into her.

It took her a distressingly long time to die.

Time enough to enjoy that brandy.

He reflected that the last thing that had made him Count Carlos Scarlioni had gone. Really, there was no need to bother putting that mask back on. He was Scaroth now.

He regarded Heidi's body, smouldering on the rug. He should have felt liberated. Instead he felt strangely sad.

'Goodbye, my dear,' he said to her. 'I'm sorry you had to die. But then, in a short while you will cease ever to have existed.'

Scaroth put down the empty glass, straightened his cuffs once more, turned on his heels, and left the library.

So, there they were, locked up with six Mona Lisas. Which was all very well if you liked that sort of thing, but it was currently the last place Romana wanted to be. For one thing, it put her rather too close to the Doctor. He was boiling with anger at her. He'd called her naive, weak-willed, and giddy, and he'd been very loud about it. Worse, he'd not once congratulated her on building a time machine out of little more than tinfoil and sticky-backed plastic.

'Whole of Paris being destroyed?' he was thundering. Her headache had returned in spades. 'What are you talking about, Romana? Is that what he threatened you with?'

'Well, can't he?' Romana pursed her lips.

'That's not the point. Paris!' The Doctor wrote the city off with a disdainful roll of his eyes. 'I've a good mind to take you straight back to the Time Academy and have you sent down. You'd be a computer programmer for the rest of your life.'

'But he said—'

'Said, said, said! They all say stuff like that.' The Doctor softened slightly. 'You have to learn to ignore it. Just think, will you? He had two alternatives, both of which he would have destroyed for himself if he'd messed around on the local scale. Either there was the time bubble…'

'But he couldn't get in that.' Duggan was trying to prove he'd been listening. 'We saw what happened to the Professor and the chicken.'

'Yes.' Romana found herself agreeing with Duggan. This was a first. 'It doesn't travel in time, it just goes forward or backwards in its own time cycle. If he'd got in it, he'd just have become a baby again. End of threat.'

'*If* he got in it!' thundered the Doctor. That was the problem with Academy students, even ones as brilliant as Romana. Just because they never thought outside the box, they assumed no one else ever did. The Doctor had never thought inside the box in his life. Oh, he remembered those tedious, awful lectures on Sidereal Time and what not. The Academy on Gallifrey taught on the noble principle of 'least said, soonest mended'. Their reasoning went something along the lines of 'We, the Time Lords of Gallifrey are so above all other life that we have mastered time travel. No one else has, and we will make jolly sure that no one else will. Because it's tricky. So, we simply need to make certain that every Gallifreyan understands why, having got the most fun toy in the universe, we must never ever play with it. Because it is, lest we forget, tricky.'

The Time Lords just couldn't understand why anyone else would want a go with time travel, for fun, friendship and maybe more. They reminded him of the French monk who discovered champagne. He was aghast at what he'd found. He frantically tried to find ways to take the bubbles out of his wine. For one thing, the bottles kept exploding. He was even more horrified to find that people loved drinking the stuff. They didn't mind that the bottles sometimes blew up in their faces. Worse, they even invented new non-explodey bottles. Reluctantly, Dom Pérignon tried a sip. And the rest is history.

Talking of bubbles and history, Romana was still missing the obvious. 'The bubble is useless. That's what I'm trying to tell you.'

'Supposing,' the Doctor said slowly, 'he stayed out of the bubble?'

Lady Romanadvoratrelundar, graduate of the Academy of Time Lords (triple first), favoured scion of the noble House of Heartshaven, and the terror of the trans-temporal debating society, stared at the Doctor and said: 'Huh?'

'Supposing,' the Doctor repeated slowly, 'he stayed out of the bubble and put everything else in it?'

'What?'

'The whole world!' The Doctor threw his arms in the air. 'What he was really trying to do was stuff the whole world in the bubble. Push the whole world back in its life cycle. Like the tiny time jumps when we first arrived.'

Romana thought about this a bit. 'Oh.'

'The cracks in time. He shifted the whole world back in time for two seconds. What he really wanted to do was shift it all back to his time. Four hundred million years ago.'

'But without a stabiliser he couldn't have been there himself to save his ship.' Romana felt relieved. 'Besides, how would he have got the power?'

The Doctor pointed through into the secret chamber, at the six Mona Lisas.

Duggan coughed. 'What do you think we've been chasing around for all this time?'

The Mona Lisas! The audacity and stupidity of the entire plan made Romana giddy. Working across history partly in order to pay a power bill that would never be sent because even the accounting department of *Électricité de France* would no longer exist to send it. Some people, sighed Romana, just didn't understand time travel. Well, it was tricky.

The Doctor brightened and gestured to the Mona Lisas almost fondly. 'He could never have sold them anyway.'

'Why not?'

'Well…' The Doctor jammed his hands in his pockets and tried desperately hard to look casual. It was as successful as an all-elephant production of *Macbeth*. 'You see, before Leonardo painted them I wrote "These are fakes" on the blank boards. In felt tip. That'd show up on any X-ray.' He looked around the room triumphantly. He may have whistled. Just a bit.

Duggan's jaw suggested he was trying to swallow a tennis ball.

'Problem solved,' the Doctor announced firmly. And then stopped grinning. 'Or it would have been if there wasn't a second alternative that someone in this room had just given him.'

He stared long and hard at Romana until she felt like moving to Belgium.

'You!' He jabbed a finger at her. 'You've given the Count the vital component he needed to just take himself back through time to his ship.'

'But I had to!'

'In direct contravention of the Time Laws.'

'The what?' At the mention of laws, Duggan had perked up.

'The Time Laws.'

'Do they count in France?'

'They count everywhere!' boomed the Doctor.

Romana was getting pretty fed up now. This was a bit rich. 'Doctor, I've never known you to be much of a respecter of the Law.'

'Ah, but…'

'No, let me finish,' Romana wasn't going to be lectured by someone who remembered the Laws of Time, Physics, Gravity and Polite Conversation only when they suited him. 'If you'd bothered to ask me before you launched into one of your broadsides—'

'Did I launch into one of my broadsides?' the Doctor appealed to Duggan.

Duggan suddenly stared very hard at one of the Mona Lisas. 'Yes,' he announced eventually.

'Well, then, I'm terribly sorry,' said the Doctor, sounding anything but.

'Keep out of this.' Romana smiled at Duggan, gratefully. She turned back to the Doctor and played her trump card. She really had thought of everything, you know. Which was rather more than he ever did. 'Doctor, when I made that component, I rigged it so that he could only go back in time for three minutes. After that, Scaroth would be catapulted back here to 1979. Now, he couldn't do any harm in that time.'

'Oh yes he could.' Thinking like a Gallifreyan, a three-minute visit was barely enough time to recite the first Observational Protocols, let alone write the answers down. For any other species in the universe, three minutes was plenty of time to cause mischief.

'Oh, what now?' said Romana.

'A very minute would be enough time to contact his ship and prevent it taking off. Which would mean he would then not be splintered in time.'

'Yes.' Romana conceded the point.

'And everything he has done in history would suddenly not have happened. The history of the human race would be totally changed, maybe even abolished.' The Doctor paused. Something was nagging at his head. Something terrible that he couldn't quite answer. So he asked a question instead. 'What are you going to do about that, then?'

Crushed, Romana looked at the door. 'We'd better get out of here very quickly.'

'Agreed,' said the Doctor. Friends again. 'How?'

'Er,' said the captain of the Arcalian Chapter Debating Team.

'I've got an idea!' The Doctor grinned.

'What?

'We'll ask Duggan.'

'I thought you wanted me to keep out of it.' Duggan sounded hurt.

'Ah, yes, but that was before,' said the Doctor.

'Duggan, please,' pleaded Romana, ever so sweetly.

With the greatest display of brute strength he'd shown so far, Duggan threw himself through the air, launching himself feet first at the door. It was a move he'd seen in a Bruce Lee movie and always fancied trying out. Bruce Lee had landed like a ninja. Duggan landed like a dropped teapot. But the door burst open, handily knocking Hermann out as it went.

'See?' The Doctor beamed at the results in approval and helped Duggan to his feet. 'I always have the best ideas, don't I?' He patted Romana. 'Sorry I shouted. It's been a bad day.'

'You didn't have to sleep in a café last night,' growled Romana.

They strode out to freedom.

Duggan had seen a lot in the last day. Chickens. Maniacs. Mona Lisas.

Now he was being held at gunpoint by an exquisitely dressed plate of calamari.

'What the devil's that?' he cried.

'The Jagaroth,' hissed Romana.

Scaroth was striding down the stairs, covering them coolly with a gun which had recently belonged to his wife. Ex-wife. 'You now see me as I truly am,' he announced.

'Very pretty, probably,' said the Doctor.

'And you will now witness the culmination of my lives' work.'

'How terribly fulfilling for you.' The Doctor missed Count Scarlioni. He had been quite a bit more fun than Scaroth, who seemed, well, rather less likely to send out for cocktails.

'For thousands upon thousands of years, my various splintered selves have worked towards this very moment.' Was that a trace of a smile creeping through those tentacles as Scaroth sauntered across the cellar? 'And now with the aid of this device, so kindly provided by the young lady –' he produced it, and for a moment adopted the air of a stage magician – 'I can make this equipment function as a fully operational time machine.'

'Well—' began Romana smugly. The Doctor trod on her shoe. She'd clearly never learned when not to gloat.

'I am fully aware of the limitations you have built into your device, my dear.' Scaroth waved this away like a small problem with the meringues.

The Doctor altered his judgement. Clearly Count Scarlioni was still very much alive inside Scaroth. He wondered about appealing to his better nature. Perhaps a friendly natter? But Scaroth continued to talk, his tone measured, even and precise. 'Believe me, your limitation will not affect the outcome in the slightest. I will return to the moment just before my ship exploded and prevent myself from pressing the button.'

With a flourish, he plugged Romana's device into the machine. The entire catacomb started to hum with energy, pouring into the pulsing spikes of the time bubble generator. The tape memory on the computer began to spin like an excited washing machine.

Scaroth looked at it all, allowing himself one last moment of pride. All this, he had caused all this.

He offered one final confidence. 'You will not be able to read the settings on these dials, by the way. They will explode as soon as they have activated. Goodbye, Doctor.'

He pressed a button and strolled into the heart of his machine, pausing only to toe the skeleton of Professor Kerensky to one side.

The bubble formed around Scaroth, last of the Jagaroth and whisked him away with a cheery wave.

Romana's device exploded and the bubble collapsed.

Silence came to the cellar.

CHAPTER SEVENTEEN
WE'LL NEVER
HAVE PARIS

This was the last day of the planet Earth. These were its very final hours. And, in the cellar of the oldest house in Paris, one man made a very important decision.

'Well –' Duggan dusted his hands and beamed – 'that's got rid of that, then. I don't know about you, but I need a drink.'

The Doctor and Romana shook their heads simultaneously.

'No.' The Doctor glanced up from trying to read the melted settings on the machine. 'We've got a journey to go on.'

'Where to?'

Romana squinted at the charred ruins and then started running.

'Four hundred million years ago!' she called as she and the Doctor dashed up the stairs.

Out of habit, Duggan followed them. 'Where?'

'Just don't ask,' yelled the Doctor.

They raced through the chambers of the Château, which seemed so empty and sad now without their master. A horrible thought struck Romana. 'But we haven't got the time or place coordinates, Doctor. Four hundred million years ago and the whole of Earth to choose from is like looking for a needle in the corn prairies.' Romana paused to lean against a Michelangelo.

'You two,' puffed Duggan. His feet hurt from all the running and kicking. 'You're both off your respective rockers.'

'So will the whole of history be if we don't get to my ship.' The Doctor was grim. He already had a slightly nauseous sensation.

'But we'll need coordinates!' Romana protested.

The Doctor threw open the doors of the Château and they tumbled into the street, the Doctor talking and running in a way that left Duggan open-mouthed with exhaustion, annoyance and admiration. 'Scaroth will leave a faint trail through time. We can possibly, just possibly, follow it if we get to the TARDIS in minutes.'

'Have you parked it nearby?' That, thought Romana, would be a help. So long as it wasn't back in that art gallery on the other side of town.

'It's back in that art gallery on the other side of town,' the Doctor admitted, starting to weave through traffic.

'Oh, wonderful.'

Romana and the Doctor found themselves stranded on a small heap of concrete between lanes of cars.

They're mad, sighed Duggan, they're absolutely mad.

There is a universal law that says that, the more you need a taxi, the less likely you are to be able to get one. This applies even more so in Paris. The rules that govern Paris taxis are fairly simple. If you're very lucky and the taxi drivers happen not to be on strike, then they will certainly be driving very, very fast. It's the only way to drive in Paris, and does not really allow for the troublesome slowing down and stopping involved in picking up passengers.

Your chances of being noticed will decrease even further if your driver has had a bad day and just doesn't fancy stopping for a tourist. Tourists in Paris often think the best way to get directions is to flag down a taxi driver and ask them. They assume this is a free service which the taxi drivers are only too happy to provide. This is based on no evidence whatsoever. Guidebooks have been scoured by exasperated taxi drivers and nowhere does this advice ever appear in print. What makes it even worse is that these tourists ask the most bizarre things. The taxi rank by the Eiffel Tower echoes to groans of despair as tourists constantly ask for directions to the Eiffel Tower. It is a state of affairs which is both miserable and also unsustainably improbable.

When people say they know all about unsustainable probability waveforms collapsing, they either understand these things instinctively, or they've been to the library, looked them up, and wished they'd bought a bigger brain. The people who understand these things instinctively are the kinds of people who go out to bars, have a good time, always get a table, rarely spill a drink, and never miss whichever bus they decide they're going home on.

One of the reasons they lead such a charmed life is because they have assessed (with blackboards) what would happen to their evening if at any point they talked about probability theory, quantum mechanics, waveform reduction, or eigenstate vectoring. The simple reason is that, if they did, they would then be definitely getting the bus home alone.

If you cornered these people in a bar, and the bar

happened to be in Paris, and you told them that the entire timeline of Paris was about to enter a thermodynamically irreversible interaction with a classical environment then they would grab their hat and start running. They would not even bother to try and catch a bus.

The Doctor was standing at a bus stop. He had given up on trying to hail a taxi. Duggan found this behaviour baffling. If the universe was ending, why were there no signs of it? Secondly, did Paris even have buses? He guessed it proved that the Doctor and Romana were English after all. Only the English would queue at a time like this.

Apparently the world was ending. The Doctor and Romana could talk of little else as they stood waiting patiently for a bus at what Duggan was fairly sure was just a lamp post.

Out of nowhere a taxi pulled up.

The Doctor beamed in delight and was effusive in his praise for the taxi drivers of Paris.

A little old man came out of nowhere, pushed past the Doctor, announced curtly, 'This m'sieur, is for me,' stepped inside and the taxi drove away.

The Doctor said some words. They weren't French.

They carried on standing at the bus stop. It started to rain.

'Do you know what, Romana,' the Doctor announced eventually. 'I don't think there are any buses in Paris.'

They started running again.

Duggan didn't have the heart to tell them that a few seconds after they had started off a bus had pulled up. He just pelted after them.

It is exactly a kilometre from the Arc du Triomphe down the Champs-Élysées. Duggan knew this because a teacher at his school had told him. He'd said that it was a useful fact. His teacher had been a tank commander during the liberation of Paris. He was defending the Arc du Triomphe when a German tank rolled into view at the end of the Champs-Élysées. Speed was of the essence. It would take time to target, sight and focus the tank gun properly. But Duggan's maths teacher remembered that it was exactly a kilometre from the Arc du Triomphe to the end of the Champs-Élysées, and so, before the enemy had had a chance to fire, the tank was reduced to scrap metal. It was a useful fact to know.

Although, Romana would have pointed out, a little breathlessly, that, actually, the distance between the Arc du Triomphe and the Champs-Élysées was 1.3 kilometres. It's an agonisingly slow run if you're weaving through traffic, have probably pulled a tendon by kicking in a door, or are worried that at any moment the world may end.

Eventually they hared off down a section of streets that a man in less of a hurry to save history would have paused in, just for a moment, to catch his breath and gasp at the beauty of it all. But Duggan didn't pause. Instead he carried on around the corner.

To find the Doctor and Romana leaning against a kiosk, catching their breath and just taking in the quaint, untidy beauty of Paris before it was all swept away.

'This really is very pretty,' gasped Romana.

The Doctor nodded.

It was a very lovely day. The sun was shining like there was no tomorrow. Which there wasn't.

A taxi bumped along the cobbled street. The Doctor waved desperately at it. The driver shrugged and drove off.

The Doctor looked around hopelessly. 'What's the matter?' he wailed. 'Is nobody interested in history any more?'

*

Only the Doctor would try and save the planet by taking them to an art gallery. That much Duggan was certain of. They finally reached the right sort of street. It was filled with tourists, all clutching bags of shopping and bunches of flowers and looks that determinedly said, 'We are enjoying dawdling and will not allow ourselves to be bustled out of the way. Not by anyone. We have quite enough of that at home. We have come to Paris for a saunter.'

Consequently, the Doctor, Romana and Duggan's progress down the street was not fast. But, judging by the Doctor's frantic pointing, they were nearly where they wanted to be.

Duggan had a nagging worry in his head, though. What was a TARDIS anyway?

In their mad dash, the Doctor, Romana and Duggan failed to notice the street artist.

Normally, Bourget earned enough from sketching tourists to stop his landlord from screaming at him. It was demeaning work, but his landlord could shout very loudly.

Stood in front of him were a family of Americans. They were all grinning broadly and saying howabout that, we're going to become a genuine work of art. It'll be a masterpiece, the father was telling them all, like a painting by Renault. He was already talking about how much he would spend on the frame, surprising as he'd haggled adroitly about the fee. Perhaps he'd noticed Bourget's hands were shaking.

Bourget tried not to look at the paper, each swift stroke cooed over as he smoothly drew the family, a little thinner, a little taller, and with fewer shopping bags. He avoided the faces. Surely it could not happen again, thought Bourget, it just couldn't. He started work on adding in a hint of the Eiffel Tower to the background. The enraptured gasps grew quieter.

'Don't worry, kids,' said the man. 'He'll do the faces in a moment. All part of the technique. Say, you will do the faces in a moment, won't you?'

Bourget finished the Eiffel Tower and idly wondered about drawing a second one. No, there was nothing for it. He had to start on the faces. He knew what would happen. He started on the head of the father first. Surely, this time it would be all right. A few strokes in and he relaxed. No clock face was appearing. Instead, yes, absolutely the head of a man. He frowned. There was something wrong about it. The jaw a bit heavy, the brow hirsute. The overall effect was oddly primitive. Apelike. He hastily started on the children. The faces appeared, all normal, stroke after stroke giving them eyes and mouths, transforming their blankness into something approaching character. And then, between one line and the next, shading became dials and the clock-hands sprouted from their noses. That's when the screaming started.

Elena was looking at Harrison, expecting a reaction from him. She was, she thought, pretty much at the end of her tether. She had shown him every beauty that Paris had to offer, and she'd known that, for some reason, the magic of it all had passed him by. Also, these heavenly little shoes she'd picked up were pinching abominably. She decided to give it one final go before writing this off as a noble attempt at an *entente cordiale*. She had, and no one could say that she hadn't, tried. Surely there'd be something in this gallery that would speak to him?

She brought him up before the last exhibit and waited for a reaction.

There was a silence which dragged, just a little.

'Well, for me,' Harrison began, a trifle uncertainly, 'one of the most curious things about this piece is its wonderful…'

He coughed and stumbled to a halt. He stared again at the work of art. He found it strangely reassuring. Suddenly he found he knew exactly what to say. 'Its wonderful afunctionalism.'

'Yes, I see what you mean.' Stunned, Elena rewarded him with a coaxing nod. 'Divorced from its function and seen purely as a piece of art, its structure of line and colour are curiously counterpointed by the redundant vestiges of its function.'

Exactly. It made Harrison think of home. And yet made him feel even more happy to be here. There was something about its sheer incongruity that was somehow tremendously cheering. He beamed, the words tumbling out of him. 'Since it has no call to be here, the art lies in the fact that it *is* here!'

Elena had brought him to M. Bertrand's gallery. At first, he'd been quite distant and mumbling, but something about that final exhibit had given him pause. Imagine that, riveted by a wooden blue box! A police box, of all things.

As they stood admiring it, three people ran past them and into the box. Which, with a snort, vanished.

'Exquisite, absolutely exquisite!' Elena gave a little gasp and clapped her hands.

Harrison nodded. Finally he'd found something in Paris that was truly beautiful.

Duggan had run into the TARDIS before he'd even had time to work out what it wasn't. Standing inside it, he was dimly aware that it wasn't entirely the shape or size he'd been expecting it to be, but there was a large bit of his brain that had simply stopped caring.

Apparently, the Mona Lisa had been stolen by a squid who was currently travelling through time to end the human race and they were chasing after it in a phone booth.

Yes. Well. Fine.

Anyway, he'd just discovered the Doctor had a robot dog and that was the most wonderful thing he'd ever seen in his life.

The Doctor and Romana busied themselves in shouting around and at a large computer thing. Duggan left them to it and made friends with the Doctor's robot dog.

'Hello little feller, what's your name, eh?'

'K-9.'

'K-9 eh? That's brilliant.'

'Query brilliance,' said the robot dog, sounding strangely pleased, as though it had just bought a new hat.

'What tricks do you do, doggy? Do you beg?'

'Negative.'

'Do you fetch?' Duggan picked up a book and threw it. The robot dog did not move.

'Doctor, I think your robot dog's stopped working,' said Duggan.

The Doctor looked up from untangling a lot of cable. 'No, no, he just bores easily,' he said and threw himself to the floor, scrabbling for some screws.

'Oh.'

Romana flashed Duggan a weak smile. She was hurriedly trying to lock the TARDIS coordinates onto the fluctuating energy signal from Scaroth's transit. It was like trying to find where a stone was thrown in a lake a long time after all the ripples have gone and the lake's dried up. What made it worse was that the Doctor was helping. As the Doctor's attempts to help normally involved setting course for the nearest supernova, it was all rather vexing. She glanced at K-9 who looked back at her with all the sympathy that a robot dog could muster.

The TARDIS hurled itself through time, the 6,000 streets

of Paris collapsing behind it. Shiny office blocks crumbled, boulevards fell apart, the Metro system heaved itself out of the ground, the romantic waters of the Seine boiled and the Eiffel Tower itself tumbled away. The present was falling into a state of uncertainty which would have got quantum physicists quite excited if there was still such a thing as quantum physics.

Every single achievement apart from one, placed itself on hold. The TARDIS fell back through time, causality unravelling like unfinished knitting, row after row of history pulling itself apart, events burning away like the fuse on a cartoon bomb, heading towards the very start of things, the one achievement that Scaroth had yet to undo.

It actually made navigating history surprisingly easy, simply because there was nowhere else left to go.

For once the TARDIS fell silent.

CHAPTER EIGHTEEN
À LA RECHERCHE DU TEMPS PERDU

There was no vegetation on the surface of the world, just a bank of mud beside a thick, lugubrious sea. It was more of a sluggish soup than a sea. It refused even to reflect the sky, because that would have been too exciting, preferring instead to glow with a deeply boring grey green. The sludge was the only dull thing about the world. Above it, the sky burnt magnificently, clouds ominous with fire. It was a Tuesday.

All in all, it was a unique landscape. One that wouldn't be seen again until it somehow sneaked from the dreams of Leonardo da Vinci and into the background of his most famous painting. Lightning skied down mountains and plunged into desolate valleys, tossing pumice into the stew-pot air.

It was a marvellous spectacle, and a real shame that there was no one there to see it.

Except that all of a sudden there was.

A man – well, almost a man – stood there, looking

laughably dapper, wearing a neat white suit which quickly became flecked with ashy smuts.

Scaroth looked around himself, pleased. He still had a little way to go but, at last, he was back where he belonged.

He set off across the rocks.

Some minutes earlier, the TARDIS had set itself down at a slight angle on the very edge of the only certain bit of Earth's history remaining.

Duggan still wasn't exactly sure what had just happened. But it all seemed a little bit unfair. If you're going to walk into a box, however wonky it is on the inside, things outside it have a duty to be the same when you leave it again.

He failed to come up with any theories as to where Paris had gone. 'What happened?'

When that didn't get him an answer, he went for 'What is this place?'

The Doctor and Romana swapped grins. There were clearly going to be a lot of questions.

Idly, Duggan picked up a stone and threw it across the plateaux. The Doctor had long ago noticed that, when a human being is confronted by a sight they don't understand, they usually throw something at it.

The Doctor swept his arms across the sullen, glowering horizon and the vast plain.

'This is, or will be, more or less the middle of the Atlantic Ocean.'

'But…' There was quite a long pause. 'We're standing on land.'

Romana realised that, in every way possible, Duggan was out of his depth.

'Duggan…' The Doctor put on his most reasonable tones. 'I promise you we are where I said we would be. Four hundred million years in Earth's past.'

'Oh,' said Duggan, testing the ground underneath his feet uncertainly.

'You can see why the Jagaroth wanted to leave.' Romana wasn't enchanted. 'Where is Scaroth?'

'Oh, he'll be here soon,' muttered the Doctor. 'After all, there's the Jagaroth ship.'

He pointed. Almost hidden in the shadow of a mountain at the edge of the plateau sat a ship like a metallic insect. You almost couldn't notice it because the mountain was so very big and looming. And yet, once you saw it, there was no looking away from the ship. There was no way in which that spaceship was even pretending to be good news.

They strolled briskly across the plain, walking on land that seemed to be torn between being rock and mud. 'That ship is the last of the Jagaroth. A vicious, callous warlike race. The universe will be well rid of them.' The Doctor did not say 'the universe won't miss them'. That seemed a bit rich. Right now he was painfully aware that time was busy working out if it could do without the human race, and figuring that it was a bit of a shame, but it could probably get by at a pinch. The Doctor also thought it would be a bit of a shame. Every innovation that Scaroth had given humanity would be wiped out. They'd have to start with a blank slate. Would they manage quite so well without on their own? To be or not to be? That was the question.

As they crunched and squelched nearer to the ship, Romana became coolly unimpressed. 'You can see why it must have exploded.' She pointed. 'Its atmospheric thrust motors are disabled. The idiots must be about to try to take off on warp drive.'

'Yes,' the Doctor agreed. In their shoes he'd probably have given it a shot. But... 'Try doing that in an atmosphere and...' The Doctor stopped speaking and started looking very worried indeed.

They crunched on for a little in gloomy silence. Eventually Duggan realised something.

'That's a spaceship!'

'Hush now,' whispered the Doctor, patting his shoulder. He crouched down, trailing a hand through the sludge and pulling up a handful which dripped and glopped back through his fingers to the ground. 'This stuff, Duggan, is the amniotic fluid from which all life on Earth must spring.' The unappetising slime trickled slowly back through his fingers. 'This is where the amino acids fuse that come slowly together to create minute cells, the cells that will eventually evolve into vegetable, animal and human life. You, Duggan.'

The Doctor poured the liquid reverentially into Duggan's hand, then hastily wiped his own hand clean on Duggan's raincoat.

'I come from that? From that soup?' Duggan flung it away hurriedly.

'Well, not that soup exactly. It is inert. There is as yet no life in it at all. It's waiting for a massive dose of radiation to start it off.' The chain of thought that had begun in Leonardo's study came to a juddering halt. The Doctor stopped wiping his hand and stared at it in horror. He'd finally worked it out. Romana had too, judging by the way she was staring at the Jagaroth ship in awe. Scaroth's first gift to the human race. 'The Jagaroth ship! It's worse than we thought. The explosion which caused Scarlioni to be splintered in time also created life on Earth. And that is about to happen. The birth of life itself.'

'Here?' Duggan looked vaguely revolted. 'While we watch?'

'Well no,' admitted the Doctor. 'If we're still watching then we'll be in dead trouble. We must stop Scaroth. If we don't make sure he remains the last of the Jagaroth, the human race will suddenly cease to exist.'

Romana spotted the figure striding across the plain towards them first. Considering he was a monocular cephalopod in a lounge suit, he looked rather suave. Apart from the gun he was pointing at them.

As he approached them at the base of the *Sephiroth*, Scaroth nodded to them. It was the polite acknowledgment one makes to party guests, saying that you will talk to them later while firmly intending not to. Instead, he turned his attention to the craft. Several million years of planning and he hadn't thought to bring a megaphone with him.

He shouted and waved his hands in the air. 'Stop, stop my brothers! In the names of the lives of all of us! Stop!'

Nothing happened.

The engine noise of the ship rose slightly.

Scaroth fired a bullet into the air. Given the flammable fug of the Earth's atmosphere, the noise and the flash were both quite impressive.

'We must stop him,' the Doctor said, rushing forward.

Scaroth stopped pointing his gun in the air and instead trained it on the Time Lord. He was more annoyed than surprised. 'Damn you, Doctor. Not now. I must stop my ship.'

When the Doctor replied, it was without any trace of the dilettante adventurer, or even the carefree wanderer. It was with the weary gravity of millions of years.

'No.'

'I am in that ship!' The hand with the gun was wavering a little. 'I am in the warp-control cabin. I must stop myself pressing that button.'

Scaroth fired the gun again, the bullet pinging off the tough metal hide of the ship.

The Doctor planted himself firmly between Scaroth and the hatch in one of the ship's legs. He shook his head ever so firmly. 'No, Scaroth. You've done it already. You've thrown the dice once. You don't get another throw.'

Scaroth knew he didn't have time for an argument. 'But I'll be splintered in time again. My people will die.'

'That's the chance you took. That's the chance you're in there taking.'

Scaroth waved frantically. He could glimpse a distant face in a filthy porthole, staring at endless screens. Me. So close. Look down, you fool. Look down and see me.

'I can save myself. I can save them all,' he cried, dashing forward.

'No,' the Doctor said it again, holding out his hands, pleading. 'The explosion that you are about to trigger is destined to give birth to the human race. The moment that your race kills itself off, another race is born. That has happened. It will happen.'

The Doctor and Scaroth stared at each other.

'What do I care for the human race?' Scaroth sneered, a little uncertainly. They'd done so much together. So many wonderful achievements. He imagined trying to explain any one of them to the other Jagaroth. What would they make of it all? Painting. Patisserie. Pyramids. They would, he realised, simply round on him demanding he got them off this dead planet and found somewhere else to invade. 'Humanity?' He sighed wistfully. 'Primitive scum. They were just the tools of my salvation.'

'The product of your destruction.'

The wretched man had a point. But Scaroth was a man against the clock. He flung the Doctor to the ground and aimed the gun at his head.

'No Scaroth.' The Doctor was begging. He wasn't fighting back. He was just lying there. Staring at him. Being right. 'History must not change. It cannot.'

Scaroth looked the Doctor in the eye, shook his head, and squeezed the trigger.

*

Duggan had hit a lot of things. Heads. Walls. Dogs. A Mini Metro.

But punching an alien in that weird squidgy face was a first. The fist sank in. The flesh wasn't as slimy and horrid as he'd expected. But nor was it solid. It was like punching a pillow filled with cutlery. He felt bits of it all slide together crunchily, and then watched as Scaroth, last of the Jagaroth, toppled onto the Doctor, the gunshot burying itself in the fuselage with a dangerous hiss.

Romana ran up, heaving Scaroth's body off the Doctor.

The Doctor stood up, dazed and deafened by the growing whine of the engines.

'Duggan!' growled the Doctor. He shook his head, trying to clear it. 'Duggan,' he repeated in a whisper.

Spare me the lecture, thought Duggan, and decided, just for the fun of it, to hit the Doctor.

The Doctor's hand grasped his own with surprising force.

The Doctor was beaming at him with every single one of his teeth.

'Duggan,' he declared, 'do you know, I think that was possibly the most important punch in history.'

Romana toed the body of Scaroth. Above them the ship's engines were building dangerously in volume, rippling the air. The hissing caused by Scaroth's bullet grew to a whine as a fuel line severed.

'What do we do now?' Romana asked.

The Doctor shrugged.

On cue, the body of Scaroth, last of the Jagaroth, vanished. One less problem.

'Scaroth's time is up,' said the Doctor. 'He's gone back to the Château.'

With nothing else to look at, they all stared at the ship. It was howling now, whipping the feeble atmosphere up into a hurricane of pumice and mud. Just visible, on one side, was a little figure, working away in the warp-control pod. It did not look up. It had problems of its own to worry about.

The Doctor saluted the oblivious figure and then turned away, crunching across the pumice.

'That ship's about to take off,' Romana said meaningfully.

'About to explode.' The Doctor didn't look back. 'Let's get out of here.'

They hurried back to the TARDIS and, for once, let history get on with its business.

At full power, the *Sephiroth* glided majestically up from the surface of the desolation. As the sphere rose, the claw-like legs tucked themselves neatly up underneath. The omens were good. A tiny fluctuation caused by a fuel leakage seemed to right itself. For a moment the sphere hovered there, glowing with energy, magnificent, expectant.

Then it shattered.

The warp field collapsed. The fragments of the ship, squeezed into place by impossible forces, finally felt free to fling themselves in burning splendour far and wide across the surface of the dead planet.

This time, nothing surprising happened.

There was no explosion. It had, despite everything, worked wonderfully. Scaroth opened his eye.

He had prepared himself nobly for this end. Awaking in the endless desolation. Perhaps time enough for a final farewell to his colleagues. Perhaps to share a single, meaningful glance with himself. To look himself in the eye, just for a soned. Or perhaps to find himself utterly alone until he faded away.

Whatever, the lack of an explosion told him all he needed

to know. That despite everything, despite that Doctor and Duggan, it had somehow worked out all right in the end.

It deserved to. After all, he had spent millions of years planning this. The Doctor just made it up on the spot. Scaroth deserved his success.

Scaroth opened his eye, finding himself in total blackness. This was it. The triumph was his. And then, as he watched, the blackness glowed. Little pinpricks appeared throughout eternity – at first a small fire, then a pyramid, statues, cars and bombs. Ghosts of history flickered into being as he flew past them. So he had failed, after all. He was falling up through the time vortex. He realised then that the three-minute limitation had fired. He was going home. To a home he wished never existed. As he drifted through the swirling centuries, his other fragments stared out at him, looking at him in fury and shame.

They couldn't understand how all their hard work had ended up counting for nothing. How could he have failed them? How could the Jagaroth have failed?

Previously, Scaroth had blamed his failure on not having enough time. Now he'd had all the time in a world, and still he'd failed.

The other splinters of the Jagaroth glared at him.

'No, no, no!' he wailed. 'It wasn't like that.'

But that wasn't the end. He knew it wasn't. He had a time machine. He could simply fire it up again, and go back. Go back over and over and over, until the entire plain was crammed with Scaroths, all waving at the spacecraft, all shouting for it to stop. This was better than the original plan. This plan would succeed. It must.

It must succeed because he knew what he was going back to. Nothing. The Château, full of valuable objects, but no Kerensky to bully to make improvements, and, of course, no Heidi. No conversation sparkling with the wine. No friendship. Just the solid, grave, cruel devotion of Hermann. Only Hermann. Hermann would understand, of course. Hermann would help.

Hermann found himself lying on the floor of the laboratory. His head hurt. Hermann made one of his lists. The list contained the order in which the Doctor, Duggan and the girl would die and the precise way in which each one would perish. He would make Duggan die last, of course. Having seen what he'd done to the others. Or perhaps the girl? That would, Hermann thought, stop her smiling.

Hermann staggered around the laboratory, trying to shake the pain from his head. Getting ready for the fight.

At first, the basement seemed so quiet and then a buzzing began, gradually filling the room. The Professor's equipment was activating.

Hermann peered at it. The time bubble was forming.

'Scaroth! Scaroth! Scaroth!'

His other selves, chanting his name, in mockery and fury.

That wasn't good enough. It just wasn't fair. He knew that he would try again. And this time he would succeed.

He could see the end of the time vortex, a bubble opening up into Paris. This time, he would fix it.

The Centuries That Divide Me Shall Be Undone.

Scaroth stepped through into the time bubble, getting ready to walk out into the real world and begin again.

Hermann stared in horror at the grotesque shape standing at the heart of the cellar. And then he did something instinctively human. He picked up the first thing that came to hand and threw it at the creature.

'No Hermann! No, it's me!' the thing cried out.

Hermann thought that a very odd thing to say. At that moment, the fish-oil lamp he'd thrown smashed into the side of the machine, igniting both instantly in an explosion that ripped up and out through the Château from the cellar to the ballrooms and the neglected galleries.

The resulting fireball could be seen from the very top of the Eiffel Tower and made a lot of appearances in photographs behind startled tourists.

Scaroth never made it out of the time bubble. He barely caught more than a last glimpse of the Mona Lisa smirking at him from the bench opposite. In a flash, it was all snatched away. Scaroth never stepped back into the world he had made home. He'd captivated all of Paris with his pithy witticisms, his cruel humour, his *bon mots*. But 'No, it's me' really weren't great last words.

But then again, they weren't really the end of Scaroth, last of the Jagaroth. With the exit of the time corridor closed, there was simply nowhere else for Scaroth to go but the void. He whirled around to seek help from his other splinters, but they had all turned their backs on him. So, with a groan, he walked on, into a darkness that had no end.

CHAPTER NINETEEN
FRENCH WITHOUT TEARS IN THE FABRIC OF SPACE-TIME

'The one nearest the wall?'

Harrison heard the angry voice and thought, 'No, not today.' He'd convinced Elena to come up the Eiffel Tower with him. Now that he'd seen the beauty of Paris, everything was so much easier. Maybe he'd never be able to talk about it as cleverly as Elena did, but that didn't matter. He could nod. He could smile. And he was doing both right now.

Harrison Mandel didn't pay the man in a scarf and the girl in a school uniform a second glance. If they were wonderfully familiar, then they were just part of the magic. He sniffed the air and really did think Paris the most beautiful place on Earth. He squeezed Elena's hand, and, joy of joys, she squeezed it back.

So they went and got on with life.

Sat miserably in his studio, the artist Bourget made his peace with his curse. He was going to take it on at its own game. Instead of trying to draw people, he would draw a clock. If that was what his hands were telling him to do, then so be it. *Chacun a son goût.* Ignoring the approaching shouts of his landlord, Bourget set out to draw the best clock he possibly could. He worked diligently, and with only a few breaks for Gauloises and brandy. In truth, it was one of the most haunting drawings of a clock the world had ever seen. This was, every stroke and line said, an instrument that firmly regulated time. Relieved, he turned his attention to the dial, shading it in.

Aghast, he dropped the charcoal, not even hearing the stick shatter on the floor.

Staring back at him from his drawing of a timepiece was the smiling face of the Mona Lisa.

With all of Paris laid out beneath him, Duggan was doing some rather serious shouting.

Romana was tuning it out. It was a glorious afternoon. Paris smelt much the same as ever. A definite, joyous bouquet wafted over from the neatly ordered boulevards, from the grand galleries, and from the merrily static lines of traffic. It was wonderful. And yet, Duggan was still shouting.

'The one nearest the wall?'

Duggan was holding a copy of the Mona Lisa in his hands. It was a very, very good copy of the Mona Lisa. And only a little soot-stained .

'Mmmm.' The Doctor shrugged a trifle apologetically. It had all been rather tricky. He'd been hoping that Duggan would be pleased. Clearly not. Maybe this hadn't been the best spot for a rendezvous. 'Well, it was the only one not damaged in the fire.'

Romana looked sadly out from the viewing platform. At the far edge of the Marais, where two of Haussman's stateliest boulevards met, was a very large hole. The Doctor had blown up a stately home, after all.

'But! But!' Duggan was still shouting and shaking the canvas. 'It's a fake! You can't hang a fake Mona Lisa in the Louvre!'

Romana still hadn't really got the hang of painting by hand. Humans seemed really terribly obsessed by it. 'How can it be a fake if Leonardo painted it?'

'With the words "This is a fake" written on it? In felt tip!' Duggan was roaring and there was a little foam on his lips.

Romana still didn't get it. 'That doesn't affect what it looks like.'

The Doctor nodded gravely.

'It doesn't matter what it looks like!' screamed Duggan, shaking the painting at them.

'Doesn't it?' the Doctor mused. 'Some people would say that was the whole point of painting.'

'But, they'll X-ray it!' Duggan's face crumpled. 'They'll find out.'

'Serve 'em right,' the Doctor grinned. 'If they need an X-ray to tell them whether a painting's any good or not, well, you might as well have painting by computer.'

'Like we have at home,' said Romana proudly. Much simpler. Much less fuss.

'Hmm,' the Doctor agreed. It was, truthfully, a bit of a puzzler they'd landed poor Duggan with. Maybe he could convince them that it was actually a secret cypher left by Leonardo. Give it a fancy name and everyone could try and solve it, the Doctor mused. But what could you call a secret code left by Leonardo da Vinci? Well, he was sure someone would come up with something that had a ring to it.

Duggan's glare had subsided into a dogged stare. 'Home,' he growled. 'Yes. Where do you two come from?'

Romana and the Doctor looked at each other as though that was the funniest joke in the world.

'From? Well…' The Doctor swept an arm out, taking in the viewing platform, the majestic ironmongery of the tower, the sweeping Paris skyline and the distant clouds. 'The best way to find out where you come from is to find out where you're going and then work backwards.'

Romana nodded seriously. No help from there apart from a slight wink.

'Then where are you going?' asked Duggan slowly.

'I don't know,' said the Doctor sadly.

'Nor do I,' Romana grinned.

'Goodbye,' announced the Doctor abruptly, and wandered off laughing.

Duggan stood alone, holding a copy of the Mona Lisa. If something funny had just happened then only she was smiling.

With an effort, Duggan stopped worrying what his chief would make of this. Instead, he looked down from the Eiffel Tower at the city glowing beneath him. There on the lawns in front of the tower were the Doctor and Romana, standing by their little blue box. They were waving up at him.

He waved back.

'Bye-bye, Duggan!' they called and tumbled laughing into the box.

The TARDIS vanished, leaving a final laugh hanging in the air.

Roaring at eternity, the small-blue, large-white box was off to new adventures…

FIN

AFTERNOTE
ON THE SEMIOTIC THICKNESS OF A PERFORMED TEXT

OR

WHILE SHAKESPEARE PLAYS CROQUET, ROMANA SAYS JUMP

City of Death is possibly the most authored and least authoritative story in the history of *Doctor Who*. Just as this book was never meant to be written by me, the original script was certainly never meant to be written by Douglas Adams.

Originally commissioned from David Fisher, *A Gamble with Time* told a rip-roaring story about a suave Count and Countess who were rigging the tables at a casino in order to fund their time-travel experiments. Taking place in the 1920s and the 1970s, the story featured a very, very limited use of location filming in Paris.

Despite the perilous state of England's and *Doctor Who's* finances in the late 1970s, Producer Graham Williams and Production Unit Manager John Nathan-Turner managed to wrangle the budget in such a way as to give them rather more time on location than Fisher's script allowed for. Which meant asking for a new draft from him in a hurry. As David Fisher was in the middle of an interesting divorce at the time, he wasn't really in any position to oblige.

So suddenly and famously, Douglas Adams, *Doctor Who*'s script editor at the time, dragged himself round to Graham Williams's house on a Thursday, sat in front of a typewriter and the two talked incessantly while Douglas typed. Sometimes the director Michael Hayes popped by to make coffee, read what had been written and satisfy himself that by Monday there would be a script for him to start work on.

There was, and what a script. There are about three people in the world who don't like *City of Death*, and they're steadily being hunted down. Thanks to ITV going on strike during its broadcast, *City of Death* remains pretty much the most-watched *Doctor Who* story of all time. Thanks to repeats, there was almost nothing else on during 1979, so it's a blessing that it's one of the best *Doctor Who* stories ever. I was 4 at the time, and even I can remember it. I had no idea what I was watching, but it kept me fascinated between *Basil Brush* and *The Generation Game*.

The thing is, what everyone was watching (over and over again) was the final, finished programme. This book is mainly based on the rehearsal scripts. The rehearsal scripts were written by Douglas Adams with ideas by Graham Williams from an idea by David Fisher. What was transmitted was slightly different. Some scenes were left out entirely in the edit, or emphases shifted around. Actors Tom Baker, Lalla Ward and Julian Glover especially took a delight in working on their lines, honing each one to a fine point. The resulting differences are surprising.

For example, whole academic papers have been written on the Doctor's approach to sexuality based on the line 'You're a beautiful woman, probably.' The original line as written was 'You're a beautiful woman. He was probably trying to summon up the courage to invite you out to dinner.'

Another famous example is that instead of the script's 'Shall we take the lift or jump?' from the Eiffel Tower, on television Romana suggests 'Shall we take the lift or fly?', a rather more poetic notion that is, curiously more fully explored in Douglas Adams's *Life, the Universe and Everything* and *So Long and Thanks for All the Fish*.

There are many other examples of this glorious refining (originally, the Doctor and Romana go looking for macaroni cheese). Many have been retained, and in other places, I've kept to the original, just because it's interesting. After all, the idea of Shakespeare playing croquet is marvellous.

The transmitted version of *City of Death* makes a lot of Paris, especially in Part Four. As Adams himself admitted, by that point in the long weekend, he was feeling quite tired. The script for Part Four is a lot shorter and the stage directions frequently suggest that a lot of running around would be quite helpful.

So, this script is heavily based on those rehearsal scripts, with borrowings from the final televised production where it helps. You'll be saddened to hear that the scripts don't contain an excised subplot. They do contain several deleted, or heavily edited scenes. Of course, I've included all of them. Douglas Adams's marvellously funny stage directions have been retained wherever possible. ('Romana picks up a vase and breaks it over the Countess's head. She goes down like a sack of turnips.' 'It should be perfectly clear that Tancredi is something out of a cuckoo clock.' 'Le Patron shrugs unconcernedly. He picks up the broken bottle neck from the table, looks at it for a moment and then slings it in the bin.') The original scripts also include a pleasing amount more fighting, with swords, fists, feet and lots of guns. That's obviously all back in. I've given the Countess a slightly bigger gun at one point, but that's about the only change. Unless I'm lying.

Along with all that come any extra amounts of detail the script offers. For example, Douglas Adams retains the

Countess's first name as Heidi, from *A Gamble with Time*. This is, of course, a goldmine. On my first day of work, I emailed a friend to say, 'The Countess has a first name! And it explains everything.' Well, it sort of does.

The script supplied two surprises. One was at the end of Part One. I'd never questioned why the Count took his face off. It just seemed to be the kind of thing *Doctor Who* monsters did at the end of Part One. But, working on this, I started to worry. Why would he do that? And, of course, the stage directions tell a different, more curious story. They begin: 'He considers his face carefully. He appears to scratch above his right eye. He pauses. He touches again, carefully.'

I read it and I wondered – could it be that the Count doesn't really know until that moment that his face is a mask with something terrible beneath it? It would explain a lot. I wondered and worried a bit, and then I got to Part Three, where the rehearsal script makes it quite clear that the Count is only now realising who he really is, wondering if it is 'perhaps a dream'. This is extraordinary. It's also slightly inconsistent, but then, as is said, the interface is unstable. Some splinters of Scaroth seem more consistently self-aware than others. It explains the enigma of the Count's marriage (although I've followed Barbara Cartland's advice and stopped outside the bedroom door). This also casts the funniest scene in *Doctor Who* history in a new light. Part Two begins with the Doctor's interrogation by the Count and Countess. What if this takes place just after the Count has discovered he's not even human? It certainly puts things in a new light.

The script, and the original storyline also solve what seems a strange dead-end in the plot. The Count puts great emphasis on needing to sell seven Mona Lisas in order to carry out his experiment. But the auction never takes place. Seemingly, after millions of years of planning, the Count just hops back in time anyway. David Fisher's original storyline makes it absolutely plain. The Count meets Romana, realises she can build him a time machine, and gets her to do it instead. Some of this survives in the transmitted version, but the rehearsal script includes a lengthy discussion between the Doctor and Romana in the cellar. Simply put, the Count meets Romana and throws his plans out the window. Well, which of us wouldn't?

A Gamble with Time also gives us a name for the hapless painter, Bourget. John Cleese himself suggested the art critics should be called Kim Bread and Helena Swanetsky (I couldn't quite honour that one). I've made a few other changes and elaborations, but all hopefully fairly minor. I mean, yes, obviously, I couldn't resist filling in the gap during Duggan and Romana's long night. She only gets one night in Paris and it seems a shame to spend all of it asleep on a chair. K-9 likewise gets a very little more to do, but sadly not much. After all, Paris is famous for its cobbled streets and presents left behind by less well-trained dogs.

In terms of research, I am indebted to the work of Francophile anthropologist Stephen Clarke (especially *Paris Revealed* and *1,000 Years of Annoying the French*, where much can be found about Baron Haussman, Dom Pérignon, and the peculiar English obsession with Paris tap water), to Tilar J. Mazzeo's survey of art smuggling in *The Hotel on Place Vendôme*, and also to the letters of Major Gaston Palewski's lover, Nancy Mitford (who lived in Paris during Count Scarlioni's era and was in shrieks throughout), and finally to Paddy Freeland, who took me round Paris. But not very far up the Eiffel Tower as I'm terrified of heights.

Finally, this book is dedicated to Douglas Adams, David Fisher and Garoth of the Jagaroth, who found his soneds were urgently needed elsewhere.

James Goss, 2015

BBC

DOCTOR WHO

THE DROSTEN'S CURSE
A.L. Kennedy

ISBN 978 1 84990 826 9

Isn't life terrible? Isn't it all going to end in tears? Won't it be good to just give up and let something else run my mind, my life?

Something distinctly odd is going on in Arbroath. It could be to do with golfers being dragged down into the bunkers at the Fetch Brothers Golf Spa Hotel, never to be seen again. It might be related to the strange twin grandchildren of the equally strange Mrs Fetch – owner of the hotel, and fascinated with octopuses. It could be the fact that people in the surrounding area suddenly know what others are thinking, without anyone saying a word.

Whatever it is, the Doctor is most at home when faced with the distinctly odd. With the help of Fetch Brothers' Junior Receptionist Bryony, he'll get to the bottom of things. Just so long as he does so in time to save Bryony from quite literally losing her mind, and the entire world from destruction.

Because something huge, ancient and alien lies hidden beneath the ground – and it's starting to wake up…

A thrilling new Doctor Who novel by award-winning novelist A.L. Kennedy, featuring the Fourth Doctor, as played by Tom Baker

BBC

DOCTOR WHO

Royal Blood
Una McCormack

ISBN 978 1 84990 992 1

The Grail is a story, a myth! It didn't exist on your world! It can't exist here!

The city-state of Varuz is failing. Duke Aurelian is the last of his line, his capital is crumbling, and the armies of his enemy, Duke Conrad, are poised beyond the mountains to invade. Aurelian is preparing to gamble everything on one last battle. So when a holy man, the Doctor, comes to Varuz from beyond the mountains, Aurelian asks for his blessing in the war.

But all is not what it seems in Varuz. The city-guard have lasers for swords, and the halls are lit by electric candlelight. Aurelian's beloved wife, Guena, and his most trusted knight, Bernhardt, seem to be plotting to overthrow their Duke, and Clara finds herself drawn into their intrigue…

Will the Doctor stop Aurelian from going to war? Will Clara's involvement in the plot against the Duke be discovered? Why is Conrad's ambassador so nervous? And who are the ancient and weary knights who arrive in Varuz claiming to be on a quest for the Holy Grail…?

An original novel featuring the Twelfth Doctor and Clara, as played by Peter Capaldi and Jenna Coleman

BBC

DOCTOR WHO

Big Bang Generation
Gary Russell

ISBN 978 1 84990 991 4

I'm an archaeologist, but probably not the one you were expecting.

Christmas 2015, Sydney, New South Wales, Australia

Imagine everyone's surprise when a time portal opens up in Sydney Cove. Imagine their shock as a massive pyramid now sits beside the Harbour Bridge, inconveniently blocking Port Jackson and glowing with energy. Imagine their fear as Cyrrus 'the mobster' Globb, Professor Horace Jaanson and an alien assassin called Kik arrive to claim the glowing pyramid. Finally imagine everyone's dismay when they are followed by a bunch of con artists out to spring their greatest grift yet.

This gang consists of Legs (the sexy comedian), Dog Boy (providing protection and firepower), Shortie (handling logistics), Da Trowel (in charge of excavation and history) and their leader, Doc (busy making sure the universe isn't destroyed in an explosion that makes the Big Bang look like a damp squib).

And when someone accidentally reawakens the Ancients of Time – which, Doc reckons, wasn't the wisest or best-judged of actions – things get a whole lot more complicated…

An original novel featuring the Twelfth Doctor, as played by Peter Capaldi

BBC

DOCTOR WHO

Deep Time
Trevor Baxendale

ISBN 978 1 84990 990 7

I do hope you're all ready to be terrified!

The Phaeron disappeared from the universe over a million years ago. They travelled among the stars using roads made from time and space, but left only relics behind. But what actually happened to the Phaeron? Some believe they were they eradicated by a superior force... Others claim they destroyed themselves.

Or were they in fact the victims of an even more hideous fate?

In the far future, humans discover the location of the last Phaeron road – and the Doctor and Clara join the mission to see where the road leads. Each member of the research team knows exactly what they're looking for – but only the Doctor knows exactly what they'll find.

Because only the Doctor knows the true secret of the Phaeron: a monstrous secret so terrible and powerful that it must be buried in the deepest grave imaginable...

An original novel featuring the Twelfth Doctor and Clara, as played by Peter Capaldi and Jenna Coleman